Beware the Solitary Drinker

Beware the Solitary Drinker

Cornelius Lehane

Poisoned Pen Press

First Edition 2002

10 9 8 7 6 5 4 3 2 1

Library of Congress Catalog Card Number: 2001098500

ISBN: 1-59058-016-8 Hardcover
ISBN: 1-59058-020-6 Trade Paperback

Poisoned Pen Press
6962 E. First Ave., Ste. 103
Scottsdale, AZ 85251
www.poisonedpenpress.com
info@poisonedpenpress.com

Printed in the United States of America

To Patrick Lehane
and
Ellen Harten Lehane

Chapter One

Five minutes after I came behind the bar for the night shift, Chuck, the day guy, came out of the manager's office, his face as white and drawn as a terminal patient's. Given his normal barroom pallor, he was a ghastly sight.

"Spotter's report," he whispered.

"Shit!" I felt the arrival of doom. "When?"

"Two weeks ago Thursday."

Trying to remember two weeks ago Thursday was like trying to recall my childhood. I couldn't remember one Thursday from another—or from a Tuesday for that matter.

"We all came back from the country," Chuck said.

That was it. I didn't have to wait for the manager's call. I now remembered. The whole day crew came in to visit near closing. I'd practically given the joint away.

"Mr. McNulty." Alphonse, the manager, addressed me with all due solemnity. He sat at his inner sanctum desk next to the liquor storage room. We both knew he was chortling and cheering behind his pompous veneer. "I want to read to you from this report." So he did. As soon as it began I remembered the weasel spotter, short, a round head, brown hair combed across a bald dome, glasses, a wimp's smile.

Alphonse read: "I ordered a double martini. The bartender, nametag Brian, poured it, took my ten dollar bill, registered three dollars on the cash register, and returned me four dollars."

Alphonse looked up. I waited for the rest. The general manager of the hotel half-sat half-leaned, against the front of the desk watching intently; the head of hotel security stood like a palace guard beside the desk. I braced myself.

"Under the circumstances," Alphonse began again, becoming almost majestic in his solemnity, "I have no choice but to request your resignation."

I wanted to stall for time. I wanted some kind of opening into the report. Actually, I didn't know what to do. "Would you read me the rest of the report?" I asked him in an anemic tone of voice.

He looked confused. "There is no more."

"That's it? … That's Thursday night?"

He nodded.

"That's all that's in the report for Thursday night?"

He nodded again.

I believed God had intervened.

"What the hell kind of spotter's report is that?"

"Enough for us to terminate you," the general manager said.

"For what?"

"For stealing."

"Where's it say I stole?"

"C'mon, McNulty. We weren't born yesterday," Alphonse shouted, his solemnity, along with his faintly European accent, bowled over for the moment by his Bensonhurst roots.

"The spotter was. Don't they give those guys eye tests?"

The entire management crew sputtered at me. I was the union steward; they hated me. The business agent from the local used to come for lunch once every couple of months until I started making him enforce the contract. No one likes a troublemaker, not even me. But I can't help it. My father was a Communist, one of the founders of the Newspaper Guild. His quixotic sense of the workers' rights and the boss's injustice rubbed off on me. It's my curse, one of the reasons why this—itself about to become history—was my twenty-fourth bartending gig.

They did fire me, and I did file a grievance. The union said they would find me another job and to forget about the grievance. Since I wouldn't forget it, they wouldn't find me a job. That was how I ended up at Oscar's on Broadway in my own neighborhood, a couple of blocks from my apartment, at 108th Street.

There, on a smoky, drunken Saturday night, I met Angelina. She came through the smoke, up to the bar, like one of those sleek and beautiful mahogany sailboats that slip soundlessly out of the fog and the early morning mist to dock at the Dockside Hotel down on the Jersey Shore—where I once tended bar in an earlier life. The four A.M. drunks were piled against the bar now that last call had sounded; no matter how many hours before that they'd spent staring silently into their glasses, now they talked, urgently, clinging to the night, fighting off tomorrow. When I leaned toward her for her order, Angelina put her hand on mine to make sure she had my attention. Tired, half-drunk myself, I wanted to brush her prettiness away, like I brushed away the other pretty brats: the waitresses-as-actresses, the business-suited innocents from Cincinnati or Iowa. I was sick of innocence and expectation. I'd been to my own four or five hundred casting calls.

That's another of my curses, thinking I'm an actor. The worst one, though, is this ability I have to watch myself when I'm pretending to something I don't really feel. That comes from my father, too. He couldn't pretend either that Hungarian workers were Trotskyists and CIA agents or that the Warsaw Pact troops' entry into Czechoslovakia constituted comradely intervention. That didn't keep him from being a Communist; it just kept him from getting any promotions or being honored at get-togethers for long-time, loyal comrades. This night, I watched myself pretend that this girl didn't bloom in front of me like the last rose of summer and that I wasn't captivated by her blue eyes. She was of that charmed and pretty school of women that men fall all over, obviously used to getting everything she wanted from men with a couple of pouts and a smile. I could fill a warehouse with pretty smiles and innocent eyes.

Pretty wasn't enough. Another link in the anchor chain from my father. "Don't homely people have a right to live too?" asked Pop. "Don't they care about attention? You're no Clark Gable yourself. Why does a girl have to be pretty? What about her heart?" One more example of that unfashionable wisdom that had made him a pariah for most of my childhood. I wanted to show this winsome waif that flirtatious smiles and innocent eyes didn't mean shit in Oscar's on Broadway at four in the morning.

"What?" I asked with no more courtesy than I'd show a truck driver from the Bronx.

"I want to tell you a joke," she said, her eyes flashing like a mischievous child's.

"This little girl wanted to know what her father's dick was, so he told her it was his dolly." Angelina sipped her rum and coke, her eyes already laughing, her voice growing drunkenly raucous. "The next morning the mother found the father rolling around screaming in pain, holding his penis. 'What happened?' the mother shouted at the little girl. 'I was playing with daddy's dolly while he was asleep, and it spit at me, so I wrung its neck.'" Angelina laughed uproariously at her joke. I went back to work.

In a few minutes, she ordered another drink, her long eyelashes fluttering over her pretty blue eyes. Locked into those eyes when I went to give her the drink, I clipped the bar with the bottom of the glass and dumped about half of it on the bar in front of her.

Batting her eyes, she watched me sop up the drink with a bar towel. "Did you spill that because you were looking at me?" she asked gleefully.

We had a drink at the bar after I closed up, then went to an after-hours joint, called the Flaming Star, and stayed until the sun came up. The Flaming Star was a warehouse on 79th Street with a dance floor as big as a tennis court, throbbing disco music, and oases of chairs and tables set about. Truly egalitarian in the worst sense of the word—the joint corrupted everyone without regard to race, creed, sex, or economic status—class, my father would say. Blacks, whites, Latins, we'd all sunk to the same level, bartenders and waitresses after work, drug dealers still at work, gamblers, musicians, assorted weirdos, all of us united in our pursuit of degeneracy. Not the place to take a nice girl on the first date.

Angelina loved the place.

"What do all these people do?" she asked. The clientele sparkled and glistened, men in everything from electric blue suits to buckskin and cowboy hats, women in waitress clothes or glittering party dresses, most of them sleek and slim and vacant eyed. At times, coked up at the Flaming Star, I'd thought I was in a roomful of mannequins.

"Nothing useful," I told her.

"But everyone's so glamorous." She envisioned movie stars and rock musicians.

"I'm not."

"No," she said. "You're grouchy and eccentric. But that's a really great way to be, too."

"What's not a great way to be?"

"A teenage girl in Springfield."

Back in the neighborhood at dawn, we walked in a secluded section of Riverside Park, down on the far side of the West Side Highway next to the river. Then, when the morning was pretty well light, we sat on the steps of Low Library, on the very top step, looking down over College Walk.

"This is very inspiring," Angelina said. "It's like visiting a castle."

The solemn, scholarly Ionic columns of Butler Library, the peace of the morning, Columbia inspired me, too. I spent many mornings sitting on the steps, trying to shore up my belief—the only one I had—in knowledge. Years before, I'd started off at Columbia College, a scholarship student, a son of the working class, on my way to a law degree to enable me to defend the oppressed, back when my father believed I would amount to something. But I'd spent much more time in the West End bar than Butler Library, and I didn't amount to much at all.

Maybe those memories haunted the Low Library steps. Maybe my belief in knowledge was that I too would know something someday—like why I'd spent my life in bars. "Dim lights, thick smoke, and loud, loud music…the only kind of life you'll ever understand."

"Why are you sitting here with a man twice your age?" I asked Angelina when I'd finished my reverie. This was at least something I could know.

"You're a father image." Her face brightened into a smile. "Why are you sitting here with a girl half your age?"

I didn't know after all.

"I'm good for your ego," she said.

"What do you want from me?"

"I want you to be my friend."

"Do you want to sleep with me?"

"I don't know." The night had taken its toll on her, young as she was; she yawned and smiled weakly; her body lost its vibrancy, like the wind gone out of the sails. Nearer exhaustion, you get closer to the truth.

My apartment wasn't far away and we didn't talk on the way there. I wanted to hug myself to sleep with Angelina. I was as foolish as I ever thought I might be, like an old dog trying to cavort with a puppy. I had to watch myself pretend on the walk home that I held onto some sort of dignity— that I didn't have a crush on her, that I wasn't as stupidly innocent and romantic as I pretended she was.

When she was in my arms in my bed, I asked her if she was sure she wanted to do this.

"I knew you'd do that," she said.

"What?"

"Want to talk about it."

"Is that bad?"

"No, it's good."

"Are you sure you want to do this?"

"No," she said. Her voice was small, as the rest of her seemed much smaller now, her thin white shoulders, her pale and graceful neck, her tiny-nippled breasts that flattened out against her chest when she lay down.

"How will you feel when we wake up?"

"Probably terrible." Her face was beautiful against the pillow, her eyelids closing toward sleep; her face even more beautiful in this repose just before sleep than it had been through the night. "It's not that I don't find you attractive or don't want to make love with you. I feel like something terrible will happen if I do."

She slept, then, chastely, beside me.

Sometime after noon, when we awoke, I regained whatever it is that passes for my composure. I told Angelina she was a sweet kid, but I didn't think we would do each other much good. She nodded solemnly.

"Were you going to fall in love with me?" she asked. Her pretty blue eyes sparkled; her expression was eager and alert, the pink freshness returned to her cheeks.

"I don't know. Do you want me to?"

"Maybe." She lowered her eyelids demurely.

In spite of myself, I was cheered by her reply. But a man of forty can't fall in love with a twenty-year-old. He already knows what little flirts they are and how fickle, and how silly it is to try to hold on to such a girl. "I'm not going to fall in love with you," I said in a tone of voice she would believe. I believed it.

"I knew you'd say that too," she said matter-of-factly.

The picture of her face against my pillow stayed with me— something in the way she looked at me, as if she knew things about me I didn't know myself.

I stumbled around for a few days mooning over her, kicking myself for passing up the opportunity to screw her when I had the chance. I blamed it on my upbringing. "Intimacy should at least be honest," said Pop. "The bedroom is not a used car lot." He must have drilled this sort of wisdom into my head while I slept because I tried not to pay any attention while I was awake.

Not a week passed before she turned up again, just before closing time, coming in out of the pouring rain, standing in the doorway shaking the water out of her hair like a wet mutt. I wondered where she'd been, whom she'd been with, but I didn't ask.

"What a pisser walking up here," she said. "It really sucks out." Then she smiled her wayward angel's smile.

She needed a place to stay for the night because she'd been locked out of her apartment. "I knew I could come to you," she said, between sips of her rum and Coke in the semi-darkness after I'd closed the bar. What did she know: that I didn't have anything else to do with my life but look after her?

She was locked out of her apartment because an irate suitor had kicked down the door. The villain was the cab driver who'd driven her from Port Authority to the Upper West Side and helped her find the address of her apartment house her first night in New York. He was Armenian or Lebanese. She wasn't sure. They'd gone on two dates in his taxi, and he had fallen in love with her. The super wanted no part of her after the maniac cab driver's visit and padlocked her apartment. She also lost her waitressing job because her uniform was locked in her room.

We ate breakfast in the greasy spoon at 106th and went to my apartment. She wanted no part of romance. Very tired, she nodded off to sleep on my couch, and whatever amorous intentions I had were doused by her sleepiness. "I'm too confused," she said before she slept.

I sat for a long time in my old stuffed easy chair sipping scotch, watching the remnants of a late-night Peter Lorre movie, remembering women I'd known, every few seconds turning to look at Angelina's face as she slept.

In the morning, she cried softly over coffee at my cluttered kitchen table, then threw herself on the couch again. "I give up," she said. "I'm staying right here. I'm your responsibility."

That afternoon we went to the Marlin Cafe, an old neighborhood bar, lately taken over in the evening by Columbia students in some subdued version of bohemianism. In the daylight, it was still a place for old men to stare into their seven ounce beer glasses. We talked for a long time; mostly she talked and I listened. She told me she was molested when she was ten and her mother never forgave her.

"'That's what ruined you,' my mother told me all my life," Angelina said. It sounded as though she believed it, too.

She was raped again when she was twelve by a friend of her mother's—though this one she had never told anyone about—and began running away from home and having sex with men when she was thirteen. She moved in with a thirty-two-year-old sculptor when she was fifteen, about the time she became a nude model.

"My mother disapproves of sleeping around almost as much as I do," she said, waving those eyelashes and smiling shyly, just after she told me the number of men she'd slept with was in the hundreds and she'd never had an orgasm. "It's so mechanical. It gets to be like shaking hands—undress, put in my diaphragm, and screw."

Angelina stayed at my apartment for a couple of weeks watching *I Love Lucy* reruns and reading fashion magazines. At night, she hung around Oscar's making friends with the regulars. She did this methodically, I realized later, checking out each man who entered the bar as if she were looking for someone.

"I think it's really nice that we're friends and not lovers," she said when we talked about it.

"Me, too. Getting laid is bad for you at my age."

"It would ruin everything if we were lovers." Her voice wavered, and she looked helplessly into my eyes. I knew she would go to bed with me if I really wanted that. For whatever reason, gratitude, habit, need, she would do it. But I shared her foreboding: I knew something terrible would happen if she did.

The regulars at Oscar's adored Angelina. She flirted with everyone, moseying from one barstool to the next, lapping up the barflies' attentions and enjoying the jealousy she created. Everyone had a crush on Angelina, and she made each of the winos feel in turn that she had a crush on him. Maybe she did.

Angelina found something to like and admire in everyone. This generosity toward her fellow suffering humanity went over extremely well with the winos, most of whom had run out of things to like about themselves years before.

Sometimes, Angelina had dates she met at the bar, and some nights she didn't come in at all. Usually, when she met a guy, she'd stay out all night, not returning to my apartment until the next day. On those days after, she was withdrawn, staring at the TV, not talking, depressed, and getting on my nerves. I hated the sound of the television.

Sometimes, her dates kept her away from the bar for a week or so, but sooner or later she'd come back for a night with the regulars. Back with a couple of new lousy jokes that everyone would laugh at. Whenever I looked up, someone's arm circling her bony shoulder, she was raucously laughing her way through the joke. The joke that was always vulgar—about balls or tits or vaginas—and never really funny.

Oscar's really became a bar late at night after the dinner crowd thinned out. Around ten-thirty, the rock and roll band set up, and the respectable people went home. Then the winos filtered in one at a time. They weren't really winos unless they drank alone. Beware the solitary drinker, the old-time bartenders had told me years before. Now, here they were, all of them—solitary drinkers.

A few of the regulars were in their twenties or thirties, but most were older, some in their sixties. Pretty much everyone had traveled many roads and had many stories to tell. As long as they told them to each other, I didn't mind.

My stock had gone up considerably because Angelina came to see me. And I have to admit my night brightened considerably each time I saw her. But Oscar's of the Upper West Side was a bar any number of women came into on their own. The women who frequented the place liked me well enough. Most women like the bartenders of the joints they drink in. But most of them didn't like Angelina. This was mostly because the men were so taken with her, and she didn't have any scruples about going to bed with men—except me. I put up with the dirty looks and snide remarks from the other women and with Angelina's outrageous act, despite my certain knowledge that her flirting and carelessness would lead to trouble, because I couldn't help wanting to have her around. As she was for the stumblebums, she was the excitement in my life. But there was more. I knew, without knowing it, that beneath the flamboyance, the craving for attention, the lewdness, and the recklessness, Angelina was as gentle as anyone I'd ever known, except maybe my mother.

Not surprisingly, Angelina's sashaying from one barfly to the next caused a good deal of jealousy, and the jealousy caused more than a few shoving matches, do-si-dos, and step-outsides. The closest we got to a fistfight was when Nigel Barthelme, one of the smitten regulars, felt called upon to defend her honor against the barbs of a certain Reuben Foster, another regular. Fed up with her antics one evening, Reuben called Angelina a slut and a prick-teasing little twat. Angelina took umbrage.

"I can't believe the assholes in this place," she said.

"It's three in the morning," I reminded her. "You're in Oscar's on Broadway. Who'd you expect, Prince Charming?"

Nigel stepped in, though. Maybe he thought he was Prince Charming. Reuben knocked him on his ass. Duffy, the doorman, grabbed Reuben while I picked up Nigel. Reuben, well into his fifties, hadn't lost his upper body strength; his torso was the size of a fifty-five-gallon drum.

"Nigel," I said as he squirmed to get back to the fight, "if you don't stop, I'm going to whack you." Something had snapped in him: he couldn't stop if he wanted; his face was twisted with hatred beyond rage. He actually scared me, but I was inside his arms so he couldn't hit me, and since I was bigger and heavier, he couldn't get me out of the way. I talked to him, my face inches away from his contorted mouth and his foul, labored breathing, trying to talk reason, and looking into his eyes that, like a blind man's, didn't look back.

"She's not a slut," Nigel screamed—a point I didn't think even Angelina would argue too strenuously.

"They're all sluts," said Reuben. He wasn't angry and he didn't show drunk, despite a half-dozen undiluted rums. On a good night, he was steady on his feet after a dozen.

"Reuben!" I bellowed, while I crushed the squirming Nigel against the partition wall, "Take a walk or I'll bar you from here, too." Reuben had to consider this threat since he'd already been barred from a couple of the other bars on our part of Broadway and was running out of places to drink.

He also liked me. "C'mon, Reuben," I said more softly, "do me a favor, take a walk for a half-hour." Grumbling about twats and sluts, he picked up his money from the bar, leaving a couple of bucks for me, and walked out. Reuben was a tough guy, and I liked having him around the bar; two or three times he'd helped me drag someone out, and once he'd pulled a drunk off-duty cop off my throat. His problem was that he hated women.

After four marriages, he hadn't learned; he'd still engage any woman, particularly a young woman, who happened into Oscar's. An aging hipster, who'd drunk in the West End with Ginsberg and Kerouac, he was a light-skinned black from an old New England family who had graduated from Oberlin College and still read novels and philosophy. He was one of the folks who made life a bit interesting at Oscar's. The college girls from Barnard and Columbia who wandered in now and again found him eccentric and charming. So did Angelina. She probably spent more time with him than with most of the other regulars, leaving him panting after her most nights there at the bar, still in fond pursuit of his biggest problem.

Nigel's brain returned to the fold a few minutes after Reuben left. I let go of him, Angelina took over comforting him, and I went back behind the bar.

Nigel Barthelme was another of Angelina's conquests. He was already part of the scene when I began working at Oscar's, having established himself as a kind of gofer. If I needed something from the liquor store to tide me over until Oscar paid the liquor distributor's bill, or the chef, Eric the Red, needed some hamburger meat from the market at 110th Street, Nigel would trot off to get it. Whenever something broke, Nigel ran to his apartment for his tool kit and came back and fixed it. But he wasn't your typical gofer. He had a good job doing something with computers in the financial district. Nor was he your typical barfly, as most of the time he drank ginger ale. He'd never really be an Oscar's regular since he considered his day job more important than his drinking.

Yet the four walls closed in on him late at night, too, like they did the rest of us. He was a night owl, and if you wanted to go out late at night on the Upper West Side, your choices were limited in 1983. Oscar befriended Nigel, word had it, because Oscar believed him to be descended from a wealthy family—and there was nothing that impressed Oscar more than wealth.

Angelina snatched poor Nigel up the first time she saw him come in the door. When he spied her that first night, he stood in the doorway gawking like he'd just fallen off the turnip truck. She looked up from her drink once, then looked up again. In no time at all, he was sitting beside her. This night, she was at first her cheerful self, then later much more serious than I was used to seeing her. Just before closing, she looped her arm about Nigel's shoulder and leaned heavily against him as they rolled out of the bar into the Broadway night. He seemed so taken with her, and she acted so differently with him than with her other conquests, that I thought she might have found something with Nigel. But he was back in the bar a couple of nights later nervously looking for her, and she was nowhere to be found. He looked for her every night for a week, asking me with fake casualness if I'd seen her.

I had seen her in actual fact because when she needed to be alone and get some sleep, she came back to my apartment, usually during the day, and curled up on the couch. But I didn't see any reason to tell Nigel this. His pining around the bar at night was bad enough; I didn't want him on my doorstep during the day also.

The time came, though, not long after this, that Angelina stayed away from the bar for quite a while and even stopped showing up at my apartment. I worried but then heard tell she'd been making the rounds farther downtown. When she finally did come back to Oscar's, she was in the chips. She bought the regulars drinks, tipped me five bucks when she bought a round, and tuned me up every half-hour from her packet of blow. She'd found a job at Hanrahan's on 65th Street, she told me, and I figured it must be a gold mine. She said she'd found herself a sugar daddy, so she would be my sugar momma.

That night, she left with Duffy the doorman. Her leaving cast a pall over the bar; the laughter and the good times gave way to steady, solitary, hard drinking, the kind usually disguised by the good time. We all shared an unspoken belief that she was throwing herself away on Duffy, but I doubt any of the rest of us planned to build her a house in the country. Even Nigel drank that night. So did I. Losing Angelina was one more failure added to a long string, so each of us, mired in the remembrance of a lifetime of losses, settled in to feel sorry for himself.

Nigel turned out to be an awful drunk, belligerent, foul-mouthed, contemptuous, and nasty to everyone. I finally threw him out around three. The next day, he was back, sheepish, contrite, diffident, wearing dark glasses instead of his coke bottles, his face even whiter than usual.

"You see now why I don't drink often," he said.

"You're one of the worst drunks I've ever seen," I assured him. "Maybe you should try drugs."

"I'm worse," Nigel said.

From then on, when Angelina did return, she and Nigel might talk or they might not, but I could tell the flame had gone out. Nigel pined after her, and she toyed with him. Still, he took it like a man, hanging on, being her friend, waiting for the day she'd come to her senses and realize he was the one for her.

During this time, too, Nigel and I took to hanging out together. Since he was often around at closing time, we'd have breakfast at the Greek greasy spoon, sometimes with Angelina, sometimes with some of the other leftovers from the bar. We regaled each other with stories of our pasts and commentaries on the state of the world and nation. Nigel liked to argue politics—bait me would be more like it. Late at night, with the greasy smoke of the Greek's grill as a backdrop, he'd pontificate like I imagined those Russian-royalty hangers-on displaced by the Bolsheviks did in the Paris cafes. An eloquent defender of privilege taking on the half-sloshed mouthpiece of the great unwashed, we bored to tears everyone around us.

Other nights, we went to my apartment or to Eric the Red's to smoke dope and listen to music, except that Nigel didn't smoke dope either. He seemed perfectly content, sitting there straight while we got stoned. He said he'd lived in the East Village in the mid-seventies when he'd been a roadie for groups like the Doobie Brothers and Aerosmith, and had been drugged out enough in those days. He did seem like a counter-culture leftover trying to go straight—a little off-kilter with the aura of having taken one trip too many.

Nigel was maybe ten years younger than me, but he seemed older. He was smaller than me, too, wore wire-rimmed glasses, and had a good-sized mustache. Maybe he was handsome but I don't think so, and maybe he was attractive to women, but I doubt that too. He wore a business suit most of the time and had an unconscious tendency to treat the rest of us, clad in our Levis and T-shirts, like the hired help. I'd never seen him infatuated with a woman before Angelina came along with her pretty blue eyes, her pouting lips, and her dirty jokes. And I suspected a good part of his interest in me had to do with keeping track of her.

As for Angelina, she settled into her gold mine near Lincoln Center and became quite well known at some of the bars farther down on the West Side, the higher-priced, glitzier places where the clientele still expected they would shine in life.

Leaving bars with strangers was a pattern for Angelina. Sometimes it was the same guy for a week or so, then for a while a different guy every night. It was dangerous to do this. I might have warned her. But it was her life, and she wouldn't have listened anyway. If she listened to warnings, she would have stayed home in Springfield.

Once she got her feet under her and adjusted to life in Fun City, she didn't need me much anymore. Finding a studio on 110th Street, between Broadway and Amsterdam, she moved out of my apartment, not really moving out after not really ever moving in. During this time, she was flush, spending like a drunken sailor, recklessly enjoying her prosperity and popularity. Dressed up, bright lipstick, colorful clothes, she would come back to the winos every couple of weeks or so, like the prodigal son, and they would take her in. She seemed desperate in some ways, but cheerful in others. She liked having money and had a lot of it.

～～～

When I saw Angelina now, it was unexpectedly—late at night in the bar or out of the blue in the early afternoon when she stopped by to have breakfast with me. I would call her, too, once in a while. I'd gotten over my crush, except when I was drunk and looking right at her, remembering how beautiful her face was against my pillow. She kept me up to date on auditions, her new discoveries and ambitions as they came and went—to open a boutique in the Village, a gallery in Soho, to sing with a piano player on the East Side—and her flirtations. She also wanted to be a bartender.

"You move so fast," she said after watching for an hour one busy Thursday night. Already a little drunk, she sat at the corner of the bar nearest the door, very alluring in a white satin shirt opened two or three buttons along her chest. "I want to go to bartending school and be like you."

"Number one, you don't want to be like me," I said. "And number two, you don't want to go to bartending school. All you learn there is how to mix drinks. You need to work behind a good bartender to become a bartender."

That's how I'd learned, the hard way, bar boy to service bartender, finally to the front bar. It wasn't the way things were done anymore. But I still had the attitude: you had to pay your dues. It rankled on me when some amateur walked behind the bar into a hundred dollar a night gig because he or she knew someone or had a pretty face.

I'd learned to pour with both hands, to make sure that the bar stations were all set up when I took over a shift, and to make sure that the bar was clean and stocked when I left a shift. I learned about working with my head up and always knowing everything that was happening at every moment. I learned how to make a good living, which means being alert for walkouts, for spotters, controlling the waiters and waitresses so they didn't become independent contractors. I learned to know who was trouble the second he or she entered the bar.

Later that night, Angelina, swaying to the music and seeming to caress the microphone with her mouth, sang a song with the band. A Tracy Nelson song that said: "It's a nickel for a donut and a dime for a dance but it's an arm and a leg for a little romance."

The band loved her. Young as she was, she could really sing the blues. They talked with her at the bar on their breaks about taking on a female vocalist. Angelina was thrilled and left around two, when the band finished up, to rehearse a couple of songs and party with the band back at their apartment.

"I won't go if you don't want me to," she said before she left. I had something going with a young fluegelhorn player who'd been at the bar for a couple of hours with some of her fellow musicians. They left; she and her girl friend had stayed. She had a cherubic face, green eyes, and dark eyebrows. Dressed in her black tux, carrying her horn, she was winsome, and impressed that I'd heard of Mendelssohn.

"It's okay," I said to Angelina.

She looked at the fluegelhorn player, who was looking at her, and said, "I'm jealous."

I knew the band and liked most of the guys. Something like the Grateful Dead, they were stuck in a time warp, all of them well past the age for playing rock and roll in a neighborhood bar. But they wrote their own songs, played with tremendous energy, loved what they were doing. Max was the leader, wild on the keyboard, a drinker, a doper, and a carouser. His father was a Presbyterian minister in Massachusetts, so sometimes late at night, when there weren't any women to chase, we would compare notes on fathers with strong belief systems. Angelina would be fascinated with him I knew, and he had fewer residual principles than I did, so I expected he would take her to bed.

I was wrong, of course. She took up with the bass player. Danny, like most bass players I've ever known, was mellow. He would play his music—usually without so much as a twitch except for running his fingers along the neck of the guitar and tapping his foot—while the rest of the band bounded around the stage like the Flying Karamazov Brothers somersaulting out of the wings to open their act. Danny leaned against his imaginary wall, his eyes closed, the bass purring out the sounds you feel in your soul, until you found yourself moving in rhythm to the rock beat of the music.

As I heard it, Danny and Max had been part of a crew running a howitzer 105 in Vietnam, both of them trying not to go deaf so they could play music again back home. A couple of years after the war, when Max arrived on the Upper West Side after ruining the family name in Barnstable, or wherever it was, he ran into his old gunner mate one afternoon on Broadway. They put together a band, called it The Hoods, and did pretty well, playing some downtown gigs at Tramps and the Bottom Line, and, of course, Oscar's three nights a week.

"Your girl friend ran off with that black bass player," Eric the Red told me, in case I'd missed it.

Eric was our Yugoslavian cook, a world traveler lifted up from sheep herding by Tito's revolution. He'd become a world-class hippie, his long black hair tied in a ponytail, sporting a stringy black beard that stood out stiffly from his chin and tapered to strings at the middle of his chest.

He'd slipped out of the kitchen to exchange my late night snack—escargot—for a healthy belt of cognac before Oscar returned to perch at the end of the bar until closing time.

"She's a real beauty. I'm sorry your heart is broken."

"She wasn't my girl friend. My heart isn't broken."

"She doesn't even talk to me," said Eric, "and mine is broken."

"I'm in love with a fluegelhorn player."

"Me, too," said Eric. "Where is she?"

"At the end of the bar."

He stroked his beard and gazed at her lovingly. "She's with a friend. We should all go to my apartment for breakfast, a joint, and Slivovitz."

We did just that. After we necked for a while on Eric's couch, I dropped the fluegelhorn player, whose name was

Cecilia, off at her apartment on 104th Street around five and ran into Angelina and Danny on Broadway, arms around each other, both of them so starry-eyed I didn't know if they'd even noticed me.

Pretty much sober myself by then, I read for a long time before I went to sleep and didn't wake up until four in the afternoon. Even though it was Thursday, I wasn't working that night because Phil, the other night guy, had asked me to switch.

I bought a steak at the market at 110th Street, and for the first time in months picked up a copy of *Variety* at the newsstand next door. I ate the steak, looked up auditions in the paper, and wondered about calling the fluegelhorn player. Instead, I went out around nine for a drink at the Terrace. Nick, the day guy, a long-time pal, was reading the next morning's *Daily News* at the corner of the bar. He slid it toward me when I sat down. The paper was open to page three, and the story he'd been reading was about the police finding Angelina's body Thursday morning in Riverside Park.

Chapter Two

I never left my barstool the entire night, just sat there with the paper in front of me, reading the story over and over again until my eyes stopped focusing. I didn't see the blood or the blows or the hands around her throat. It wasn't her death I imagined, but her terrifying anticipation of death, like a nightmare that turns you rigid, when you're so scared your voice won't work to scream, and you wake up finally in cold sweat but into familiarity and relief. But not for Angelina—no waking from her terror. She died with her scream frozen in her throat.

David, the night bartender, kept tuning me up with blow, so I woke up sick and terribly nervous Friday afternoon in Betsy Blumberg's bed. I'd been sleeping and waking fitfully during the morning, trying to make myself sleep instead of thinking about Angelina. The coke boiled inside me; I couldn't stand myself. I needed a Valium, and I needed to fuck Betsy. Good old Betsy came through on both counts.

She was in love with David Beattie, the bartender at the Terrace, but, on the frequent nights he found someone else to sleep with, she took whoever was left at the bar at closing time home with her for comfort; once in a while it was me. This morning—or afternoon—after we had fucked ferociously, and I had almost pulled her hair out while her nails dug long scratches into my back, I went back to sleep in her arms. When

I woke once more, we fucked again. Then she cooked me eggs and a steak.

"Today has been wild," said Betsy. She looked coy and pleased, sitting across her dinette table from me, her blue bathrobe carelessly tied so when she moved slightly it opened at the top, baring her breast. "You're becoming my number one beau."

"What about David?"

"He's a pig, and even when he does come here, he doesn't spend all afternoon…you know—" She smiled again.

"I know what?"

"You know…."

"What?"

"Fucking me. He doesn't spend all afternoon fucking me." Her smile was lascivious.

"The last time I was here I couldn't get it up," I reminded her.

"You made up for it." She rested her chin in her hands, elbows on the table, and looked longingly in my direction.

"I don't want to be your beau, Betsy."

"I know."

I concentrated on eating.

"I'm really sorry about Angelina," Betsy said tentatively. "The poor kid."

I didn't know why I'd spent the night with Betsy. I didn't know why I had to get laid the day after Angelina was killed. Bottomless pits were opening up just beneath my consciousness.

⌐⌐⌐

That night, a police sergeant introduced himself to me at the bar. Oscar clocked him the moment he entered. The first thing Oscar had said when I got to work was that the broad getting herself killed was going to get his place closed. Now, with a knowing grimace, he nodded toward the man in the door and buried his face in *The Racing Form*.

The cop introduced himself as Detective Sergeant Pat Sheehan. He had sandy hair, bluish eyes, stood a good few inches over six feet, and gave the impression that he had a perfect right to do whatever it was he might be doing, despite the chilling pall his presence cast over the bar. He might just as well have driven a squad car through the door.

He didn't order a drink or show me a badge, just settled like a searchlight into my eyes. "A woman named Angelina Carter was murdered in Riverside Park Thursday morning. Did you know her?"

"I'm sort of busy right now," I said politely. I was pretending that if I went back to work, he would go away.

Oscar squirmed and bounced on his stool at the other end of the bar, trying to hear everything and be inconspicuous at the same time. The cop looked at him. Everyone looked at him because he kept thumping around like a percolator.

"Can someone take over for you for a few minutes?" the cop said. "You are McNulty?"

I nodded and called Oscar, who sprang off his stool, then tried to act nonchalant as he came behind the bar.

"How do you know me?" I asked Sheehan when we sat down at a table. Except for his feet, which kept up a non-stop tapping under the table, he seemed at ease, uninterested in the impression he was making or in establishing any kind of rapport. He was intimidating without trying to be. I didn't know if he thought me the best witness or the prime suspect.

"You're the beneficiary on her life insurance policy."

"I'm what?"

"She had a five thousand dollar life insurance policy from the restaurant where she worked. She named you beneficiary." He sat back in his chair, tilted his head to the side, and watched me from this vantage.

"Why did she do that?" I didn't want money from Angelina being dead.

"You won't get the money until we find the killer."

"I don't want the money." When I said this, it occurred to me he might think I killed her for the money. "What do you want from me?"

"What can you tell me?"

"Nothing. I don't know who did it."

"Tell me anything you know, anything you think might be helpful." His face held an open, guileless expression you might mistake for simplicity, but his questioning was purposeful and measured.

"I don't know anything."

"When did you see her last?"

I wanted to tell him, but Oscar had sworn me to secrecy. It was a stupid delusion of Oscar's that the cops wouldn't figure out that she'd been in the bar. But at that moment Oscar carried more weight in my life than Sergeant Sheehan. "I don't remember," I said.

"Was she in here Wednesday night?"

"I don't remember."

He looked me in the eye long enough for me to avert my gaze. "Do you want the person who did this to be caught?"

I didn't want to tell him the truth, which was that I really didn't care. It wasn't going to help Angelina—so I didn't say anything.

He waited, looking me in the eye whenever I looked up at him, his expression patient.

"Were you in love with her?" he asked, really taking me by surprise. He looked right into my face when he asked, and I'm sure my face registered the changes I went through like a computer screen.

"I wasn't in love with her," I said, but my voice wavered.

Oscar had been rubbing the same section of the bar with the bar rag for about ten minutes watching us. When Sheehan left, Oscar came out from behind the bar. "What did you tell him?"

"I told him you did it."

Oscar didn't get immediately that I was kidding. His eyes went wide and his face lost some of its color. For all I knew, he had done it.

"I didn't tell him anything, Oscar. But he'll be back. Someone else will tell him she was here."

"We can say no," said Oscar, still scheming. This was the same Oscar who, when he burned the top of the Quiche Lorraine in the broiler, served it upside down on a bed of lettuce. "It'll be their word against ours."

The cop found me again the next morning at my apartment. It was almost noon but I'd drunk too much and hadn't gone to bed until six. My health was going downhill fast. If I didn't let my system flush itself out, I'd start shaking soon. Drinking in the morning to stop the shakes—a new horizon loomed. Looking at Sheehan through the peephole in the door, I imagined what had happened. He discovered that Angelina used to live with me, that everyone in the neighborhood thought we had something going. He'd found out she'd been in the bar talking to me most of the night I said she hadn't been there. Next, he'd check the FBI records and find out my father was a Communist. Everyone knows Communists never tell the truth.

"Sorry," he said when I opened the door. "I thought you'd be up by now." Once more, he had me at a disadvantage; this time, I was embarrassed because I was so obviously hung over. He seemed chipper, despite a probable lack of sleep, wearing the same rumpled gray suit but a fresh blue shirt, with a red knit tie replacing the blue knit tie of the night before. He didn't seem to like me very much.

"Everyone lies to me," said Detective Sergeant Sheehan.

"You haven't heard anything yet," I warned him. "Wait till you talk to Oscar."

"She was in the bar that night."

I nodded.

"Who was she with?"

"No one."

"Who did she leave with?"

"I don't know."

"Yes you do; she came over to say goodbye before she left with the band. Who'd you leave with?"

"That's personal."

"Did you see her after she left the bar?"

"No."

"Did you call her?"

"No."

"Did you go to her apartment?"

"No."

"Did she come to your apartment?"

"No."

"Did you look for her?"

"No."

"Who did she spend time with besides you?" Sheehan didn't smile or change his expression, which suggested he was already looking ahead to something and losing interest in me. Still, he questioned relentlessly, and I felt like a fraud.

"I'm going to find answers." Sheehan pulled himself up taller, seeming to take up most of my small foyer. "I'm going to know everyone who was in the bar and where they went after the bar closed. I'll know your personal business, too. I don't understand why you think it's cool to protect a murderer."

"Bartender's code. We only care whether they're good tippers."

When Sheehan left, I tried to figure out for myself what I was doing. I acted out of habit. Not helping the cops was something I'd learned growing up in Flatbush when the FBI crashed through the neighborhood telling everyone my father was a traitor.

When I arrived at work that night, Saturday night, I found Oscar at his corner of the bar with Sergeant Sheehan. Oscar spoke with a Spanish accent, had black hair, thick black eyebrows, and a pug's face. He told enormous lies and was impressed by financial successes like doctors and lawyers, and especially business men, some of whom, remembering him from the West End Bar during their college days, stopped by once in a while to say hello. He didn't mind gangsters but hated drug dealers, blacks, and cops. With Sheehan he was having trouble. I could tell by his gestures and the workings of his face muscles that he was telling bigger and bigger lies to get out of the lie he'd just been caught in. Oscar was talking about a lieutenant he thought he knew, while trying to ascertain if Sheehan was on the take so he might arrange something to keep his joint out of the murder case, so he wouldn't lose his liquor license.

If you carry yourself the right way as a bartender, after a while people forget you're there no matter what kind of secrets they're talking about.

"I don't care about your club," Sheehan said. "I just want one guy."

"I know, I know," said Oscar. "Me, too."

"Look, Oscar. I'm not on the take. I'm not after your joint. I just want the perpetrator."

Oscar wasn't so much unwilling to tell the truth—he just didn't recognize it. He refused to conform his view of things to someone else's idea of reality.

"The first time she was ever here," Oscar said, his thick eyebrows bobbing enthusiastically.

"She was a regular, almost every night," Sheehan said.

"She came in but never hung around." The eyebrows stopped.

"She was a friend of the bartender."

"He never paid attention to her." The eyebrows crept down over his eyelids.

"She used to live with him."

"He never let on." Oscar's eyes squinted closed.

When Sheehan left, Oscar leaned over the bar. "You got to tell the truth," Oscar said. "Tell him everything you know, or he'll have the place closed. He's a big man in the cops, a chief or something. You can't fool around with him."

"He's a sergeant."

"Yeh, but he's in charge of things—he's a big guy from downtown." Gazing out from under those eyebrows like he was peering out from under a rock, Oscar made sure no one was listening. "He knows who did it," he whispered.

"Who?"

"Reuben."

"Did the cop say that?"

"He didn't have to say. I know."

I didn't believe Oscar, but I began to wonder if Reuben did kill Angelina. He seemed capable of it. Most of Oscar's clientele—bitter, angry men, with lifetimes full of unresolved grievances—seemed capable of murder. Already, I knew two of our regulars were murderers, Sam the Hammer and Boss Abbott. There wasn't any reason to believe Angelina's killer frequented Oscar's. But Sheehan seemed to think it was as good a bet as any that the killer was one of Oscar's lost souls.

Standing behind the bar near closing time, I'd begun sifting through Oscar's rogues gallery for any hint that one of them had it in for Angelina when Nigel walked in with Carl van Sagan, just ahead of the nightly crew drifting back home for last call. Nigel looked like I felt, shaken and drawn, like he might be hung over. If he'd been drinking the night before, I was glad I'd missed it. With those thick glasses magnifying the grief in his eyes, he looked at me for sympathy, but I didn't want to talk to him, or anyone else, about Angelina. Nigel drank a ginger ale. Carl had scotch.

"Duffy showed up yet?" Carl asked. I'd known Carl for years. We'd been watching basketball games together at various corner bars since Earl Monroe began playing for the Knicks. Though we'd each left the neighborhood a few times, we'd always gravitated back. When I saw him now, it felt like we'd grown up together. Carl was my age but a bit heftier. He drank a good deal more than was good for him, but was a peaceful man and a thinker. He also possessed an amazingly expressive face. On his peaceful days, something in the cast of his eyes reminded me of Snoopy; on the days when the hustle of life in the Big Apple became too much for him, he thundered and blustered around the neighborhood like Captain Haddock. When he was thoughtful, he wrinkled his forehead, pursed his lips, and took on an owl-like guise.

He usually relieved Duffy the doorman at midnight, but tonight was his night off. Carl had trouble keeping track of what day it was because his shift started at midnight. The first week on the job he was off on Saturday, so he got drunk in Oscar's with me Friday night. When he went into work Saturday night, Duffy was mad as hell.

"What are you doing here now?" Duffy bellowed at him. "And where were you yesterday?"

"You sure this is your night off?" I asked Carl.

"No. But I don't give a shit." He took a sip of his drink and grimaced. He was in one of his Captain Haddock moods. "We're all being investigated."

"You, too."

"All the doormen on West End Avenue. We're watchdogs for the community."

"What did you see?"

"I saw Angelina."

"Did you tell the police?"

"No." He looked defiantly at Nigel.

Nigel had a higher opinion of law enforcement than the rest of us since he seemed to think of himself as a member of respectable society, so I, too, expected him to complain. But he didn't, just played with the lime section floating in his ginger ale.

Sam the Hammer, hunched into his Yankee windbreaker, drank coffee at the end of the bar next to Oscar, who was doping out the races for the next day at Belmont.

"They busted Boss," he told no one in particular. "They're closing his numbers joints."

We all sympathized in the way the neighbors might if Mrs. Murphy's plumbing went awry.

"Did he forget to pay someone?" Carl asked.

"The girl getting murdered," Sam said, still not looking up, as if he might not be talking to us after all. "They got to do something."

Everyone clammed up and looked at his drink when he said this. We hadn't talked much about Angelina, but she was on my mind, not far from the surface most of the time. I figured it was like that for everyone else, too.

Sam didn't have much to say beyond that; he was a guy who kept his own counsel, anyway. Distinguished in a certain New York City ne'er-do-well style, Sam wore his hair in a slicked-down, fifties DA, even though it was turning gray, as were his eyebrows and his salt and pepper walrus mustache. He knew about crime, Sam did. That is, he knew who did it most of the time—knew them personally. He might know who killed Angelina. But Sam was closed-mouthed; he would say what he wanted to say. If you asked him anything beyond this, he'd snort, hunch up further into his jacket, and might not speak to you again for a couple of days.

One of the reasons Sam came into Oscar's was because he liked Carl van Sagan. Carl was a writer, a poet who worked midnights as a doorman to support his muse. Sam told stories to Carl that I got to hear because I was the bartender. He wanted Carl to tell him how to write a book.

"A book about characters," Sam told Carl. "I know some real characters."

Carl raised an eyebrow.

"You're a writer, right?"

Carl nodded.

"Can you make any money at that?"

"I'm hoping to sell one of my poems to the movies," Carl said.

Nodding his head, pursing his lips, Sam looked Carl over. "I suppose not…"

Carl hitched up his glasses, wrinkled his forehead, which he did when he was interested in what was being said, and which gave him that owl-like look, and bought Sam a drink. The only time Sam drank was under such auspices.

"I just want to know how you write it down," Sam said after sipping his beer, the foam decorating his mustache as he turned to look at Carl with some earnestness. "I mean, do you got to start when the guy's born?"

His first character was Nick. "I told him they're going to build a statue of him in Greece. When those guys get off the plane there, he'll be right in front of them." Nick, it turned out, was a handicapper who went to the track with Sam, but who only gave tips to Greeks. "They love him," Sam said.

Carl wrinkled up his forehead, cleaned his glasses, and ordered another scotch. Sam wanted coffee.

When I got back with the drinks, they were talking about capital punishment.

Sam was in favor of it. "If I go back again, it'll be the third time," Sam said over his coffee cup. "That means for keeps. I'd rather be dead."

Listening to Sam talk to Carl, I found out how he'd gotten to jail in the first place. It was back in the Fifties when he thought he was a hot shot and went to work running numbers for Boss.

"Three guys jumped me in an alley behind the Terminal Bar down on 10th Avenue. They were going to kill me. They threw me against a loading dock. I looked down and there was a hammer. God must have put that hammer there. I picked it up and clobbered the guy closest to me.

"The cops came in the Terminal an hour later. They said, 'Hey, you with the hat on.' I did nine years for manslaughter."

Now he sat beside Oscar, who tried to ignore him. Sam was one of the many customers, like Reuben and all the Eritrean and Namibian refugees, Oscar didn't like. But he left them alone when they came in to see me. Oscar wouldn't fire me, even though he didn't like me either. He believed in the pre-eminence of the bartender, having been one himself, so he was afraid he'd lose all of the customers if I left.

This night, as I refilled Sam's coffee cup, he reached into the pocket of his Yankee jacket and handed me a napkin with "Briar Patch 2nd" written on it.

Oscar, looking over my shoulder, said he lost his shirt on the last tip Sam gave him. His dark eyes filled with sadness. He was in a mood to lament. "Someone being killed is the worst thing that can happen to a bar," he told us all.

Sam said there were shirts for sale at 96th Street, and crying towels too.

All of this was on the surface. No one said how sad it was that Angelina was dead. We didn't try to comfort one another. These were hard guys; they'd already suffered through the holes in their hearts. But, every few minutes, talk would stop. The men would stare into their glasses or at the bottles lining the back wall. Oscar would rattle the pages of *The Racing Form*. These moments, I knew, were for Angelina. We did miss her after all.

Later, after I'd done last call, I poured a final coffee for Sam and some for me and took a chance. "What do you think happened to Angelina?" I asked. It wasn't a question to ask Sam, and, up to this point, I'd been working pretty hard on pretending to myself I didn't care who killed her, so I was a little bit surprised at myself.

"She was crazy," Sam said. "You can't do those kinds of things."

"What things?"

"The weirdos."

I walked away from him to the other end of the bar. I felt that pang you get when you discover something terribly embarrassing about someone close to you. Sam seemed to think I knew what he meant, and I was too embarrassed for Angelina to ask.

At the end of the bar near the door, Nigel and Carl talked quietly. I heard Carl say she must have a family.

They're sending her body back to Springfield," Nigel said.

"That's gruesome," said Reuben across the semi-darkness from a couple of bar stools away. "It's just a fucking body now. What difference does it make what you do with it?" He was drunk and ugly, trying to provoke Nigel.

"Cut it out, Reuben," I said.

"That's what we all are. Nothing special—rot in a couple of days. In a week no one will remember her. You," he said to Nigel. "When you die, no one will remember the next day."

I sent Reuben home.

"Maybe we should send flowers," someone said from the darkness. Whoever it was, his words were slurred, so it took us a while to get his meaning. But, despite this heroic effort at community, it wouldn't work. The winos came anonymously to the bar precisely because there were no obligations. They wouldn't send flowers; they wouldn't go to her funeral if it was down the street. They wouldn't go to my funeral.

Carl van Sagan was thoughtful. He'd liked Angelina, too. Sometimes, after the bar closed, she and I stopped off to visit him in his little booth off the lobby in the big West End Avenue building where he worked.

"I think we should go to her funeral," Carl said.

"What did you say?" I asked, my first response to words that take me by surprise, even when I've heard them perfectly.

It took quite a while, until well after closing, till everyone was gone except Carl, for me to give in. I thought, at first, Angelina would go away from my life now that she was dead. Nothing connected me to her. But I couldn't get rid of the feeling that I owed her. I thought maybe I was supposed to have loved her after all and taken care of her—that my hard heart had helped kill her.

The next afternoon, Carl and I, both wearing borrowed suits, went to Springfield on a Peter Pan bus. We took a cab from the bus depot to a funeral home just outside the city in a town called Chicopee that looked like a set from a 1950s movie. I recognized a bank and a gas station, a liquor store and a bar. I saw a used furniture store, then a street of storefronts with drab displays behind foggy plate glass windows. In a men's apparel store, the mannequins wore fedora hats and loose fitting double breasted worsteds, as if they had been dressed shortly after World War II and hadn't changed since. This was what Chicopee felt like—frozen since World War II.

The cab entered a traffic circle of the every man for himself variety. Beyond it, a bridge crossed a quiet river; next to the bridge, a red brick mill, a vestige of the New England textile era, stretched out along the riverbank. We turned right and passed the Hotel and Restaurant Workers Union office. It, too, was in a storefront, next to a store that sold surgical equipment. The funeral home was a large, old house a short way up a hill. When the cabbie dropped us off, he promised to pick us up again in an hour and take us to a restaurant in walking distance of the bus depot.

A directory with a black background and gold borders listed Angelina's name. When I read it, I wished I hadn't come. I had to just stand there thinking about her being dead. I couldn't make the idea of it go away anymore. Carl walked ahead of me into the viewing room and up to the casket. He stood with his head down. I stood beside him, holding myself still to keep from running away. I didn't want to pray, and I didn't want to look at Angelina's dead body.

On our way in, we'd passed two women, one young, one older, sitting in the front row of chairs. All of the other chairs were empty. I didn't know how long we should stand in front of the casket. I didn't know what to do when I stopped standing there either.

Carl shifted on his feet beside me; finally, I turned and walked over to the older woman and asked if she was Angelina's mother.

"I knew Angelina in the city," I told her. "She was a good person. I'm sorry she's dead."

"Thank you," the woman said. Her eyes were expression-less; they seemed almost cold. I wondered if she felt responsible for her daughter's death.

"My other daughter, Janet," she said turning to the young woman next to her.

"Brian McNulty," I said, shaking her hand. This sister wasn't anything like Angelina. Very businesslike in her tailored suit that seemed very obviously not borrowed, she shook hands like a salesman. But her eyes were red-rimmed and puffy, her face pale and drawn.

"Did you know Angelina well?" she asked.

"Not very well," I said, while Carl mumbled his name to Mrs. Carter.

"Nice of you to come all the way from the city," the mother said.

Carl nodded, smiling, then thought better of it and wiped the smile off his face.

"She used to come into my bar," I said.

"Oh," said her sister in a tone that made me feel unwholesome.

"She sang there with a band sometimes," I mumbled.

"And you, Mr. —"

"Carl."

"Mr. Carl."

"Not Mr. Carl," Carl said. He was more flustered than I was.

"How did you know my sister, Carl?"

"From the bar…We were friends…She was really talented." Carl spoke earnestly and meant what he said, but it was lost on her.

Distaste dripped from sister Janet's words; brooding anger smoldered in her eyes. Yet I couldn't help noticing that, though this sister wasn't at all like Angelina, she was attractive in her own right. Nicely built, shapely, nice legs. But she didn't do anything with it—at least not for us. She carried herself with a mixture of elegance and aloofness, as if she'd been bred for respectability, her tone and manner suggesting she knew we were part of the seamier side of her sister's life. Her politeness was vague. I felt like a delivery man.

The mother, short and stocky, her hair tied in an efficient looking bun, her dark blue suit serviceable and nondescript, kept the empty expression on her face. I knew from Angelina that she was an office clerk, and she looked like one—the kind who goes by the book and can't bend the rules and takes it personally if you haven't paid your electric bill on time.

Some other, mostly younger people began arriving then, probably high school friends of Angelina's. Later, as Carl and I sat in the back row on cushioned folding chairs staring straight in front of us, guys in suits came in and with them women who looked accustomed to wearing high heels. These were friends of the sister. Janet hugged each of them in a way that suggested she was glad they came but felt funny about the hugging. None of them seemed the hugging sort either.

We shook hands with mother and daughter once more before we left. The mother smiled tightly. But something had changed in the daughter. She seemed more interested in me. Her eyes, still red and puffy, were almost friendly. "I'd like to talk a minute," she said. "I'll walk out with you."

She walked with Carl and me out onto the porch of the funeral parlor. A black car with a taxi light on the roof idled at the curb. Carl and I glanced at each other, then looked longingly at the cab.

"I'm coming to New York in a few days to pick up whatever might remain of Angelina's things," Janet Carter said. "Might I call you?"

"Me? Sure...I guess," I said.

A beseeching look, an entreaty, tears starting up in the corners of her eyes. I didn't like this. Carl was eyeing the cab like he might make a run for it. Janet Carter looked at me with those pain-filled eyes. "Poor, little Angel—" she began, then turned away, sobbing, her shoulders shuddering.

I patted her awkwardly on the back. "I'm sorry," I said. I didn't know what she wanted. I suppose at that moment she didn't either. But I couldn't turn her down, whatever it was.

I gave her my phone number and the phone number and address for Oscar's and left her standing, sniffling, on the porch. There was something about her, too, even in her sniffling. Strength, maybe. Determination not to give in to her sorrow? Anger? I couldn't tell. I wasn't sure I wanted to see this Miss Carter again. But I wasn't sure I didn't want to see her.

‿ ‿ ‿

At dinner in a surprisingly good German restaurant near the bus depot, Carl and I drank Wurtzburger drafts, direct from Germany, and ate weiner schnitzel.

When we were finished, Carl's expression turned owlish, so I expected something serious. "It would be better if Angelina's sister didn't come to New York," he said.

"Oh?"

He fidgeted a bit with what was left on his plate, then sloshed the beer around in his stein. "There's something you should know about Angelina," he said in a determined voice. "She acted in some movies for Boss and Rocky—" His eyes softened with sympathy. Maybe the shock I felt registered on my face. It was the shock of finding out what I couldn't believe but knew immediately must be true as soon as I heard the words.

Cheap sixteen-millimeter flicks made in the cellar of 811 West End Avenue. I knew about Rocky's flicks. I'd even, in my innocence, thought I was the one who first told Angelina about them. We'd sat in that cellar on a sagging filthy couch in the shadows of the giant boilers watching them once. A girl slapped around by two guys, until her tits hung out of her dress and the guys became frenzied like starving dogs and devoured her while she writhed, tied to the bed, panting, bleeding from her mouth.

When we walked home afterward, I told Angelina I didn't know why there were movies like that.

"Men get off on them," she said.

"I don't."

"It's better for men to watch that than to do it," she said. "Men are into really sick things."

I hadn't gone back. But I guessed now that Angelina had …or maybe she'd already been there, just protected me from knowing she was more depraved than I thought.

Rocky, when not a movie mogul, was the super of the building Carl worked in. He came into Oscar's every night, except the one night a week he went to visit his girlfriend in Staten Island, and drank anywhere from eight to a dozen Dewars. He'd been doing it for twenty years, Oscar told me. I marveled each night that his rotted liver didn't explode right in front of me. Reuben told me once that the day after Rocky got married he came home and found his wife in bed with someone else. "Right in his own bed," Oscar said, as if he'd been there. Reuben repeated it, "Right in his own bed." All of Reuben's unfaithful wives, it seemed, had enough savoir faire to use someone else's bed. Rocky had gone to sea after that, worked in the engine rooms of the big ships, studied during his sober times, eventually landed up in New York a stationary engineer peddling sadomasochistic bondage flicks on the side. Other women had acted for him, I knew, none as pretty as Angelina though. I couldn't guess why any woman would go near him. He was grimy, leering, missing half his teeth, mumbling and drooling and slurring words when he was drunk. He wore the same clothes all week and the cellar smelled of urine from the bottles he pissed in when he was too drunk to get off the couch. Yet other women had gone to him—and now Angelina.

ᔑᔑᔑ

On the way back to the city in the dim and shadowy light of the Peter Pan bus, Carl seemed much wiser than I was as he talked about Angelina. I discovered she visited him on many nights and spoke to him for hours at a time, sometimes all night long, in his booth off the lobby of 811. I was surprised by how much he knew about her.

"She wanted to do things," Carl said. "She wanted to be a singer. I told her to take lessons, and she did. She was really serious." Carl was serious also. He wrote for hours every night, had been to writing workshops, had published poems in small magazines. I admired him because he was his own barometer of success. I was even impressed that he liked me; it made me feel that I might not be altogether full of shit.

"Why did she have such a fucked up thing for men?" I asked, even though the answer no longer made any difference.

"She said she felt closer to you than anyone she'd ever known."

"I don't know what that means."

"It's what she said. It means she hadn't given up. She said you and I were the only men friends she had and that we'd changed her way of looking at men."

"Great," I said. "Do you think that's what got her killed?"

"I don't know."

"Do you know who killed her?"

"No. She couldn't stay away from fucked-up men. The part of her she could control, she worked hard on to become something. She really was quite remarkable. But the other part she couldn't do anything about."

Chapter Three

I was off Monday, the day after we got back from the wake in Springfield. On Tuesday night, about half an hour after I got to work, Janet Carter appeared. I saw her through the window walking down Broadway to the bar. She held herself straight when she walked, her arms swinging by her side, taking long strides, her shoulders back. She wore gray slacks and a black jacket that on a man would be called a sports jacket.

My mind dreaded the sight of her. She meant trouble, no question about it. Yet my heart quickened. I kept my eye on her from the moment I spotted her, lest by some chance she not come in after all. When she opened the door, conversation stopped and heads turned.

"Good evening," she said, holding out her hand like a businessman again. "Do you remember me?"

Sitting herself down on a corner barstool, she took stock of the place with what I sensed was mild disapproval, then looked at me questioningly. "Do you always work behind the bar?"

"I'm the bartender."

"Oh." She looked confused. "I thought you owned the bar."

I didn't know why she would think that.

"You said I should come to your bar. I thought you meant you owned it."

I poured her a dark rum and grapefruit juice and braced myself. She'd put on a good bit of make-up, but it didn't hide the reddened eyes and the puffiness beneath. She had a professional kind of presence. I wouldn't say it was a false front. But it was automatic: a smile, a handshake, a way of giving her full attention, as if what you said must be really important. I didn't know what she did for a living. But she was polished, used to making her way in some area that used to be a man's world. Much of this style was muted by the toll Angelina's death had taken on her. But, like I said, how she presented herself was automatic. She was charming without trying, without even thinking about it.

"I'm not sure this is the right place to find out much about your sister," I said. "I didn't know her that well. She took singing lessons, I know. She worked further downtown.... You'd probably find out more about her down there." I was tiptoeing around because I didn't want big sister Janet to find out too much about Angelina's habits in Sin City, and I especially didn't want one of Oscar's blabbermouths to spill the beans about Rocky's porno flicks.

"Angelina was here the night she died," Janet said by way of establishing that she was settling in for a while. "Who were her friends? Did anyone here now know her?"

"She wasn't here that long," I said, groping for an answer that sounded like it said something without actually doing so. I'd become an oracle—except I taught untruth. "People knew her, I guess. I don't know who all were friends."

"Do you know if she had a boyfriend?"

"I think she was sort of shopping around."

"Did she try you for size?" Janet Carter arched an appraising eyebrow.

Even though I didn't say anything, she seemed to have her answer. I began to think a red light lit up on my forehead when I toyed with the truth.

Nigel picked that moment to arrive. He was a pretty good yacker so, while I would have preferred Carl, Nigel would do, certainly better than Reuben or Oscar or Sam the Hammer. Self-effacing as usual, and in much better shape than the last time I'd seen him, Nigel perked up immediately—as all of the regulars would—as soon as he spied the new and pretty female face at the bar.

Janet Carter carried herself well, and her body fit nicely into her more relaxed clothes, her breasts straining just so slightly against her silk blouse that was open along her neck, her jacket tapered along her hips. She was good to look at, though some hardness in her manner suggested not easily touchable. She flashed him a brief smile, and Nigel beamed.

"He knew your sister," I told Janet, and Nigel's face dropped like I'd kneed him in the balls.

I didn't blame him. One of the advantages a bartender has is control of the conversation—he can get two people next to one another talking or arguing then walk away to the end of the bar. For them, committed more or less to their chosen barstools, walking away is not so easy.

I hoped Nigel would keep her busy with small talk, so she wouldn't get a chance to pump the regulars for any real information. He usually had a lot to say. Every situation that came up reminded him of something that had happened to him in the past. His stories weren't boring, but they somehow never related to him, the teller. If he told of getting stoned with the Allman Brothers or driving from Chicago to Minneapolis with Jerry Garcia, you thought it was exciting or interesting but it did nothing to alter your opinion of Nigel who was telling the story. He still seemed wimpy and uninteresting.

But my plan didn't work. She got away from him, managing to accost Reuben and Duffy, the Boss, and even Oscar. She created discomfort, not unlike Sheehan, as she went from one bar stool to the next. She paid no attention to the clear differences in class and style, not seeming to notice how the winos reacted—as if the madam of the house had descended into the servants' quarters.

"All of these men knew Angelina," she said well into the night when she came to rest on her barstool after floating from one end of the bar to the other for a couple of hours. She didn't seem concerned that I'd misled her. "Everyone is so nice."

Ignoring her sociable smile, I watched instead the sadness and rage hiding in her dark eyes.

"Did you find out all you need to know?" I asked, suspecting she hadn't found out much.

"I'm not really sure what I found out." Her expression grew quizzical as she thought over what she'd heard. "Everyone talks in riddles." She'd just spoken to Sam, and before that Oscar, so the longer she thought it over the less sure she would be.

Just like god damn Sheehan to pick that moment—when I thought I might hustle her out of the joint—to saunter in and sit down beside her.

"Hello, McNulty," he said, wiping at the bar in front of him with his fingers as if it might be sticky. "Had a couple of days off?" I waited for him to acknowledge that the bar was clean. "Went to the girl's funeral I understand." He leaned forward onto his elbows. "Nice gesture...See anyone from the neighborhood?"

Janet hadn't taken her eyes off Sheehan since he sat down, so it didn't take him long to sense her interest. Turning to her with a more engaging manner than I thought him capable of, he held out his hand and said, "I'm Detective Pat Sheehan."

"I'm Janet Carter. Are you investigating my sister's murder?"

"Yes. I am," he said. He looked her over in an appraising sort of way that I thought she should find offensive, but she didn't seem to notice, or care if she did notice.

She didn't take her eyes off his face. Her own face was rigid.

"I'm surprised to see you in New York. In fact, I've just finished reading a statement you gave to the Springfield police this morning."

"Do you know who killed her?"

"No."

"I want to find out," Janet said. Her voice shook, and she seemed to freeze over. It was rage—anger so deep and brooding that it surprised me. She'd been wearing a pretty convincing mask, this poised professional from Massachusetts. For that moment, she seemed as tough as Sheehan.

"So do we," said Sheehan. "Maybe you could convince McNulty here and his cronies to cooperate."

When she turned to look at me, the rage was still in her eyes, but it wasn't directed against me as I expected it to be; it went inward. She went after herself, a look of bitterness you might associate with failure or despair or self-hate. She might fit into Oscar's after all.

Sheehan stood up and without speaking to me walked to the end of the bar toward Oscar, said something to him, then left the bar without looking at me again.

When he left, Janet nursed a drink and brooded for a long time. She seemed to have lost interest in conversation but did tell me she'd be in town for a couple of days, staying at a hotel in the Sixties, the Empire, next to Hanrahan's.

Trying to cheer her up with a bit of New York City lore, I told her it was the hotel the ballet dancers stay in when they come to town to dance at Lincoln Center. I'd always wanted to work at Hanrahan's, mainly because of the ballet dancers, but also because of the name. Its full name was Hanrahan's Baloon. Legend has it that they told Hanrahan, who'd just put the name of his new joint—Hanrahan's Saloon—in lights, that he couldn't use the word saloon because saloons are against the law in New York. So Hanrahan, rather than paying for a completely new sign, changed the S to B.

Janet said she picked the hotel because Hanrahan's was the last place Angelina worked, and went back to nursing her drink.

Around one, I put her in a cab right in front of Oscar's, and, under the delusion I worked for the Visitor's Bureau, asked her to have lunch with me the next day.

She seemed surprised and thought about it for a minute before she said yes, her response bringing a sparkle of light to her eyes and a flush of color to her cheeks.

"I'll pick you up at the hotel around two," I said.

"Isn't that a little late?"

"I thought it was early myself."

☙☙☙

We ate lunch at an American Restaurant in the Seventies, one of a chain of Upper West Side Greek coffee shops, a kind of upscale greasy spoon. On the walk up Broadway, I pointed out the Ansonia Hotel, one of the West Side's most intriguing buildings, which was across the street from the Central Bank building where my socialist dentist had his office.

After Janet's lunch and my breakfast, we walked to Central Park. This time, I showed her the Dakota, where John Lennon once lived—realizing, when her face crumbled, that I wasn't doing a very good job of steering her away from thoughts of death and murder.

Next, I pointed out the Inn on the Park, where I'd once worked. The inn has white Christmas lights in the trees all year round, lots of floor to ceiling windows, sparkling chandeliers, and crystal vases with fresh flowers every day. We stood for a long time looking at it.

"It's beautiful," she said. There were tears in her eyes.

"It's a shit hole," I told her. "I used to make piña coladas in a five gallon pail, using the bar boy's broom handle to stir them, the same broom I used to chase the rats out of the garden..."

She wasn't shocked by my outburst, just looked at me curiously, as if not sure why I'd say such a thing. I wasn't sure myself, except I didn't like that she was impressed by the glitter. I wanted her to know what it was like behind the glitter.

Janet Carter, dressed for an afternoon walk in slacks and a dress shirt with a sweater over it, had an air of casual, well-groomed confidence that I normally didn't like. There was something vacant in how she was also, as if an important part of her was somewhere else. Me, I felt left over from the night before, red-eyed and murky of mind, flabby and out of sorts.

When we walked across Strawberry Fields, this profound sadness caught up with me: for Angelina, for John Lennon, for the day not long after John Lennon was murdered that a couple of thousand of us stood in front of the Dakota singing "Give Peace a Chance."

For that moment, tasting sadness, climbing a grassy hill in the cool sun of a New York City autumn, for that moment, I felt unbearably lonely; I felt sad for everyone, and hopeless, and I shivered from fear that rippled through me like a chill.

"Why'd you come to New York?" I asked Janet, who, head down, her own expression far from cheerful, climbed the hill beside me.

"I don't know—to get whatever my sister left behind, I guess." She started to say more but stopped, as if she couldn't make up her mind what she should say if she did go on.

"I was afraid Angelina would be killed in New York…" she said suddenly, out of nowhere. We stopped on the hill and she faced me, her expression stony, her body going rigid. "…I tried to stop her. I feel like it's my fault…I feel like it's my fault she was murdered."

"How could it be your fault?"

"I told her not to come."

"You told her not to come, and she came anyway."

"I had a premonition—"

"Premonitions don't mean anything," I said—not something you should say to a visibly distraught, not-far-from-the-edge premonition believer.

"No," she said, all too calmly. "Angelina and I were really close. We had premonitions about what might happen to one another. It happened enough times that we both believed them."

This businesslike and self-assured professional woman had come unstrung for the moment. I was embarrassed for her and turned away. I didn't want to hear about premonitions. If there were such things, why didn't Angelina have a premonition about going to the park with someone who was going to murder her?

"I need to find out for myself what happened," Janet said to my back. It seemed that once she got started explaining herself, she needed to keep going until she was sure I understood.

So I understood: guilt and anger brought her here. She came to the city to wear out whatever guilt she had.

"You can wait just as well in Massachusetts and find out what happened to your sister. You don't need to be here."

"I know I should be here...." Her eyes reddened, so she began walking away from me. After a few steps, she straightened her shoulders and turned around. "I have to find out what happened. I knew my sister better than anyone. I'd be able to help...I'd know things others wouldn't know. I'd do anything to find her killer. Anything." Her voice shook with anger; her eyes flashed with challenge.

"Why? What good will it do if you do find the killer? It won't bring her back. Angelina will still be dead."

Janet Carter turned on me. "How can you say that? You don't care about finding the killer? You wouldn't rip him apart? You wouldn't kill him with your own hands if you knew?...What kind of man are you?"

I started walking.

In a little while, she caught up with me. "I'm sorry," she said. "I feel so horribly awful...I can't bear it...I don't know what to do."

"I'm sorry, too. I don't know what you do with this kind of sadness. But I do know what you shouldn't do, and that's come down here and start rummaging around looking for someone who might be a killer. You're not going to find whoever it is—and even supposing you're able to, the odds are the murderer will find out about you long before you find him—or her—so you could get yourself murdered. The good offensive guy beats the defensive guy because the offensive guy knows where he's going and the other guy doesn't."

Janet, purposeful again, sized me up. "I'm not a fool. That analogy doesn't make sense." She glared at me. But, this time, something behind the glare reached out to me. It was as if she asked for help. The expression reminded me of Angelina; that was her expression too.

"Let the cops handle it. This is the kind of case cops solve. If your sister was black and got murdered in Brooklyn, it might be a different story. But she's young and white and pretty, and got killed in a neighborhood where people with money live, so the murder is a big deal for the papers. Then it becomes a big deal for the cops. They'll find a murderer."

"God, you're so cynical—"

Here was this attitude again: Ms. Success. She'd done okay in life, why couldn't everyone? The cops not care about poor black people? Who'd believe such a thing? Angelina wasn't like that. Angelina knew all along what was on the other side of the glitter.

We'd completed our trek to the top of the hill, so Janet sat down on a bench we found there. "I like to walk," she said. A combination of words and action I thought was at least as contradictory as my basketball analogy.

"If you think the police will find who killed my sister, why did that detective say you wouldn't help him?"

"Number one, I don't know much he won't find out anyway. And number two, I don't know what he's looking for."

"What does that mean?"

"It has to do with being cynical."

Janet looked at me significantly. "You know more about Angelina than you told him or you're telling me. Why won't you tell me about my sister? Don't you trust me either?" Her tone wasn't angry, but she looked into my eyes the way Sheehan did until I stopped looking at her.

"If you won't tell me about her, I'll tell you." She liked to talk, this big sister from Massachusetts. Under the blue sky, in the declining autumn sun, on a park bench above the Sheep Meadow, Janet Carter blurted out her story.

"My father took care of me before he died. He left money for me to go to college in a trust fund. He didn't leave anything for Angelina...He never really cared about her. ...Angelina didn't even remember him because he left my mother right after she was born, so my mother wouldn't let him see Angelina after he did that." She sighed.

"They had a pretty stormy relationship. My mother is very demanding and high strung—and I guess my father had a temper. Angelina came along when they already hated each other. My father left us and said he wasn't Angelina's father. That's how the poor kid started out in life, something for my mother and father to fight over.

"Was he? Was your father Angelina's father?"

"My mother said he was, and there weren't any other men in her life. My mother doesn't like men very much, so I'm sure he was. He just hated my mother so much he didn't want to believe it—so he ignored Angelina." Janet looked down at the stubble of grass beneath her feet.

"He loved me, though. He began telling me when I was five that I would go to college. Then, after they broke up, he told me that whenever I saw him, all through grade school. My mother really hated that."

Janet raised her eyes. "A big part of their problem was my mother really thought she married beneath her. She thought she was the perfect everything. She thought my father should have a better job and make more money. She went nuts when she discovered he'd saved so much money for me. He worked in the post office. Then he died when I was sixteen.... My father was the only thing in my life I didn't share with Angelina. I regret that now...I should have...She always wanted to be with him, but I liked having him for myself." Tears seeped from the corners of Janet's eyes, so I left her with her memories for the moment and watched the edge of the city beyond the park.

She gathered herself together after a few minutes and started in again. The older sister by almost ten years, she'd more or less raised her baby sister until she went to college. Some of what she told me I knew already from Angelina: the molestation that was the centerpiece of her life. But Janet told me something Angelina hadn't.

"I know this is impossible to believe but the boy who molested Angelina wasn't a terrible ogre…I mean, he was an ogre…but he wasn't a pervert who jumped her as she walked down the street. Angelina knew him. He was a college student who met her in the park. It was past the dying days of the Sixties, past the end of the hippie days when everyone loved everyone. But Angelina loved what she knew of the Sixties and wanted so much to be grown up and part of it. When she was four or five, she wore love beads and peasant dresses. By the time she was ten, with lipstick, she was so pretty—a real baby doll—and she was stunning. Although you wouldn't mistake that she was a child.

"For months, Angelina talked about her friend in the park. No one paid much attention. And then, she began calling him her boyfriend…I was the one who knew he'd done it …All of a sudden, she was in a tiff, mad at her boyfriend, but too grown up about it…It was too much like a jealous woman's anger. I got Angelina to tell me because I already knew…That's how close I was to her. I could feel what she felt."

"How did she feel about being raped?"

Janet started and lost her footing. She seemed troubled by the word. "I guess she didn't think she was raped…She thought she had a boyfriend."

"Didn't anyone explain the difference to her? Did she get counseling?"

"No. My mother said she didn't need it…It was the boy who was sick. I guess he was sick. He was from a really respectable family, my mother said…His father worked things out with my mother…He went into some kind of hospital, I guess, after it happened. We never talked about him again. I imagine the whole thing ruined his life."

"Angelina's, too."

Janet kept her thoughts to herself for a minute, watching the buildings and the traffic on the far side of the park, as I did.

"So you think this closeness will work a second time? You'll intuit who the murderer is? You'll get a premonition?"

"I'm not saying that…My sister and I were very close, Brian…I'm not going to let anyone forget what happened to her…I'd know things that other people wouldn't know…I might see something no one else would see."

"Why don't you know what she did in New York then?"

Again, she looked startled. For a moment, she hemmed and hawed. "I do… At least I know some things about what she did here. She wrote to me…" She looked me straight in the eye. "Actually, I knew of you before I ever saw you…"

The spell broke. I'd been conned. Now, I didn't like this Janet Carter at all, this superior-acting upper-crust lady from Massachusetts, this pillar of respectability.

"I suppose I should have told you," she said in what must be her most professional tone.

"I don't give a fuck what you tell me. This is New York… No one tells anyone the truth…You get used to it." I'd let my guard down and Janet Carter got a couple of steps ahead of me. Lots of fancy footwork. Pop would tell me I was out of my element, like with the kid con men on Flatbush Avenue when I was growing up. "Life made them sly and cunning and tough," Pop said the times I told him I'd been swindled. "You wouldn't want their lives." Why this maxim applied to a proper young lady from Springfield, I wasn't sure. But I knew now she chose carefully what she told me; she didn't innocently gush out her life story.

"Why did Angelina come to New York?" I asked.

This time, I'd caught her off guard, and her eyes that had been looking into mine shied away for a second. "I'm not sure…She wanted to become something, an actress, a singer…"

I'd had enough. "Why don't you sit down with Sheehan and tell him everything you know?" I said. "That might get him moving in the right direction." I had no reason to spar any longer with Janet Carter, I decided. She had her own agenda.

She smiled a superior smile. "Why don't you?" And walked away.

⌐⌐⌐

That night, Janet was in Oscar's again. Not particularly interested in me, except for ordering a beer now and again, most of the time paid for by one of the winos, she spent the evening in casual conversation with the regulars. For most of the first part of the night, with Ozzie Jackson. He kept crying and was too drunk to talk, even though he kept sputtering a language of some sort at Janet. I could tell by the bewildered way she looked about her she had no idea what he was talking about.

Ozzie Jackson hailed from Arkansas or Alabama—I get them mixed up—and did something downtown that made him a lot of money. Word had it that he was an executive at Manufacturers Hanover. He'd never said what he did, and I'd never asked. He spoke in a Southern accent, waved his glass around when he spoke, said "har, har" fairly often, called me a "son of a gun" fifteen times a night. With his horn-rimmed glasses, his sandy hair and cowlick, and his friendly Southern face, he had a startled look about him, something like a bird, eyes darting, body tensed, ready to scatter, feathers fluttering, at the slightest sound. He looked almost boyish before he got himself sloppy drunk, and a lot more respectable than he actually was. I don't think I'd ever seen him leave the bar sober.

In all the months I'd worked at Oscar's, I never saw Ozzie sit down either. He drank his Jack Daniels standing up and talked standing up, most of the time incoherently.

Then one night—the night he first met Angelina—he told me about his wife. "You old son-of-a-gun," said Ozzie when I'd given him his drink on the house.

"That's on us," I said.

"You old son-of-a-gun," Ozzie said again, waving his glass in my direction.

"How've you been, Ozzie," I asked, even though I knew that no attempt at conversation would persuade Ozzie to talk sense.

Yet this time was different. Angelina had just left the bar, stopping to kiss me on the cheek on the way out. I thought this might be why he was son-of-a-gunning me, but there was really no telling what he meant. I stood in front of him for a few minutes while he har har harred and called me an old son-of-a-gun a couple of more times.

Then, speaking perfectly clearly, he said, "I married a girl who was fifteen."

"Good for you, Ozzie," I said.

"She died when she was sixteen."

This was all he told me; he went back to talking gibberish and never mentioned it again.

But he really took a shine to Angelina, treated her like a princess, buying her drinks all night any night she chose a barstool next to him. She liked to talk to him, too, sitting beside him while, one foot on the railing and his arm on the back of her chair, he leaned toward her, laughing and listening, calling her an old son-of-a-gun, talking nonsense, and buying her drinks. Now, I wondered if he was telling Janet about Angelina or about his wife. She'd probably never know.

Learning things about people when their defenses are down and their brains addled is a little like the priest hearing confession. At least according to the old school, it went this way. Telling secrets learned over the bar violated a public trust. If someone got stupidly drunk the night before, you didn't bring it up the next day unless he did. If Reuben got himself slapped by one of the Barnard girls, you didn't gossip about it. If Betsy, a little tipsy, necked at the corner of the bar with a stranger, she wouldn't be reminded of it the next day. The Boss could drop his coke vial in the men's room; if I found it, it was discreetly returned. Sam the Hammer was not reminded that the absolutely sure thing in the fourth race ran out of the money. If Carl hadn't made a payment on his tab in three or four weeks, nothing was said when he needed a drink. You take up the stick deaf and leave it dumb, the old bartenders said.

~ ~ ~

Somewhere during this night, when Janet Carter had so clearly lost interest in me, I found myself trying to get it back. I started after her with no more forethought than I used in taking a few hits from the Boss's coke vial or a couple of shots of tequila with Eric the Red as the night waned.

This particular combination left me more talkative than usual and more enamored of Janet Carter than might be wise. She wore lipstick this night, which she hadn't that afternoon, and the red of her lips made her eyes a darker and a more sparkling brown. She wore a dress also, a pretty flowery dress that drifted and floated around her legs when she walked— not at all like the crisp blue suit that was all straight lines and stiff material or the sexless slacks and blouse she wore in the afternoon.

She stayed until closing time, winding up sitting between me and Eric the Red, sipping a beer, while we had a couple of after-closing drinks. I sat close to her and felt her leg brush against mine and smelled the flower water scent she gave off. Though I was surprised she stayed with us, I understood why she'd put off being alone. I also understood that, for the moment, she wanted to talk about something other than Angelina.

She began to talk about New York. Visitors do this a lot, almost by way of apology for all the nasty things they said to their friends and neighbors before they got here. On this night, tourist Janet said Springfield was culturally deprived, and she liked New York because there were plays and museums, concerts and the ballet, things that people in Spring-field didn't care about. It was an old factory town filled with boring factory workers.

She probably didn't mean to be offensive. But I thought she was condescending and reminded her that factory workers, busting their asses to keep alive, didn't get the chance to do the things she'd experienced.

"You're making me sound like an elitist." She looked from Eric to me. Eric, pretty well sloshed to begin with, leaned toward her, as if to commiserate.

Leaning away from him, she moved closer to me, looking sincere and almost relaxed for the first time since I met her; the tautness gone from her face; her mouth soft and sensuous instead of tight-lipped. "I'm not," she insisted. "I believe everyone should have opportunities and help. But you don't get something for nothing. People who have advantages worked hard to get where they are."

"You don't think folks work hard in factories? They don't work as hard as your crew—those plastic people in expensive suits, shoring up capitalism and eating quiche and guacamole?"

Eric growled agreement.

Janet and I argued for an hour. She accused me of cynicism and bitterness and having no respect for people who were successful. Her spirit showed through. She liked arguing more than I did, enjoyed the exchange of ideas, so to speak. I don't like arguing. I'm not particularly fond of my beliefs; I just can't get rid of them. They came from my father and follow me like a specter.

"You can't say that no one in all of business cares about their employees. You can't say no rich person cares at all about poor people."

"I just did. If they really cared, they'd do something. They don't care about anything but making money—"

"Now, wait just a minute," said Janet. "I happen to know you're wrong. I work for a large commercial bank and we're devoted to serving our community. We raise money for charities. We support education and cultural activities. Our employees go into the schools on their lunch hours to help poor children learn to read—" She was taking a breath for a second wind when Eric interrupted her.

In his eagerness for the discussion and frustrated by not having the language to get his thoughts out, snarling and growling and gesturing with his thick hands, he lunged at her like Quasimodo's younger brother. In guttural tones, pounding on the bar and staring into her eyes, tapping her shoulder when she tried to look away, he explained how Tito had taken the land from the banks and given it to the farmers like his father. "There would be no schools for the peasants if not for Tito," he said, as if this might explain everything. "I could never read or write...I could not come to America."

Still, slightly tipsy in an Upper West Side neighborhood bar, long after four in the morning, sitting between a confirmed Titoist and an American cynical anti-establishmentist, Janet held her own pretty well, refusing to give up her reasonable positions. "You can't hate the whole establishment," she told me with finality.

I did. But what was the point in telling her, who, it turned out, made a pretty good living as public relations director for a Massachusetts banking corporation? I should have known better. You don't talk about religion or politics if you want to stay sane as a bartender. But here I go again. I'm the only bartender in Manhattan who gets red-baited. I couldn't wait to tell Pop I'd spent the evening trying to convert a banker to socialism. Well, if nothing else, I consoled myself, it took her mind off her sister's murder for a while.

But not for long. Over breakfast at Tom's, under her prodding, I did tell her more of what I knew about Angelina's life in New York and how she might have gotten herself killed by taking too many chances on too many people. I told Janet her sister was a lost and lonely girl driven by compulsions having to do with men and sex that she couldn't control. She did dangerous things, picking up men in bars almost every night; and the bars were filled with men who hated women; that was how most of the drinkers got there. They hated women for being pretty and not belonging to them. Some were driven crazy because a girl like Angelina wouldn't sleep with them, others because she would, and still others because she slept with someone else. The bars of New York were filled with suspects. Then, I told Janet, honestly, I didn't know much about Angelina's life, except what I knew from Oscar's.

"But you could find out…" Janet said eagerly. She leaned across the table toward me. I tried to back up into the corner of the booth. But she was having none of it. "You know these neighborhoods. You know the nightlife and who the players are. You could find out a great deal."

"And why would I do that?"

Into the restaurant, at this moment, came Max and Danny. They stopped beside the booth to say hello but didn't sit down with us. I asked if they were playing at Oscar's tomorrow night. Max said yes.

"They're the ones my sister left the bar with the night she was killed," Janet said as they walked away. "Have you asked them about what happened?"

I told her I hadn't, but I thought the police had talked to them.

"Do you think they'd talk with me?" Practically quivering with excitement, she craned her neck to look over at them, then back at me.

"You'll have to ask them."

She squirmed in her seat for another minute or two and kept looking over at them. They sat across from one another in a booth and didn't seem to have much to say. Max had his long legs stretched out into the aisle. He looked bored. They both looked sober.

"I'm afraid to go ask them," Janet said. "What should I do?"

"Go back to Massachusetts."

This was enough. She got up and walked over to their table. Max looked up for a minute or two while she stood nervously in front of them, explaining who she was and that she wanted to know about her sister. Max didn't move, but Danny slid over to let her sit down.

When I'd told Janet about Angelina, I'd made it a point
not to mention the porno flicks, nor did I tell her I'd seen
Angelina with Danny. I didn't tell her about the porno flicks
because I couldn't bring myself to say it. As for not telling
her about Danny, I was pretty sure no one else saw him with
Angelina, so I wasn't going to be the one to blow the whistle.
The cops would pick him up as soon as they knew. Black junkies
make good suspects. They're always guilty of something.

Janet talked with Danny and Max for five or ten minutes
before I wandered over. Max made room for me. I didn't
interrupt, just listened. Max did the talking. Angelina would
have been great with the band, he said. They'd even worked
out a couple of arrangements that night. They'd smoked a
joint and had some beer. But nobody got wasted. He didn't
think Angelina even drank anything. Danny said she didn't.

"When did she leave your place?" Janet asked. Max looked
at Danny. Maybe Max didn't stiffen. Maybe Danny didn't
look at me. I was on my fourth cup of the Greek's coffee,
which is about the hallucinating level anyway. I could have
imagined it all. Danny looked back down at his uneaten eggs.
Max said she left around five. Maybe four thirty.

"Did she say where she was going?" Janet asked.

"I thought she was going home," Max said. Danny began
eating his eggs but he looked at me once more. He chewed
his eggs like they were alive and he had to wrestle them down
before he could swallow. It might have been my imagination,
too, but I thought Janet listened most intently to Danny Stone,
who had only spoken a few words.

⌐⌐⌐

While we stood waiting for a cab on Broadway, Janet took
my arm in her hands and made me look at her. Her face was
tired and soft. In her weariness, she resembled Angelina again;
some of her little sister's vulnerability showed through. "I know
you were kind to Angelina, and I'm very grateful." She didn't let
go of my arm, just stood there while her eyes filled with tears
again. "I know you think there's nothing you can do…

"But you could…I know it's terrible to ask when you've already said no…but I have to go back to Massachusetts to work tomorrow…" She stopped talking to get her voice under control again. She steeled herself. I could see the resolve flow into her eyes pushing the tears aside. "The men in the restaurant…the band. They weren't telling me everything. I could see it in their eyes.…In the bar, too, I could tell.…Those men knew things about Angelina they wouldn't tell me.…I'm sure they wouldn't tell the police either—but they'd tell you."

"Maybe they would. Maybe they wouldn't. What good would it do?"

"It would mean someone cared enough to find out what happened to Angelina, that everyone didn't forget she existed, like her life meant nothing—that whoever did this would pay."

"Like in vengeance?"

"Yes, vengeance—" She tried to spit the word out so it sounded bitter and hate-filled, so it would carry her rage and hate out into the night. But it didn't work. The word sounded flat and empty to me.

Again, I said, "Angelina will still be dead."

She stared at me while her own eyes went empty in her head. I wanted her to say something. This wasn't how I wanted this to end up. I started to speak, but it wouldn't do any good. She held back her tears but didn't trust her emotions enough to say anything, just stuck out her hand for another banker's handshake and walked away.

⌐ ⌐ ⌐

After I watched her cab head downtown into what was left of the Broadway night, I walked uptown on my way home. Near 110th Street, I noticed a group of men on one of the benches in the island in the middle of Broadway. I thought they were the usual bag people and bums who hung out on the streets panhandling, so I fished around in my pockets for some quarters for when they came upon me.

Instead, this voice from the Broadway bums cried, "Hey Brian." Sam the Hammer sat on a bench with the Boss. I went over.

The Boss, who is small and thin and has a kind of olive complexion that might make him Latin or Arab or Greek or even Black, did not get up. He sat on the park bench in the middle of Broadway as if he were in his office sitting behind a desk.

"You're a good guy, McNulty," the Boss said.

Uncomfortable because I didn't know what he was up to and embarrassed because I did in a weird way enjoy his praise, I waited.

"This little girl's murder was a terrible thing…such a pretty thing…really wild about you, too." The Boss didn't look at me when he spoke. This made me nervous, as did his manner of speaking, because he went off on tangents and became elliptical. He left big clumps of information out of what he was saying when you weren't really sure what he was talking about in the first place. "I like you, McNulty. These other guys don't know.…They talk like they know something. You told that guy it was smoke.…Smoke he told him," the Boss said to Sam and chuckled.

I didn't know what the Boss was talking about, but I knew, as sure as I stood there, that he was warning me.

"A shoe salesman," the Boss said and chuckled again. This one, I remembered. One of the college kids had discovered the Boss was connected, as they say, and was drunk enough to bother him. He asked me if it was true, and I told him I thought the Boss was a shoe salesman. The Boss had overheard.

"I'm fifty-three," the Boss said. "A man of peace.…They all come to me.…I tell them I'm a man of peace." He looked at me through his half-closed eyes for confirmation, so I agreed with him.

"The cops think I know something. What do I know?" This time he waited for an answer with his eyes closed.

"I don't know what you know," I said.

He chuckled good-naturedly. "They all want to know what I do."

"I don't know what you do," I said. He laughed once more, taking out his coke vial, shoving some up his nose with his little spoon. He handed it to me, but I said no, I wanted to sleep.

"You're smart," he said, "because you don't ask questions and you don't know answers." He seemed finished when he said this, leaning back on the bench, letting his eyes droop, drifting away into his own thoughts.

"I'm going to bed," I said, taking the opportunity to edge away.

"Good-night, McNulty," said the Boss.

Chapter Four

The next morning—afternoon to everyone else—when I walked out of the shadows of 110th Street into the sunlight and bustle of Broadway on my way to Tom's at 112th for breakfast, a park bench in the middle of Broadway called to me once more.

This time, Danny Stone sat on the bench, alone on the island except for an old lady in a gray overcoat who had parked her shopping bags beside him and was rooting through the garbage barrel. Danny looked like he'd been up all night. This wasn't a meeting I wanted. Danny knew I'd seen him with Angelina. I didn't know if he'd pretend I hadn't seen him or ask me to lie. I didn't know what I'd say or do in either case; too much strategy was involved, certainly too much strategy before breakfast.

"I'm going to eat," I told Danny. "Wanna come with?"

"I want to talk to you about something." His eyes were cold, his face serious, his manner chilling, as if he'd discovered some wrong I'd done him and was here to do something about it. "Let's walk." He started west across Broadway.

"Where you going?"

"To the park."

I froze. My face must have registered the shock I felt, because when he looked at me his did. We'd both made the same connection. He stared, as if the Grim Reaper were lurking behind me. "Maybe you should eat something," he said, changing direction and heading for Tom's.

As we crossed Broadway, I got the sense of something unusual. Broadway's a busy street, teeming with cars and cabs, trucks, buses, vans, baby carriages and strollers, and, because 110th Street is where the 24th Precinct ends and the 26th begins, more often than not, you see a couple of squad cars nosing around. But this morning, there were too many cop cars, marked and unmarked, from the two-four and the two-six, on either side of 110th Street and both sides of Broadway, doing that slow crawl they do when they're looking for some-one. I noticed the cops the way you sometimes notice something out of the ordinary: it registers but you don't remark on it.

At Tom's, Danny sat across from me drinking a cup of coffee that he'd put five teaspoons of sugar into. I played with my fork, drank my coffee, looked everywhere in the restaurant except at him, racking my brain for a piece of small talk so I could stop sitting there looking like I expected him to murder me as soon as I finished breakfast.

"You got a good appetite," he said after my eggs and sausage arrived. I kept eating. I didn't have to talk if I was eating.

"You know what I want to talk about?" His expression was less angry. It was more like impassive; I couldn't tell what he felt.

I said no, but I was afraid I did.

"Angelina…"

I didn't look at him but I felt his eyes on me all the same. "What about her?"

"Finish eating and let's get out of here." We were in a booth next to a plate glass window that faced 112th Street. Danny's reflection in the window when he stopped looking at me to stare out of it seemed sad rather than anxious. I'd never been afraid of Danny, whether he was drunk or sober, which was not something I'd say about most of Oscar's patrons. We'd spent a lot of time talking about mostly nothing on the slow nights during the band's breaks. I liked him for how good he was at what he did. He played for the pure joy of it, not because he thought he was going to be famous or rich or successful; he got off on the music; it was enough all by itself. My liking him was instinctive, built up of watching him through many things over a long time. You knew when someone was genuine. You called him a good guy when you talked about him. You knew he'd do the right thing.

Watching his reflection in the window, I remembered one time when Oscar was getting antsy about a friend of Danny's who sat nodding out at a table near the band. "I don't want these tough guy junkies coming in here," Oscar said. He was trying to get Danny to tell the guy to leave so he wouldn't have to.

"There's no such thing as a tough junkie," Danny told him. He went over, gently touched the junkie's shoulder, and nodded toward the door. The guy got up without a word and tiptoed out.

Drinking my third cup of Tom's coffee, I remembered hanging out with Danny when he opened for groups at the Lone Star or played downtown at the Bottom Line and Tramps. During the band's breaks, when the other guys were seeking out the sleek chicks, the assistant record producers, and the cool people in the audience, Danny wandered over to sit with me and whoever I brought with me. It was cool to be a friend of the band, but I would have been glad to see Danny if he'd been taking a break from washing dishes in the back. We were on some kind of wavelength that didn't require a whole lot of explanation.

One night, a drunk Dominican guy I was trying to eighty-six reached under his sport coat toward his belt line at the center of his back just as I came around the bar after him. Everyone in the joint knew what he was reaching for and froze, including me. As soon as he reached, I saw the gun come out, the explosion from the barrel, another bartender dead because some jerk-off drunk thought he'd been insulted. No one moved to help, except Danny. Danny slipped behind the guy where he could see his back and shook his head: no gun. I wanted to pulverize the guy, smash his face in, he'd scared me so much. But Danny wouldn't let me; instead he helped me walk the jerk outside and calmed him, like a good trainer with a frightened horse.

Now, in Tom's, I began to wonder if I really knew what Danny was capable of. I'd been happy for him that night I saw him with Angelina, happy for her too. In my romantic reverie, I saw Angelina and Danny become a couple. They were both troubled people. Angelina was too pretty and too sexy, and maybe she'd never be able to keep away from men. She also drank compulsively. Probably we were all drunks, but her drinking was the kind that led sooner or later to skid row and the shakes. Danny had worse problems: too much downtown, the monkey on his back. I'd never seen him sick, but in the way I came to know those things, I knew he was shooting smack every day just to stay even. Yet, in my foolish way, I wanted happiness for them. I wanted them to make records, play the great clubs of the world, when they were a little older settle down and raise kids together.

Instead, Angelina was dead, and maybe Danny murdered her. For a long time, I'd been around people who did not nice things to other people. None of them ever hurt me. I guess I believed that even if Danny had killed Angelina, he wouldn't kill me.

When we came out of Tom's, I noticed right away the cruisers were still there: two parked in the bus stop on the east side of Broadway, an unmarked car around the corner on 110th; a couple cruising uptown; another cruising downtown. They gave me the willies.

Danny and I walked to the end of 110th Street, then over an embankment that led down to Riverside Drive. A half dozen rats lay sunning themselves on the side of the hill. The sight of them scared me. If the city had to have rats, they should at least hide; they shouldn't be brazen, lying in the sun, they should run and hide when people came by. Something was terribly wrong with a place where the rats didn't have to hide. Like the drug dealers and the numbers joints and the illegal after-hours clubs and the crazy people from the SROs, they shouldn't be so readily visible, so out of control. It made me feel like no one was in charge—that we were all like the animals in the wild with only our wits to rely on.

I followed Danny across Riverside Drive to the street level of the park where the toddler playgrounds were and the path the joggers and bicyclists used. A stone staircase led down to another level where there were trees and grass and trails and benches. Below this was another level where the asphalt basketball courts were and beyond the courts more lawn and trees until you came upon Robert Moses's attempt to kill two birds with one stone—the West Side Highway. If you followed the right path, you went under a bridge to the lowest level of the park, the quietest and scariest part, the pathway next to the river that I had shown Angelina the first time I met her. It was down there they'd found her body.

I wanted to ask Danny what happened that night with Angelina. I tried to piece it together: A moment of passion… rage…despair. Maybe Angelina told him about her past—all the men. Maybe it drove him crazy. I didn't know what happened, but I knew the kinds of things pain and passion drove people to. I missed Angelina enough to bring tears to my eyes whenever I remembered her. But I didn't hate Danny if he'd done this. I felt sorry for him…sorry for Angelina…sorry for everyone. Something I must have gotten from my mother—understanding too much…feeling sorry for everyone.

I noticed the wispy white clouds high up in the blue sky. The air was limpid, not humid; there was warmth from the sun, but the trees cast long shadows even that early in the afternoon. It was a perfect fall day. What I noticed most was the quiet, like a hush, except for the cars passing on Riverside Drive, but even those sounds were muffled.

As we walked along the asphalt on the joggers' trail and I waited for Danny to tell me what it was that he would tell me, I heard squealing tires and turned my head in time to see a parade of squad cars whipping around the awkward turn at 110th to head downtown on Riverside. A couple of the cars took off down Riverside and turned into the park a block or so below us. Some others pulled up alongside the low iron fence that separated the roadway from the thin swath of park along the road.

Danny started to say something, so I turned to him. The pupils of his eyes were pinpoints. From the sun or from drugs, I wondered. The whites were yellowish and streaked with tiny red veins. He looked at me while I fidgeted beside him. But, before he could say anything, the quiet afternoon exploded into the noise of men running, of shouts and pounding feet. Danny turned and ran, while shouts followed him and popping sounds. Men in suits and men in windbreakers, with badges hanging from their lapels, foul-mouthed men, yelling "Police," "Stop," "Cocksucker" and "Motherfucker," came from everywhere.

In an instant, Danny lay on the ground, his face mashed into the blacktop walk; one cop knelt on his back pressing a revolver against his head, another stood over him with his gun pointed at him.

When I went toward Danny, following some instinct that told me to help him, I was pushed hard from behind, hard enough to snap my neck like a whiplash, and then slammed against the stone wall next to the asphalt path. Two burly, red-faced men waved leather wallets with badges pinned to them in front of my eyes. They leaned me against the wall to frisk me. Since I didn't have a gun, knife, or even a wallet, the pickings were pretty slim. I scraped my fingers on the rough surface of the wall, looking down into the park, picturing prison yards.

"You guys are nuts," I said when I finally got my breath. A chunk of anger big enough to choke me rose in my throat: fucking storm troopers.

"What's your name?" the largest one asked, his blue eyes squinting against the sun while he tried to stare me down. For the moment, I was too mad to be intimidated.

"McNulty," I said. "What's yours? And your badge number?"

"Looka this, Charley," he roared to his partner. "A solid fucking citizen."

"Up yours," I said, continuing along the diplomatic track.

As a couple of the other cops gathered round, the oaf said he'd take off his gun belt and badge and have it out with me right there. Then one of the cops recognized me. He was a little, dark-haired guy, who was probably Puerto Rican or Dominican. He was from the 24th Precinct and recognized me. "This guy's okay," he said very softly. "He's a bartender over on Broadway." The other cops mumbled and growled like a pack of dogs being pulled off the scent. The little cop spoke carefully and diffidently, as if he recognized that being Latin he wasn't exactly one of the boys either.

The big blue-eyed cop left me to go harass Danny. The group of cops around him had picked him up and bounced him on the ground a couple of times. Then another cop came over carrying a Marlboro box from which he'd taken a set of works. He held it in Danny's face.

"Smart ass, right?" he said. "You think we're fucking idiots?"

"Read him his rights," one of the cooler heads suggested.

"Don't say anything, Danny," I said. "I'll find you a lawyer."

"Shut the fuck up," the blue-eyed cop shouted, coming toward me again.

All the cops were sweating, huffing and puffing, stomping around, coming down from the excitement. They reminded me of trained guard dogs, baring teeth, holding themselves back from biting you because they've been trained. But you're not quite sure they'll be able to hold themselves back because they've also been made vicious. That's what the cops felt like—on edge—if you poked one of them he would come right at you, teeth snapping.

The cops hustled Danny into one of the cars. Since the Puerto Rican cop had put in a good word for me, the cops—except for the blue-eyed one—were okay with me, kind of gruffly polite.

"Where are you taking him?" I asked the cops putting Danny into the car but no one answered.

"Where are they taking him?" I asked one of the other cops.

"Two-six," he said.

They lost interest in me. I stood around for a couple of minutes while the cops finished up their business after Danny was gone. No one said anything else to me, so I left, walking slowly back up the blacktop path.

Peter Finch was a criminal lawyer who drank semi-regularly in the Terrace and on a rare occasion in Oscar's. He was a red-diaper baby like me, and maybe a Communist himself; I'd never asked. He used to be a civil rights lawyer in the South back in the Sixties. I didn't know him all that well, but we'd tucked away a few together more than once, so I stopped at the Terrace to ask Nick if it made sense to call him for Danny. Nick made the call and put me on with Peter. It turned out he knew Danny well enough to want to help. He said he'd find out why they grabbed him and what it might take to get him out of the slammer.

I suspected I already knew why they arrested Danny, but since I wasn't sure, I didn't want to say. I said something awkwardly about lawyer's fees and left it at that.

"Let me find out," Peter said. "You can buy me a drink. I'll talk money with Danny if I can do anything."

I ordered a beer and collected my thoughts.

〜〜〜

That night at work, Sheehan showed up again. He wanted to know what I was doing with Danny in the park.

"Why'd you go down there with him?" Sheehan said. "You tired of living?"

"Sometimes," I said. "Why did you arrest him?"

"What'd he say to you?"

I didn't answer.

"Did he tell you he killed the girl?" Taking in Sheehan's steely blue eyes, I realized I didn't like blue-eyed cops. They were worse than brown-eyed cops, I decided, or gray-eyed cops, or even one-eyed cops.

Angelina had been strangled by a pair of strong hands, Sheehan told me. Her own hands were tied behind her back with her pink sweater. A footprint now being analyzed, probably Danny's, was picked up alongside the path. A witness puts Danny and Angelina together on West End Avenue around five. The coroner puts her death between five and seven that morning.

"Your friend sounds like a real nice guy," said Sheehan. "How well do you know him?" Sheehan asked questions whether he got answers or not. But I didn't feel at all bad about not answering him anymore since my fling in the park with his fellow-workers.

"I'm busy," I said. "I don't want to talk to you. If you want me, you can arrest me." I said this in my surliest bartender tone, walked away from him, and began washing glasses.

When Sheehan left, I could see I'd gone up another notch in the estimation of the regulars. Every once in a while this happened: when I threw out a troublemaker, broke up a fight, or went home with a pretty customer. The winos grew friendlier and more animated, giving me a wink or a nod, patting me on the back as I walked by, as if I'd been wearing their colors.

Not Sam the Hammer though. This time, he happened to be sitting at the bar in front of the sink and looked up from the coffee mug he'd had his eyes glued to while the cop was there.

"I did that once," Sam said. "I told them: 'Book me or release me'—so they booked me."

Around one, Carl van Sagan and Nigel playing chess at the corner of the bar and Eric the Red watching them, Sam drinking coffee at the other end, Oscar came in to announce that Danny was in jail for killing Angelina. Oscar usually was the last to get the news.

"I knew he was no good," said Oscar, casting an accusing glance my way. "I told you he's on drugs....I don't want them coming in here....I told you, none of them—"

Oscar was prepared to go on with his tirade, a variation on his usual theme that I, McNulty, attracted too many unsavory types to Oscar's. Normally, when he got on his respectability kick, he looked to Nigel for affirmation. But, this time, something in Nigel's expression slowed him down. Nigel's face took me aback too: the pain and sorrow in his eyes, as if he was taking on Danny's trouble for him.

I wanted to tell Oscar he was wrong, too. But what could I say? That Danny was a good guy, and even if he had killed Angelina, it would have been a terrible mistake, something he would never forgive himself for, the result of abuse and war and drugs and all the ways life had beaten on him? You had to believe in your own purity to demand vengeance. I couldn't muster it up. A too-real sense of my own horrors got in the way.

"He didn't do it," I said.

Oscar's jaw dropped. Everyone turned to look at me, waiting for me to say something else. I waited myself to hear what I'd say next. How did I know Danny didn't do it? I had no idea. Something told me he hadn't done it, some piece of information that clicked when I heard it, then went out of my mind before I could put things together. It was useless to try to explain this, so I walked away.

Later, when Nigel left and everyone else had gone about his business, such as it was, Carl leaned closer to me as I poured his drink. I'd been wondering if he'd seen Danny and Angelina, as I had, and maybe was the person who dropped the dime.

He must have read my mind. "Danny wasn't the only person with Angelina that night," he said.

"How do you know?"

"I saw her and somebody walking on West End Avenue."

"How do you know it wasn't Danny?"

"I don't know for sure. I didn't really pay attention. But I think the guy was white…and maybe wearing a suit."

"Don't you know? Didn't you recognize him? Didn't you talk to her?"

Carl's eyes were sad like Snoopy's. "I didn't pay attention," he said. "If I'd known he was going to murder her, I'd have run up for a look."

"I guess so," I said absently. "But that doesn't mean Danny didn't get to her later. Maybe he freaked out because she'd left him for someone else."

"Maybe." Carl's eyes were still sad and his expression sagging after a long night of drinking scotch, yet he seemed to possess a patient sort of wisdom.

"Did you tell the cops?"

Carl shook his head. "What am I gonna say? Maybe I saw somebody, but I don't know what he looked like. If I told them that, they'd say, 'Could it have been Danny.' I'd say 'no.' They'd say 'How do you know if you don't know what the person looked like?' It's a waste of time telling the cops. Still, I'd want to know who that person walking with her was."

"And who called the police to say she was with Danny."

We looked at each other for a few seconds. "You're starting to sound like a detective," Carl said. He'd finished his drink and was nudging his glass toward me, lest I neglect my primary role in his life. "Maybe Oscar would give you a raise if you cracked the case."

"I don't want to crack a case. You read too many books. Why would I want to catch a murderer?" I dropped some ice cubes in his glass with one hand and poured with the other.

"Maybe you believe in justice. Maybe you don't want Danny to get screwed. More than likely, though, it has to do with Angelina's sister, who seems to be your type. Whatever the reason, you're the man for the job."

"Catching the murderer?"

"Precisely."

"What if I get killed? Murderers kill people."

"Unarguably true," Carl said, taking a healthy slug of his scotch. "You'd have to be careful."

"Why would I do that? Why don't you?"

"You have more at stake than I do. You, in fact, have taken responsibility for the two people most heavily involved. But I'd like to be kept informed."

Reuben arrived and behind him the rest of the last-call winos, drifting in from the other joints along Broadway that had sense enough to close up before four. This was the time of night when I made my living. I concentrated on my work, forcing myself to move faster and faster, planning far ahead so I never had to stop to think, just run, my fingers flying on the cash register keys, holding the liquor bottle in one hand, soda gun with the other, using the calluses between my thumb and forefinger to twist the caps off the beer bottles, glad-handing the guys I liked, making a joke, taking a joke, scooping money off the bar, sliding a beer past three or four regulars to Eric the Red at the end of the bar, keeping Oscar in Budweisers. High-speed life on Broadway.

Carl joined the winos in the chase, settling in to serious drinking and the serious thoughts behind the booze. I kept his scotch full, charging him for every fourth or fifth drink, until he no longer noticed what I did. The booze hit its mark. He fought whatever battle it was with whatever held him captive, and, for that moment, after that ninth or tenth scotch, he had it on the run. He was coming out on top and would stagger off with the other winos into the Broadway night sure he had won, only to wake in the morning to find he hadn't after all. Whatever it was he thought he'd fought off would still be there, perched on the bedpost, waiting for the night and the scotch and the next battle.

I drank a couple of beers while closing up, then sat in the darkness at the bar. When I'd been there for a half-hour, I heard tapping on the window. It was Peter Finch.

"I don't suppose I could get a drink this late," he said shyly. Not one of the winos, he didn't know how things worked late at night. He thought I closed up the bar and went home.

I gave him a scotch on the rocks. He looked shaken. "I didn't know it was murder," he said after his first swallow. "Thanks a lot."

Taller than me—and thinner—in pretty good shape, his light colored hair thinning in front, his face pale and thin, Peter always seemed serious and thoughtful, even more so now. "I stopped the interrogation," he said. "They're holding him on a drug charge, not murder."

"What happened? What did he say? Why did they arrest him?"

"Someone called the police this morning…said he saw Danny with the girl around four or five in the morning the night—or morning—she was killed. Danny said he was here that night. He thought you could tell me something that can help him."

"I don't know anything that would help him. The only thing I can tell you is Carl might have seen her with someone else that same night after I saw Danny with Angelina."

Peter's eyes sprang open. "With Danny? Danny said he wasn't with Angelina that night."

I shrugged.

Whatever energy had been holding his face up gave out on him. "Shit," Peter said, downing the rest of his scotch in one swallow.

Chapter Five

A couple of mornings later I woke up once more in Betsy Blumberg's bed. We'd hooked up at the Terrace in the early hours of the morning, drinking brandy at the bar and snorting coke in the ladies room in the basement. On one of the trips to the cellar, we began necking in the ladies room. Later, we staggered off into the night, wrestled each other down the street and into her building, where I opened her blouse and unbuckled her bra in the elevator while she opened my fly. We fondled our way to the fourteenth floor and fucked on the rug inside her apartment door before we were out of our clothes.

"I thought you had a new girlfriend," Betsy said in the morning as we ate bagels that she'd gone out to the corner for before I'd even pulled myself out of her bed.

I didn't say anything, though I knew what she was talking about.

Betsy grumbled, "Angelina's sister. I've seen you with her—a high-class broad."

"She's very nice," I said. "But she's gone back to Massachusetts."

"What a thing to say! I saw you moon around after her, and all you can say is that she's nice?" Betsy regarded me sadly. "You acted differently around her. I bet you haven't even noticed. When she came into the bar that time, she was the most important person there for you. It's never like that when I walk into anywhere."

"You just haven't found your niche yet, Betsy."

"I don't think I have one," she said even more sadly.

Betsy was easy, but not at all in the negative sense of the word. She was one of the good people who make it easy to get along with them, who don't have prerequisites for friendship. It's a way of being I like, one of the reasons I prefer the winos to many of the solid citizens I've run into. And I didn't feel dishonest about sometimes fucking her because she knew I really did care for her.

Why I was thinking this, sitting across a bagel from Betsy Blumberg, had to do with something I'd thought of the night before then lost in the fog: Betsy would know about men in the neighborhood.

"Do you think Danny murdered Angelina?" I asked her.

She looked at me strangely. "Don't the police think he did?"

"Do you?"

She wrinkled her eyebrows and seemed to think about it.

"Do you think he's capable of it?" I asked when she didn't say anything.

"Every man I've ever met has seemed capable of murder."

"Including Danny?"

"I guess," she said thoughtfully. "But I wouldn't think he'd kill Angelina; they were too much alike."

"Who do you think would?"

"Someone who had a weird idea of her. Men made her into things. She was something different for everyone, like one of those women who make a living acting out men's fantasies."

"Why not Danny, then?"

"He's like her, the both of them like they weren't nearly hard enough for the city. Despite being cool and all that stuff, they were babies. Besides, Danny didn't have hang-ups about women. Women like him. He's really natural about sex. Not hung up on it, if you know what I mean."

Hung up on it myself, I wasn't sure I did. My own fetishes rose before me: tiny feet and slim-legged girls in summer dresses. What was Angelina in my fantasies?

Betsy might have a point, but I wasn't about to get involved in other people's sex fantasies; this was too sordid and unpleasant a pursuit even for me. Privacy was a reasonable right. Still, I wondered what sex fantasies Angelina knew about. I thought about who in the neighborhood she might have slept with. Thinking this over, I got my internal cameras going and began a newsreel of how she looked with some of Oscar's regulars. The whole process turned perverted enough to make me stop. But Betsy was onto something. Perverted sex had everything to do with Angelina's life; it must have something to do with her death.

Betsy, munching on her bagel, looked thoughtful. Like lots of people who didn't make any pretenses to be so, she was smart. Why was she so unhappy then? Why didn't David fall in love with her?

"How well did you get to know Angelina?" I asked.

She looked at me nervously before she answered. "Not so well and then pretty well. She was needy and loving and really vulnerable." Betsy laughed. "So needy she made me feel together and in control…" No longer munching, Betsy stared at me like I knew a terrible secret about her. "…We were lovers," she said in a whisper.

"Oh?"

"I thought you knew."

"How would I know?"

"I thought you knew by the way you looked.…I thought Angelina would have told you. I thought that was why you were asking me about her.…I thought she would tell you everything."

"I guess not."

Betsy and I went over all the men in the neighborhood. I trusted her instincts, not that I thought she could intuit who the murderer was, but that, like Angelina, she knew about men and what they wanted. She thought that the Boss, Oscar, Rocky, Reuben, Danny, Eric, Carl, Duffy, and Nigel were possible murderers.

"That certainly narrows the field."

"You asked."

"What about me?"

She looked into my eyes. "No, not you." Her answer was serious and her voice kind. I was touched by what she said. All too aware of my own depravities, I needed someone to think kindly of me.

"And Ozzie, too," she added as an afterthought.

"Ozzie?"

"She had an affair with Ozzie."

"With Ozzie?" Ozzie!? Why did anything surprise me? Jesus, Ozzie! I didn't want to picture beetle-eyed, Alabama-accented, tow-haired Ozzie naked with Angelina. I couldn't conjure him up as a lover of anyone. But with no encouragement from me, my mind's eye pictured a naked Ozzie with an erection. It was repulsive. Yet he'd had a fifteen-year-old wife. Why not replace her with Angelina? His wife died. Why not reenact it with Angelina? It was crazy. But maybe Ozzie was. It made its own perverted sense. Not only could I now picture Ozzie as a naked lover, I could picture him as a murderer.

"There's another thing," Betsy said. "That night in the Terrace, after Angelina was killed, before I knew about it and before you came in, Ozzie was in the bar and he was completely ossified. He could barely stand up. I think he was delirious. He was always talking to himself anyway, but this time he kept looking up with this horror on his face and talking to an empty barstool as if someone was there."

"The ghost of Banquo?"

"Who?"

"A play I was in once. Never mind."

"Nigel and Carl carried him home. Maybe he told them what he was afraid of."

⌐⌐⌐

That night, Friday night, Janet Carter appeared in Oscar's, about a half-hour after I got to work. Stopping what I was doing, I looked at her for a long time. She fidgeted with her purse, danced around the barstool before she sat down, began to say something three or four times before she finally ordered a bourbon and water in a snippy, challenging tone as if I might not give it to her if she didn't sound determined.

"It's nice to see you," I said.

The tension drained from her face, and she almost smiled. "I came back," she announced. She didn't need to say why she'd come; it was written on her face. She could barely contain her eagerness. "Can you tell me what happened?"

I didn't answer, instead made myself busy around the bar while she sipped her drink. She wasn't really a drinker, even though she came on like one. She drank the drinkers' drinks and seemed to be one of the boys, but if you watched carefully, which none of the regulars ever did, you'd notice that even on the nights she stayed until closing, she never drank more than two or three drinks.

"If you don't want to tell me, I'll ask someone else. They arrested that person Danny that we saw in the restaurant. Then they let him go again. Is that what happened?"

I didn't know where she got her information, probably some contact in Springfield with the police grapevine. "Nothing happened. They arrested Danny on a drug charge. They haven't charged him with killing Angelina."

"But he did, didn't he—he killed her."

I held back an instinctive rush to tell her she didn't know what she was talking about and shouldn't be throwing accusations around. Some wisdom told me trying to set the record would be a waste of time. Something about the way she came on bothered me. It was her eagerness: she was bloodthirsty.

"You feel vindicated that they found someone to pin the murder on, right?"

This I said in pretty nasty tone and it knocked her back a couple of notches. "I don't feel vindicated at all…" she stammered. "…I feel worse than I felt before I knew who killed Angelina."

I felt a rush of anger, but once more yanked it back. "It's just as well."

"What does that mean?"

"It doesn't mean anything."

Like the cops, she'd settle for wishful thinking that got the case solved. Like them, she wouldn't look at anything that might spoil the flimsy truth she'd latched on to. Once more, I wasn't sure I liked her very much after all. She wanted me to lie just as she did. That's what she came in for. Join her in letting Danny take the rap. He'd take the jolt. We'd each forgive ourselves for betraying Angelina: He'd take the rap for all of us. If I went along, some flickering light in her eyes told me, we could spend some time together on this trip to the city, some final mourning and consoling, maybe leading to some comforting in the sack. Yet something in those same eyes, some hope or fear or yearning, wasn't letting her go. Part of her needed to get to the real stuff, too.

"Can't you just say you were wrong?" She challenged me with her dark brown eyes.

"You want me to say he's guilty?"

Her eyes and her face broke rank, even her posture began to sag. She couldn't get rid of the doubt, so she tried anger again. "How can you keep thinking he didn't do it? What's he to you? What's with you? Some kind of white guilt?"

"I don't know whether he's a murderer or not."

"You're a fool—" I thought she was going to stomp out. But she didn't go. Then the light went on inside my head. Stranger things have happened, but not to me. Exactly at this moment—the exit line given, the exit not taken—I caught up with the piece of information I'd been trying to remember. I knew why I thought Danny hadn't killed Angelina.

The picture I had in my mind of Danny and Angelina on Broadway, arms around each other, the sky turning pale behind them, stayed with me. Since the night I told Oscar that Danny didn't kill Angelina, every time I thought about it, this picture came back, and each time I knew he didn't do it. It would have been stupid to tell anyone, but I was more convinced after Sheehan told me the evidence against Danny than I had been before. But I didn't know why.

Now, with Janet sitting sadly in front of me, with me sadly waiting for her to go, the picture of Danny and Angelina came once more: They were walking north on Broadway just past the Olympia Theater and the Academy Florist, about to cross 107th Street. Angelina was leaning against Danny, her arms around Danny's waist, Danny's hand resting on Angelina's shoulder, the back of his black hand against the ivory white skin of her shoulder—his black hand against her white shoulder. Angelina wasn't wearing a sweater.

I put my hand on top of Janet's. "If you wait till midnight, I'll get Michael to cover the bar, and we'll go talk to Carl. I think I can convince you Danny Stone didn't kill Angelina."

She waited. She had just enough doubt to need to hear me out. But she didn't talk to me anymore while she waited.

＊＊＊

We found Carl van Sagan sitting in his cubicle off the faded marble lobby of 811 West End Avenue. He was reading about ants.

"Ants from the same family are different sizes," he told us, as if we'd asked. "Some are ten times bigger than others in the family."

"Oh," Janet said. She seemed a lot more interested than I was. But he hadn't gotten to the good part.

"When the big one is carrying a leaf, the little one rides on top watching out for flies—the enemy."

"I never knew that," Janet said.

I was willing to bet most people didn't.

"Flies drop larvae on the ants which bore in and eat them from the inside. If it wasn't for flies, ants would take over the world." Carl looked up from his book, like a preacher from his pulpit.

"It sort of gives you a new perspective," I volunteered.

"Let's get down to business," Janet said, looking from Carl to me and getting fidgety. "I don't know what I'm doing here. I must be crazy."

I told Janet about the sweater. Carl told her about seeing Angelina with someone he was pretty sure wasn't Danny. She was wearing a pink sweater. Janet listened, her face clouding over as her doubts grew.

"How can you be sure? What if you just didn't see the sweater."

"I can see them clearly," I said.

"I noticed because I'd seen her earlier with only a T-shirt with straps," Carl said. "I would have noticed her pretty neck and shoulders this time, too. She was wearing a sweater…and the guy she was with wasn't Danny." Carl's sad eyes carried such earnestness that I could tell Janet already believed him. He had this way, when he was giving advice or encouraging you to do something, of making you feel that he was seeing things from your point of view and not trying to talk you into something.

"Why didn't you tell this to the police?" she asked quietly.

Carl didn't answer but indicated by his expression that perhaps I would field the question. But I wasn't about to try to explain the complexities of police-citizen relations when the citizen was not in the mainstream of modern life to Ms. Respectable.

"We'll tell his lawyer," I said finally. "He'll figure out what to do with the information."

Carl seemed relieved that I'd provided a cover, but I could tell he was also a bit shaken, since anything that lifted him from his basic anonymity bothered him. To compensate, I spread a couple of lines of coke out onto his desk.

"Just like Sherlock Holmes," he said.

"What?"

"Sherlock Holmes did cocaine....The seven per cent solution." Carl followed my movements as I chopped the powder. "I don't normally do this stuff."

"Well, don't start on my account. This shit cost a hundred and twenty bucks a gram."

In the meantime, Janet had snapped up my piece of straw, hitched up her sleeves, snorted to clear her nose, and bent to the task. I hadn't really counted her in.

"I thought she was straight," Carl said as she swooshed up a line, leaving nary a grain. He took his place behind her. "Actually, I like the stuff," he said.

I didn't know if I did. Cocaine matched up too well with selfishness and greed. We all used to smoke the herb together, even went out of our way to find someone to share with. This snowy stuff I tried to keep for myself, telling my friends I didn't have it when I did. Doing too much of it, not keeping track on purpose. Maybe the fun was gone.

"Everybody's always willing to do coke," I told Carl.

The coke hit me. Janet sparkled in front of me. Carl was a great guy. The cubbyhole office became an enchanted villa. As Janet's gaze swept around the tiny room, her eyes caught up with mine. We smiled at each other. Our eyes locked. She was so alive, so wired. I moved closer to her, then stood beside her so that if she moved, if she wanted to, we could touch each other.

This electric attraction sparkled in the air. Carl babbled on about ants while Janet and I kept looking at each other. I got more and more excited because I could feel her wanting me to kiss her. This whole love affair and seduction took place without a word being spoken. The ardor flared and in a little while leveled off in the high plains. We were even a little shy with each other as we came down a bit.

When things calmed sufficiently, Carl and Janet got back on the trail.

"If your friend Danny didn't kill Angelina, we have to do something," said Janet.

I had the distinct thought in the back of my mind that things weren't as simple as, at this moment, we all seemed to think they were. But I plowed ahead anyway. "Could the guy you saw Angelina with that night have been Ozzie?"

Carl's face froze; he turned white. I thought he was about to keel over from cocaine death. Instead, he said, "Of course."

"It could have been?"

"It could. I wouldn't swear to it, but it could've been."

The coke that had heated my blood to boiling moments before now turned the blood cold. We stood in that room in an eerie silence.

Ozzie lived in one of the big apartment buildings just east of Broadway on 110th Street. A bunch of people lived there: Betsy, Nigel, Duffy. It was where Angelina had lived in a sublet efficiency apartment.

Now was the time for some action, I decided. The first thing was to talk to Danny. It was time for him to come clean, at least with me. Peter had gotten bail set on the drug charge and the band came up with the money, so Danny was back playing music. On Friday nights, he played with a jazz band at a club on Amsterdam in the Nineties.

Janet insisted on coming with me. I didn't know whether she was getting me deeper into this thing, or I was dragging her in. We argued for a few minutes on the corner, then when I looked her up and down a couple of times and she looked back, I realized something was happening here and I didn't want to let go of her just yet. We picked up one of the hordes of empty cabs pouring back down Broadway after the night trip north from downtown and were whooshed over to the club at 94th Street before I had time to think of what I would do or say when we caught up with Danny.

Arriving in the middle of a set, Janet and I sat at the bar and listened to the music. The jazz sounds were mellow: piano, horn, drums, and Danny on bass, the club almost somber. Danny leaned against the wall with his eyes closed, the way he usually played. But something was calmer about him, the sound and the setting were perfect for him. After listening just a few minutes, I realized Danny was a jazzman; rock and roll was a sideline.

When the set ended, without having let on he knew we were there, Danny walked slowly to where we sat at the bar. Shaking hands with me, he looked at Janet. His face was calm and impassive. Maybe the music soothed him, or maybe he was high. Janet jumped off her barstool; she looked ready to spring into action, just barely held back. She kept looking at me as if to say I should do something faster and looking at Danny as if to apologize for my slowness.

"Can we talk?" I asked him. He led us to a table.

"This is my story," I said as soon as I sat down. "I saw you and Angelina the night she was murdered." Danny stiffened and looked away from me. Then he looked back. "But Carl van Sagan also saw someone with her after that, after she was with you." Danny's expression didn't change. "Angelina's hands were tied with her sweater when they found her body. She didn't have a sweater when I saw her with you."

"We don't think you killed her," Janet said. I was as surprised as Danny. Janet sat on the edge of her chair, and her voice was so tense she squeaked.

There were lines of pain in Danny's face and his expression remained inscrutable. He seemed sort of empty. "What do you want with me?" he asked.

"Did you see Ozzie that night?"

"Yeh, in the lobby of Angelina's building on our way back....I thought it was either you or him who told the cops."

"You saw me, too?"

"On Broadway. I didn't know if you were mad because I'd hooked up with Angelina. You didn't say hello." His expression didn't change but he looked me in the eye.

"What about Ozzie? Did Angelina talk to him?"

"Angelina didn't want to see him."

"Did he see you?"

"I don't know."

"Why didn't Angelina want to see him?" Janet leaned toward Danny, hanging on his words. He seemed both interested and disturbed by her intensity.

"She didn't say." He paid more attention to the glass of ginger ale he was drinking than he did to Janet.

But she lost none of her intensity. "The police think they found your footprint in the park."

Danny shook his head. "Maybe they did. I was there. We walked in the park." He looked at me again, and now there was something in his expression—maybe hope. "But Angelina didn't have a sweater. She wore my jacket."

"Did you go to her apartment?"

"No. I thought we were going to. She changed her mind when we got to her block."

"Why? Could it have been seeing Ozzie that changed her mind?"

"No. I think she decided before we saw him. She said she'd come to my place in the afternoon."

"Did she see anyone else?"

" I don't know....I don't think so."

"Why did you go to the park?" Janet asked him. "Isn't it dangerous to go in the park at night?"

"Not then. It was almost morning. She wanted to go there...to look at the river. She said she went there a lot to look at the river."

Danny went back to work. Janet and I took turns in our respective rest rooms with my folder of blow. After, she sat in the chair next to me, pulling her silky dress up over her knees and crossing her legs. I had all I could do to keep my hands off her thigh. While I wriggled in my seat, she smiled flirtatiously, put her arm through mine and leaned toward me so her breast brushed against the muscle of my arm and her bare leg pressed against me. I let my hand drop to touch her leg. She didn't wear stockings, so I rested my hand against the cool white skin of her thigh. Later, when I touched her breasts, she looked into my eyes and then held my hands against them.

When we waited, arms around each other, on the sidewalk in front of the club for a cab, she said, "I want to make sure that you know that you touched me because I wanted you to."

The driver of the cab that streaked kitty-corner across Amsterdam Avenue and skidded into the gutter in front of us turned out to be Ntango, an Eritrean refugee, one of the regulars who came with the other exiles late at night to Oscar's. He was stoned and as usual glad to see me, speaking in his low monotone mumble and calling me "Mr. Brian" in a Peter Lorre tone of voice. We chatted about life on the Upper West Side, good times at Oscar's, and the trials of driving a cab. He refused payment for the fare, so I wrapped up half of what was left of my blow in a piece of paper from Janet's notebook and gave him that.

Ntango worked a horse hire, which meant that he got his cab for a flat fee, paid it off with what he made in fares, and kept the rest, a rung up the ladder, he maintained, from the fleet cab he used to drive. He'd also gotten hooked into a dispatcher and insisted that Janet call him whenever she needed a cab. He said this while holding the door open for her and bowing graciously.

"He's quite charming," Janet said as he sped away. "Wise and sad. What's Eritrea?"

I didn't want to talk about Ntango. As fine a person as he was, he had too much trouble about him, reminding me of the oppressed and suffering of the earth. At this particular moment, most everyone he'd ever known in childhood, who hadn't already been killed in the Ethiopean war, was starving to death. I didn't want to think about those things. I didn't want Janet to think about those things. I wanted to be reckless and happy and joyful. Who needed to think about pained and whacked out Ntango, hurtling through the streets of New York in his cab, dodging memories of his mom and dad, sisters and brothers, dying alongside the dirt roads of northern Ethiopia?

"He's also the most beautiful man I've ever seen," Janet said.

"All the Eritreans are," I told her. "Powerful argument in favor of miscegenation."

Inside my apartment door, Janet looked around her. "I don't know if I should be doing this," she mumbled.

"I think you're beautiful," I said. She made a little mumble-murmur of pleasure and nestled against me. We kissed in the doorway, and I realized it was for the first time. In some kind of ecstasy of kisses and caresses we made our way to the bed. I took off her underclothes from beneath her silky dress and unloosed her breasts from her blouse and bra. She was all smooth and firm: her breasts, the muscles rippling along her thighs, her hips, the softness and firmness of her ass. When I entered her, I reached back and caressed the taut muscles of her thighs. We stopped for a moment while she wiggled out of some more of her clothes. Then, I came at her from the back, holding her breasts in my hand pushing against her, entering her again. Once more, we stopped. This time, I lowered my head to between her legs and caressed her with my tongue. She came twice. When I sat up, she kissed me wetly all over my mouth. Once more, I entered her, rising and falling in her while she held me in a bear grip with her legs until I exploded. When we were finished, I was panting. Lying beside her, I wanted her just as much as I'd wanted her before we'd started. I just couldn't do it again. Not right then, but there was no let up on the wanting. Could it always be like that for her? I was afraid to ask in case it was. She didn't cuddle afterward, just withdrew into her own space. Not at all shy about her nakedness, she just lay on top of the bed while I looked at her.

Around noon I woke up, ready for her again and reaching for her, but she wasn't in the bed. She'd gathered her things and dressed. I got the feeling she was trying to leave before I woke. I got up and put my arms around her. She stood stiffly, resisting when I pulled her toward me.

"I wish we hadn't done that." She stood still, letting my hand rest on her shoulder, waiting, stiffly, lifelessly.

"It wasn't frivolous," I told her. I knew what I felt, but it was way too early to say that.

"This was a mistake," she said, her voice as stiff and cold as her stance. "I hope you don't think it means anything....I'm really confused right now. I don't think you should have taken advantage of that."

I'd started to pull her toward me, to hug her, but felt so much resistance I drew back.

She took a few steps back and looked at me directly. "Did you ever make love with my sister?"

I didn't answer.

"I want to know," she demanded. Having already made up the answer, she was furious, so her voice shook with her anger.

"It's not any of your business."

"You have to tell me."

We stared at each other for a solid minute, but I didn't say anything.

"I don't know anything about you. You're forty years old. You didn't just drop off a shelf. Were you ever married?"

"Yes."

"Do you have any kids?"

"A son."

"Where?"

"In Brooklyn."

"Do you see him?"

"Yes."

Her eyes softened with sympathy. But it wasn't much help. Like feeling sorry for Ntango. Pissing against the tide.

"It must be sad not being with your child."

When I opened the door for her to leave, I said again that what happened hadn't been frivolous. She wasn't listening. Instead, she was looking at a wrinkled, torn piece of paper that had been stuck under my door. The writing was almost illegible, done with a flat pointed lead pencil. The note said, "Brian, Meet me at the Dublin House tonight."

We both looked at the note.

"Who's that from?" Janet asked, suspicion frosting her voice.

"I don't know."

"How can you not know? Of course you know."

"How the fuck would I know? There's no name."

"Who leaves you notes?"

"No one."

"Is that from a woman?"

"I told you I don't know who it's from."

"Was some other woman supposed to be here?"

"No."

"What kind of friends do you have who write notes without signing them?"

"Who said it was a friend?"

When Janet left, I felt a silence and an emptiness to my apartment that I wasn't used to. I'd been in the apartment for years. It was roomy and almost bright. I thought it the most comfortable and safest place in the world, a haven from the clang and rush of the city. Now, when Janet walked out the door, it seemed empty. I stood in my own foyer looking at my own apartment wondering where everyone had gone.

When I read the note again, I knew it had to do with Angelina's murder.

Chapter Six

I knew the Dublin House because Carl and I used to go there to watch Knick games back in the days of Clyde and the Pearl. You walked up a couple of stone steps and in through an old oak door. Once inside, you came upon your classic gin mill, long, straight, dark, mahogany bar, dim lights, worn plastic booths, the television and the juke box mumbling forth at the same time, both too low for anyone to hear, no one giving a shit anyway. Almost everyone up in years, if not in years at least in miles, all but one or two of them men, all hunched over pilsner glasses, the beer glowing from the lights behind the bar, glowing golden in the dimness as if lit by its own internal light.

Not only had the note not given a name, it hadn't given a time. Night on the Upper West Side meant something though, so I asked Michael to take over the bar and got to the Dublin House around eleven-thirty. I didn't know anyone at the bar, and with only a nodding acquaintance with the bartender, I had no reason to ask if anyone was looking for me. I ordered a draft beer—the Dublin House being one of the dying breed of legitimate bars that cleaned its beer lines once a week—and sat back to wait, like a boy on a blind date. On my second beer, I realized I might actually be in trouble, lured there by someone who might want to do me harm. Just as I ordered my third, Sam the Hammer appeared in the doorway.

I ordered him a light beer.

"What are you doing here?" he said.

I looked at him for a sign that he had sent me the note. There was none in his expression. He drank the beer, wiped the foam off his walrus mustache.

"You're looking for trouble," Sam said. "Pissing off the wrong people. So I got something for you you're maybe gonna need. When I leave, you keep the bag on the floor."

"You want another beer?"

"No," Sam said. He left half his beer behind him and walked out.

I kept in touch with the bag by kicking it now and again. When I finished my beer, I ordered another for good measure. I wasn't any good at this shamusing, but I thought I should wait a longer time after Sam left to throw off suspicion. Suspicion of what by whom—I hadn't a clue.

The bag, which I peeked into as I walked up Broadway after a few feints to make sure no one followed me, contained a wad of newspapers wrapped around something like it might be wrapped around a fish. I peeled the newspapers back and found a gun—a nice black gun with a handle like the cowboy guns I used to play with as a kid. This gun was heavy, had a revolver kind of chamber, and a very short barrel.

When I got back to my apartment, I spent about an hour trying different hiding places for it: under my pillow, but I was afraid it would shoot accidentally and blow my head off; under the mattress, but I imagined that like the princess with the pea I could feel it through the springs; in my top bureau drawer, but anyone could find it there. All of this searching I did at a frantic pace, as if at any moment the cops would break down the door and arrest me or the gun would start going off by itself and chase me around the room.

I finally hid it behind some books in my bookcase. I looked at the bookcase, and the gun's location behind *War and Peace*, from every angle, and was positive that anyone at all could spot it from the front door, though the bookcase was clear across the room and partially blocked by a wall. But it would have to do. I went back to work.

The next afternoon, gunless, I went in search of Sam the Hammer to find out what kind of trouble he thought I was in and what I should do with the gun. In the lobby of my building, between the outside door and the inside door, I ran into Detective Sheehan and almost fainted. I had all I could do to keep from turning myself in before he even opened his mouth.

He stopped in his tracks and stared at me. "What's the matter, McNulty?" he said. "You look like you've seen a ghost."

I couldn't speak for a moment. My mind whirred. All I could think of was the gun. "I'm sick," I said. "Something I ate."

"Probably at Oscar's," Sheehan said. "I made the mistake of eating there once myself." I laughed, but he was serious. "I was looking for you." He looked me over with more curiosity than sympathy, like a doctor might. "Are you well enough to talk?"

"I'm not sure."

"Maybe we can go in your apartment. You can rest and talk at the same time."

"No…" I stammered. "…I mean, I'd rather go for a walk—get some air."

Sheehan looked at the door, looked at me. His eyes narrowed, and he became cautious. Every move he made told me I couldn't have made him more suspicious if I was carrying the god-damn gun in my hand.

"Is someone in your apartment?" Sheehan seemed to belly up to me although he hadn't moved.

"No. I just don't want to be inside right now."

"McNulty, you're the worst liar I've ever come across. If I didn't know where my wife was, I'd break down your door."

"I don't know your wife."

"Keep it that way. Let's walk." He assumed his tough guy policeman attitude, speaking harshly now, more out of the side of his mouth than before.

We walked out of my apartment and west along 110th Street toward the hill that led down to Riverside Drive. As always, I looked for the rats as we climbed down the hill, but the day being gloomy they must have chosen to stay inside. We crossed Riverside Drive and sat down on one of the benches in the tiny playground at 108th Street.

"I understand you're playing amateur detective," Sheehan growled louder than he needed to for me to hear him, his shoulders back and his chest puffed out to let me know he was ready for a fight if one came along. "You and the murdered girl's sister."

"I'm a bartender."

He picked a stick up off the ground and played with it. "She called to tell us Danny Stone didn't kill her sister. She said you knew who did."

"She talks a lot doesn't she?" I said. If Janet had been there, I would have pushed her into the sandbox.

"Who?" Sheehan asked, his tone loud and harsh enough to make me lean back away from him.

"I don't know."

"I'm tired of fucking around with you, McNulty." Sheehan poked the ground with his stick until it snapped; then, his cold blue eyes bored into mine. "You're not as smart as you think you are. I know this neighborhood. I know a lot more than you do. I'm also a lot tougher than you, and lots of the people you deal with are a lot tougher than you and nastier than you think they are."

"Look, man," I said. "I'm tired of all this, too. I don't know what she told you. All I have is suspicions…they don't mean anything. I just thought Danny didn't do it. I don't know who did. It could have been half the people I know."

"Stick to pouring drinks." Sheehan's tone was still tough, but the tension was gone from his face and, with the way his eyes wrinkled in the corners, he looked almost friendly. "You dig and you dig. Pretty soon you turn up something. Then you'll know too much."

I looked as levelly as I could into his eyes, finding something there, I guess, because I crossed up my instincts. "A neighborhood guy named Ozzie was waiting in the lobby of Angelina's building late the night she was killed."

Sheehan nodded.

～～～

That night at work was slow even for a Sunday, but I was jumping around the place like it was four deep at the bar. To calm my nerves, I played cribbage with Carl, who sipped beers while he waited for Sam to show. I didn't tell Carl about Sam and the gun. I felt like Shirley MacLaine in that movie where she keeps trying to hide the stiff, Harry.

Carl carefully poured some beer from his bottle of Beck's into his glass, holding the bottle in one hand and the glass, slightly tilted, in the other. In spite of his portliness, he was precise in his movements, almost dainty, and his beer pouring was a carefully performed ritual that he savored almost as much as the beer. This night, he was particularly deliberate. I sensed that, taking note of my jitteriness, he tried to be a calming influence. "What have you been doing about tracking down murderers?"

"Trying to forget about it."

"You know, for Sherlock Holmes it was the only thing worth doing. The rest of the time he spent getting high because he was so jaded by life."

"That's one approach, all right," I said, watching Carl turn another corner with his cribbage board peg. "—staying fucked up all the time."

"Like Ozzie." Carl took a long swallow of his beer.

He'd put his finger on something I'd known without knowing. I hadn't seen Ozzie since we'd made him a suspect, but for the week or so since Angelina's murder, he'd been drunk morning, noon, and night. Now, it was a tip-off; then, it hadn't meant much. The winos had their ups and downs. One week, they'd be perched at the bar drinking ginger ale. Another week, I'd have to peel them off the floor every night.

Normality was drinking every night, but steady enough to walk home and coherent enough to say goodnight. Ozzie hadn't been either of these for a week. He was already so drunk he couldn't talk when he came in. I'd give him a dropper full of Jack Daniels in each drink, charging him for every third one. But he wouldn't notice. St. Brian of the drunks, that's me.

Now, a more sinister light shone on poor old Ozzie.

"You and Nigel took Ozzie home from the Terrace the night after Angelina was killed," I reminded Carl.

"Did I?" He raised an eyebrow.

"Did he say anything suspicious?"

Carl thought this over. He didn't really remember taking him home that particular night; nor did he remember anything strange about Ozzie or anything Ozzie said on any night he might have taken him home.

"That's great," I said.

"You're the detective. I'm a doorman."

"And a poet. Poets are supposed to notice things."

Carl swallowed a couple of times, puffing himself up in his irritation: a Captain Haddock mood was coming on. "In preparation for my 'Ode to a Drunk Walking Home,' I presume?"

Nigel showed up about then—sober among the late night wasted. It was, I admit, cheering to see him. He made me feel almost normal.

At breakfast at the Greek's, I asked him the same question I'd asked Carl about Ozzie. He didn't remember either.

"Try to remember, damn it," I said. "Ozzie saw ghosts that night. He's been drunk for a solid week since then."

"He was drunk long before that," Nigel pointed out, his expression superior, his tone disapproving. "He just babbled that night like he does every night. I don't remember what he said. He's unintelligible."

My seriousness, accented by my tiredness and the hopelessness I usually felt when I was sober at the end of a shift at

Oscar's, rubbed off on Nigel. Night and tiredness seemed to be catching up with him, too. I watched his energy and enthusiasm wither.

"He's pathetic," Nigel said. "Falling apart....Killing himself."

"He may have been with Angelina the night she was killed. Danny saw him in the lobby of her building that night."

Nigel jerked forward like he'd been kicked in the ass. "Why would he be with her?"

"They'd had an affair."

"You're crazy!" Nigel shouted. "Not Ozzie...she couldn't have." He was so flabbergasted he was spitting. I knew how he felt.

"Angelina," I reminded him, "was not the most discriminating young lady."

Nigel didn't say anything. Since he didn't drink coffee or eat meat, he was sitting across from me in this upper Manhattan all-night greasy spoon sadly eating from a tiny bowl of rice pudding.

"What did you see the night Angelina was killed?" I prodded him. "Where were you? Did you see Angelina? Did you see Ozzie?"

Nigel stopped playing with his rice pudding. He took off his glasses, rubbed his eyes, then looked at me. His eyes looked weird and I wanted him to put the glasses back on. "Ironically, the night Angelina was killed, I was in Connecticut visiting my father for the first time in more than ten years."

Some people talked easily about their pasts, but Nigel wasn't one of them. His reluctance bothered me, so I labored over finding out, asking question after question, grilling him, while attempting to seem casual, drinking cup after cup of the Greek's wired mud. Nigel didn't sleep at night; we'd done this many nights before. But then it had been stories about being a roadie, about the rock and roll bands and traveling around the country. Now, when I tried to take him back home, he balked. I did get out of him that his father was a corporate executive with an office in the city and that Nigel had grown up on a large estate in Stamford, Connecticut.

"I'm sure this disappoints you," Nigel said. "You've been befriending a capitalist."

He had me. I was shocked. My own peculiar reaction was to feel sorry for him. I'd feel awful if I woke up and found myself rich. I couldn't handle the responsibility—or the guilt. But I tried not to hold it against him. Nigel seemed to have repudiated his past.

"You're fortunate. Your son worships you. He'll even hang around your seedy bar just to be with you. Whatever it is that you are, he's proud of you. The only time my father ever thought about me was when he feared I would ruin the family name."

Talk about Kevin always brought me down off my high horse. Knowing how little I deserved his hero worship made me as humble as a saint. Kevin got along well with everyone on his nights in the city when he sneaked out of my apartment to come down to Oscar's and hang out, but he liked Eric and Nigel best, Nigel in all likelihood because he was the only one besides Kevin who was sober that time of night.

"Have you rejected riches in favor of poverty?"

"Almost," Nigel said ruefully. "Being rich isn't what you think. But I doubt I could persuade you of that."

"Probably not."

"You're a Marxist. You should know the rich are as much pawns of the system as the poor. The employers as much pawns as their employees."

He was right. He wasn't going to persuade me of anything.

"My father destroyed our family making sure he stayed rich. I have no family. My parents are divorced....I'm here.... Until a week ago, I hadn't seen either of my parents since I was a kid."

"Why'd you go see your father last week, after all this time?"

"Family business."

Only rich people have family business. The rest of us have problems and things we have to do, but never any family business.

"I've been debating this," I told Nigel. "Should I go see Ozzie myself?"

"Tonight?"

"No, not tonight. I thought I might catch him when he got home from work tomorrow while he was still relatively sober." That might not work either, since he'd probably hit the first bar he came to downtown after work and be drunk before he got uptown.

Nigel sat spooning up his rice pudding and letting it plop back into the bowl. "Talk to Ozzie if you want.…But I don't think old Oz would make much of a witness."

ᔑ ᔑ ᔑ

I called Janet Carter at her hotel the next day. I wasn't sure she'd still be there, or, if she were, if she would talk to me. She was. She'd decided to take a few days' leave from her job. I asked her to have lunch. Her tone was cold, and I sensed she was about to say no. So I told her the note we'd found under my door had been from Sam the Hammer.

"What did he want?"

"I don't want to talk about it over the phone."

Her tone brightened a bit, and she whispered something excitedly.

"I can't hear you," I said.

"Can you tell me everything at lunch?"

"Everything," I said.

As eager as a pup, she sat across from me at the Terrace. I told her Sam had given me a gun.

Her eyes widened. The excitement colored her cheeks pink and sparked from her dark eyes. "We must be getting close," she said seriously.

"To what?" I counted back five cups of coffee to explain my jitteriness to myself.

"To the killer."

"You may be close. I don't have any idea."

"Someone thinks you do."

"Sam does."

"He must know something."

It hadn't registered with her that if Sam wanted to tell me something, he would have. The gun was all he would tell me. I ate my omelet and brooded.

"It's even more important now that we find him." Janet looked into my eyes compassionately.

"Who?"

"The killer. We have to find him before he kills you."

⌐ ⌐ ⌐

Once more, I crossed up my instinct, which told me to go looking for Ozzie. Instead, I went with Janet to look for Sam. We found him at La Rosita, a hole in the wall Cuban-Chinese, sipping espresso and going over *The Racing Form* with his friend the Greek. He barely nodded to me.

"Go ahead," Janet said. "Go ask him." I was sitting at the counter staring in front of me. Janet was on the stool next to me leaning against me breathing in my ear. We were like two kids afraid of the grown-up.

"No, not now." I raised my shoulder to push her back from me.

We waited, so I drank another cup of coffee, this one espresso, while Janet sulked.

"You drink too much coffee," Janet said.

Sam knew I wanted to talk to him. But he sat with the Greek for another twenty minutes, then more or less shooed him away, saying he would see him on the bus to Yonkers.

He sat down next to Janet and looked at me across her. "Nosey must run in your family," he told Janet.

"Why did you say that?" she asked.

"Why'd you say that?" Sam mimicked, then sat in silence for quite a while.

"Who should I be afraid of?" I asked.

Sitting hunched into his Yankee jacket, Sam looked me over. "The girl talked too much"—nodding toward Janet—"just like her."

"About what?"

Sam was fighting some battle with himself, trying to tell without telling. He was a hoodlum whatever else he was, with whatever code of honor a hoodlum has—a hoodlum and a gentleman, as they say. Usually, I could decipher his messages, but I couldn't make sense of this one. What did Angelina know?

"About movies…" Sam sounded disgusted with me and with himself when he said it. Then he left.

I thought this one through while Janet chattered at me. Her approach to difficulty was to talk at it, mine was to keep quiet.

"What about movies," Janet asked.

"I don't know."

"You do, too." She spun me around on my stool to face her.

She was right. I did know. The porno flicks Carl had told me about. I was getting too close to the Boss. But what could Angelina have known or talked about that would hurt the Boss?

"Wait here," I told Janet. Then, I ran down the street to 811 West End. Duffy stood like a sentry next to the door.

"Do a lot of kids come in and out here?" I asked him.

"For music lessons," he said, not blinking an eye.

"At night, too?"

He nodded, rising and falling on his heels, staring straight ahead. "Be careful, McNulty." He looked at me without sympathy.

Janet was standing in front of La Rosita when I got back.

"You trust this guy Sheehan?" I asked her.

She began to squirm, averting her eyes, coming back at me then too eagerly. She was easy enough to trap. "What do you mean?"

"You talked to him."

"Well, he asked me questions." Her dander rose. "He's the police. You're so damned suspicious of everyone. All these crooks you know don't tell you anything. I only talked to him."

"Calm down....I just want to know what I asked. Do you trust him?"

"I think so. I think he really wants to find out who killed my sister."

"Call him. Tell him to meet us someplace downtown."

Sheehan met us at a coffee shop on Broadway just below Columbus Circle. On the walls were pictures of the old Miss Rheingold ads that used to be all over the subways, memorabilia of my youth. Sheehan sat at a booth with his hat on the table in front of him. Once more, I was walking into 1955, though in one concession to the contemporary world, the menu had a lunch special named after Mayor Koch. I ate a hamburger and drank more coffee. Sheehan didn't look smug exactly; he looked officious, like it was about time that I came to my senses and recognized the authority of the state.

I told him about Angelina, the Boss, the movies, and what I suspected about the children. I'd tried to prepare Janet on the subway ride downtown. It wasn't enough. The truth of her sister's life shook her. Spread out in front of me now, it looked putrid also, desperate and sad, terrifying at the end.

"You think the Boss killed her?" Sheehan asked when I was finished. His tone was intimidating, telling me I'd better have a good answer.

"I'm just passing on some information."

Janet jumped into the conversation with both feet. "Why don't you arrest him on the pornography charge; then, you can search that place..." Wrapped up in her own ideas, she spoke too quickly to notice that Sheehan gave no sign of sharing her enthusiasm.

"That's not so easy." Sheehan shifted uncomfortably in the booth that was too small for him, avoiding Janet's eyes, not hiding very well the irritation curling the corners of his mouth. "That's not my jurisdiction. And your information isn't good enough for me to pass along."

What he meant was the tangled internal relationships between vice and homicide; he had to figure whose toes he might step on. "We already picked the Boss up and leaned on him. We didn't find out anything."

"If someone's doing something illegal, don't you arrest them?" Janet asked.

"You gave me some information. It's hearsay, right—supposition?"

Janet nodded.

"Ask your friend McNulty here. I thought you kind of people believed in all that civil liberties shit." Bearing down now, he seemed to tower over us, though he hadn't left his seat. "When we have some hard evidence, we'll move. Let us handle it, okay?"

"Fine," I said, pulling myself out of the booth, and Janet with me. We left Sheehan unfolding himself from the booth, gesturing impatiently for the waitress.

⌐ ⌐ ⌐

Janet stared in front of her, silent and sad, on the ride uptown on the train. I couldn't think of anything to say that might make her feel better.

At the 96th Street station, in the quiet while the local waited for the express, she asked, "Do you think she was a prostitute?"

I was thinking about other things: about the cop, about the Boss, about Ozzie. The whole thing was making me angry. I was mad that I kept giving Sheehan information.

"She was pretty. She was a commodity. Everything's for sale. Prostitution is one of the pillars of the national character."

Janet's eyes were icy. "Don't tell me your goddamn politics. I'm talking about my sister. Don't you have any feelings?"

Janet was determined that we should force Sheehan to arrest the Boss. I told her things didn't work that way and we should just drop it. But she kept talking at me—relentlessly. First, she accused me of corrupting her sister, of exploiting her. She said I was a coward and a liar, a drunk, and a bum. On and on, she went, until I discovered I'd agreed to sneak into Rocky's cellar to steal one of the porno flicks as evidence that would force Sheehan to arrest the Boss.

I had to be nuts. The only saving grace was that Rocky lived alone and was totally predictable. I asked Jim, the day guy at Oscar's, to stay until ten-thirty that night. This wasn't really fair because I could come in, work the back half of the shift and make all the money, which came at the end of the night. But I'd tightened Jim up a few times in the past, and for reasons of his own, he got a charge out of deferring to me, probably because I'd started bartending when he was in diapers.

Rocky would be sucking scotches beginning like clockwork shortly after nine. Duffy would be on the door. My best hope was to convince Carl to go in early and get rid of Duffy, so Carl would be on the door if anything came down.

"I really don't think you should do this," Carl said.

"Me neither. I got myself into this because she said she'd do it herself anyway. Look, I'll just run in, grab one of the movies, and slip out. Who would go into the basement besides you and Rocky?"

"You may not like what you find out," Carl warned me. Everyone's idea of peace was to stay ignorant.

"That's like people are afraid to go to doctors if they think they have cancer."

"I never go to doctors," Carl said.

"Switch with Duffy, will you? I don't trust him not to tell Rocky or the Boss."

"You'd get hurt," Carl said.

"That's why I want you there."

Carl agreed finally, when he saw that I was desperate. Actually, I used the same approach on him that Janet used on me. If he didn't help, I'd go in when Duffy was there. He very unhappily told me that he owed Duffy a couple of hours anyway for coming in late one night the week before. We agreed Carl would get there at ten. I would get there at ten-fifteen, do the deed, and be at work by ten-thirty so I would be covered if anyone asked.

The giant brass and glass lobby door of 811 was almost always open that time of night because tenants were going in and out every few minutes. Carl watched the door and ran the elevator, so I waited in the doorway across the street until I saw one of the tenants enter, then followed a few seconds behind him. I caught a glimpse of Carl as he peeked out the closing elevator door. He tried for a smile of encouragement, but actually looked like he was sticking his head out of the elevator to throw up.

I knew this was ridiculous, slinking around like the Continental Op, but on I went to the far end of the lobby and through the door that led to the service elevator—a conveyance I'd learned to operate when I used to go with Carl to smoke dope in the cellar. It was the only elevator to the cellar; the only other way was a stairway that they kept locked. If I kept the elevator with me, someone might wonder who was in the cellar, but no one would be able to get down to find out without either ringing the bell for the elevator or getting the key from Carl. Sam the Hammer would have called it a sure thing. Thinking about Sam, I remembered the gun, wondering if this were the kind of caper he had in mind when he gave it to me. I'd forgotten all about it; it never even occurred to me that I should have it with me. The idea of it sent shivers down my back and turned the cartilage in my knees to sponge.

Hyper-alert, I heard and measured every creak and groan of the elevator chains. When the creaking stopped and the elevator thudded softly to a stop, I opened the iron grill, peered into the murkiness of the cellar, then made my way stealthily toward the rumble of the boilers. Why I tiptoed across the cellar if I was certain no one was in the basement might have been a mystery itself had I thought of it. But I didn't think; I'd become a creature of cunning and wits and senses, all instinct. I crept toward the cabinet in the makeshift lounge of sagging couches behind the boilers where Rocky kept the films and his movie projector. I didn't have a flashlight or anything to pry open a lock with if that were necessary, this B&E thing not being my first line of work. It occurred to me that people in the business probably did an apprenticeship before they went off on their own, as there was not much room for mistakes during on-the-job training.

Maybe the cabinet wasn't locked. And if no one was in the cellar, there was no reason not to turn on the lights. If I could only find the light switch…

Someone saved me the trouble. In a glare of light that will stand in my memory as bright as the Second Coming, the boiler room lit up like Yankee Stadium. I was caught between first and second and the pitcher still had the ball.

Actually, only one little light bulb went on; it swung jauntily from its own wire a foot or so above the head of the Boss and his goon—who had remembered to bring his gun. The Boss smiled placidly; the goon stared grimly.

"Barkeep. Barkeep," said the Boss, clucking a little and shaking his head, like he was the principal and I was the kid gone bad. This parasitic, degenerate sucker of society's blood, purveyor of filth, corrupter of children, pilferer of the quarters and dollars of the poor, this boil-like symptom of society's systemic corruption, *he* was clucking like a duck and shaking his head at me.

"I told you to pour drinks," he said sadly. His eyes looked completely closed. I wondered how he knew it was me.

My insides crashed in a lump somewhere around my ankles. Frozen to the spot, I stared, as if it might all go away if I looked long enough. This feeling of absolute awfulness that I'd felt only once before in my life—when I knew my mother was dead—this feeling of irreparable doom jolted through me like high-voltage electricity, standing my hair up straight and wobbling my knees.

"Hello Boss," I said when I could talk. "What are you doing here?"

"People think it's fine to take things that don't belong to them," the Boss said. "Tell stories about a person's business. I treat you like a gentleman....I treat everyone like a gentleman who knows how to act like one." His little weasel eyes opened a crack and bored into mine. "When was I not a gentleman?"

He phrased the question broadly, I thought. Certainly, I could guess at some times when he wasn't. But, all in all, he had always acted well around me. He talked pleasantly, tuned me up, tipped well, paid me compliments on my bartending and my intelligence, talked to me about his sons, introduced me to his wife. I didn't know whom he had extorted or beaten or stolen from, or even murdered—or if he had done any of these things; it seemed hard to believe he would, but then I couldn't imagine anyone would. Yet Angelina was still dead, and the guy with him still held a gun. Maybe it was already out of the Boss's hands. He wouldn't kill me if it was up to him, but it wasn't anymore. The boys from Jersey had sent this other thug over to take care of it.

"Look, Boss, you've always been okay with me," I began.

He looked hurt; his eyelids drooped again, his nodding slowed from self-righteousness to martyrdom, his lips pursed and his clucking stopped. "Why do you do this?"

"I don't know what you mean."

His eyes flickered open and anger sparked from them; his face hardened, and he seemed capable of all the evil I'd ever imagined for him. Then the elevator bell rang like a shot. We all jumped. I was amazed the gun didn't go off.

"Take it up," the Boss told the goon.

The goon looked at me and then at the Boss. "I don't know how," he said.

The Boss shook his head, then looked at me. "Take him up," he said, nodding toward the goon, who looked like he'd been dressed for the job by Damon Runyon. Dark jacket.

Black shirt. White tie. Baggy black pants. Small and skinny. He wasn't young either. While he followed me to the elevator through the dank, murky cellar, I decided I could take him. Somehow I could do it. I had the feeling in my bones, a rush of excitement like a hit of coke. The shot of adrenaline. I thought I could take him, but decided to wait. I wanted to see who rang the bell. Maybe it was the cops.

I drove the rickety elevator up one floor, opened the iron grating, waited for the big outside door to open. There stood Carl—and Janet Carter.

Things get to a point where they can't get any worse; then, they do.

"What's taking you so long," Carl asked in a jittery voice. Not nearly as jittery as it was about to become, though. He looked at the man behind me; he looked at me. Understanding and fear registered on his face, but then as he stared at the goon a couple of puffs of anger rose to the surface from the Captain Haddock side.

"What did you find?" Janet asked excitedly, not grasping the significance of the character behind me. "Do you have them? Did you look at any of them?" When I didn't answer, she looked at Carl. Seeing his face, she looked back at me. She noticed the man and the gun. She screamed.

"In," the man said. I could tell that Carl, who had just snorted a couple of times like a bull, made him nervous.

"Now everybody's here," the Boss said when we got back to the boiler room. His manner was obsequious, like the worst kind of funeral director. "Good evening, miss. As I told your friend here before, I am very sorry about your sister." Through their narrow slits his eyes burned into hers. "Not me," he said. "I told him."

"Let her go," I said. "She'll go back home and forget about all this."

"See, you are a gentleman," said the Boss. He moved slowly and spoke softly, turning toward me when he spoke. He was smaller than I had thought too. I judged the Boss and the goon together didn't make up one of Carl. "We would all like to keep the lady out of this. But what does she know?"

"She doesn't know anything," I said.

"All of you take things that don't belong to you and don't mind your own business. She knows everything you know. Just tell me now what do you want? You want movies, take them." He handed a packet to Janet. "To watch them at home? To give them as gifts? Once I had a movie of your sister—a work of art. Now I had to burn it. You want all the movies to burn up?"

Janet stared at him. Her face was white, but she stood straight and held herself firmly. He knew what we wanted the movies for; he'd known we would be there. Of course the cops wouldn't come to our rescue. I didn't know if she'd figured it out, but I had.

"We made a mistake," I told the Boss. "We talked to someone we shouldn't have….Maybe we didn't know who was a gentleman."

Still unruffled, his eyes slits once more, the Boss smiled. "We're all gentlemen," he said. "Perhaps you didn't know how things work."

"I guess not."

"Too bad," said the Boss. "You look for one thing, you find something else. We'll have to leave here now, all together."

"Maybe we can work something out," I said.

Carl, who had been speechless since we met at the elevator, perked up. "You don't have to kill us," he said in what I gathered he thought was a reasonable tone, though he sounded to me a bit argumentative for the position we were in. He was fully into one of his Captain Haddock moods and under normal conditions not to be trifled with. These, however, were far from normal conditions.

"We're good secret-keepers," I agreed. "The bartender's code: 'I enter my friend's house deaf; I leave dumb.'"

The Boss liked that. "You were always a gentleman," he said. "Too bad."

As we walked solemnly to the elevator, Carl in front muttering to himself, Janet clutching my arm, I got an idea. Putting my head close to hers, I whispered a two-sentence plan. "Now lean against Carl in the elevator and tell him," I said.

I could see Carl's body puff up a bit more when she told him. The plan unfolded quickly when the elevator bounced to a stop at the main floor. Since Janet and I were to get off first, we jumped ahead. Carl whacked the lever that sent the elevator bouncing and grumbling back toward the cellar. Then, he jumped. The elevator was already a couple of feet below the floor when the goon and the Boss realized what was happening. In their panic to get out, they forgot about us, and when they did clamber up out of the elevator well, they instinctively looked back for a quick second at the gaping cavern created by the descending elevator. In that split second, Carl let out a roar, jumped forward, and shoved. The goon followed the elevator into the abyss.

The Boss, looking more dapper than ever, stepped back from the hole, peered over at his departing colleague, dusted off his hands as if that was a phase of his life that no longer mattered, then, his eyes wide open, smiled at Carl.

"Nice!" he said.

I had no idea what to do next now that we seemed to have captured a gangster and a gunman. Actually, I wanted to call the whole thing off. Janet, however, was not to be thrown off the scent.

"Who killed my sister?" she asked the Boss, looking into the elevator shaft. "Did he?"

The "he" in question was remarkably quiet. I expected him to yell. But it occurred to me that folks in his line of work would not want to see anyone who might choose to help them.

"Not us," the Boss said.

"Who?" I asked.

He shook his head. "You should know."

With much talk about gentlemanliness and peace, we reached a Mexican standoff with the Boss. He recognized that our interest was in who killed Angelina and not his varied nefarious activities. We'd stumbled onto an operation we would forget about. The Boss would persuade the gentleman in the elevator well that there would be no hard feelings. We would stay alive. Life would return to its everyday sordidness.

Chapter Seven

"Why would you believe him?" Janet asked after the Boss and his henchman left—the latter nursing lumps and bruises and limping along behind—and we sat shaking together in Carl's small cubicle off the lobby.

"He's a gentleman," Carl reminded her.

"He was willing to kill us for what we found out." She looked from me to Carl and back to me. "How do you know he'll leave us alone?"

"Life on a darkling plain..." Carl said.

He was right. The ground shifted beneath my feet; ignorant armies clashed by night. The world wasn't safe at all.

When I got behind the bar, an hour late, I poured myself a shot of tequila, washing it down with a beer.

"All sorts of people looking for you," Oscar said to jangle my nerves again as soon as he sensed they might be settling. He and Sam sat next to one another at the end of the bar, each with his own copy of *The Racing Form*.

"Who?"

"Big guy.... Tough.... Very tough." Oscar looked carefully around him, as if the tough giant might be lurking in the dining room behind the partition.

"Who?" I asked again. Sam the Hammer swatted his hand in Oscar's direction, brushing him away. So Oscar zipped off to clear some tables and get in the waitress's way.

"What a night," I said.

"Don't tell me," said Sam. He stared angrily at *The Racing Form*, as if it had done something terrible to him, which it probably had.

My nerves let go when the tequila hit. I snapped. The tequila worked on me like Popeye's spinach. I'd had one riddle too many. I no longer cared; I'd had enough. I was ready to kill Sam, Oscar, and the rest of the fucking winos.

"Why the gun?" I growled at Sam through my teeth, my face an inch from his.

He didn't say anything. Dummied up is the proper expression.

"For the Boss?"

"That was your idea." He looked at me contemptuously. "Use it to blow your fucking brains out."

"Did the Boss have Angelina killed?"

He looked straight at me, no longer seeing, his face blank. I felt like I'd disappeared. Fortunately, I was rescued by a loud feminine voice.

"I've been looking for you for days," Betsy Blumberg shrilled at me. "Have you forgotten I exist?" Already half-sloshed, she was starting to look a little disheveled, her mouth gone a bit slack, her lipstick smeared, wisps of hair loose from her ponytail. I hadn't noticed her at the bar when I came in. I really was glad to see her.

"I have some news, but I got a good mind not to tell you. I'm sick and tired of you never-come-back, never-call men."

"It's okay, Betsy." I patted her hand that rested on the bar. Just this was enough; she didn't need a whole lot of kindness, just a drop now and then.

"I missed you. Should I wait for you tonight?"

I was tempted to say yes. Janet had gone back to her hotel, depressed and disappointed, taking a cab downtown. The cab, in fact, had been Ntango's. He was parked outside Oscar's when we got there. Janet wouldn't come into the bar when I asked her. She didn't want to see me later. This time, I was sure she'd head back to Springfield, though she'd told me she'd taken the whole week off.

I wanted to spend the night with Betsy, but it wasn't a good idea. I needed to spend some time sober, thinking things through. Also, tomorrow was my Saturday to go to Brooklyn to see Kevin. Yet I didn't have the heart to tell Betsy to go away. While I tried to figure this one out, I caught a glimpse of a drunk staggering up Broadway. He was on the far side of the street, hunched down into his jacket—staggering furtively, if such a thing is possible.

"That's Ozzie," I said out loud, as if that would explain everything. "I'll be right back."

I dashed out of the bar, calling him. When he looked up, I felt like I'd turned into Dr. Death on my sprint across the street. He held both arms up to ward me off. I looked in my own hands for the scythe.

"Ozzie," I said. "You okay?" His eyes and his mouth formed a silent scream of terror. Startled-looking, birdlike Ozzie looked like that bird after he'd gotten caught in a hard and heavy downpour: He couldn't quite get himself into the air the way his instincts told him he should, and he didn't know what had gone wrong.

Is this what a murderer becomes? I wondered. Why would anyone bother to punish Ozzie? He'd already done it himself, a worse punishment than any judge could dole out. "Take it easy, Ozzie. It's me, Brian. I'm a friend."

For a moment he looked like he believed me. He reached out for my hand, catching my sleeve instead and holding on. The terror melted from his eyes. I put my arm around his shoulder.

"You need a cab to get home," I said. "But later, I need to talk to you."

He nodded dumbly.

"About Angelina."

He nodded again.

"Did you kill her?"

He looked into my eyes, rolling his head solemnly from side to side. "I know," he said. Then, once more, his eyes froze with terror. Someone else came up on us. God damn Nigel, with his lopsided grin. The cab I'd flagged down sat idling at the curb. I wanted to get Ozzie into it before the driver realized he was drunk and took off.

"Grab that cab, Nigel," I said.

"Old Oz needs some help getting home? I'll take him along with me." Nigel's good nature and cheerfulness was a rebuke to us weaklings worshipping at the altar of demon rum.

"Better take the cab."

"I can hold him. He'd like the exercise. Wouldn't you, Ozzie?"

Ozzie had crumbled in the meantime. He looked like the condemned man who loses his nerve walking the final hallway to the death chamber: his knees buckle and he shits in his pants. Nigel held Ozzie up. He was surprisingly strong, holding Ozzie effortlessly with one arm. Nigel had a lot of experience walking drunks home. He and I were the neighborhood good Samaritans. The cab took off.

"I'm working or I'd go with you," I told Nigel.

He waved me off with his free hand, hoisted Ozzie up against him with the other, talking encouragingly as Ozzie lifted one wavering foot and then the other.

"Maybe you can get him to talk about things on the way home."

By this time, Ozzie's head had drooped so far that his chin rested on his chest. Nigel looked at him and shook his head. "I doubt it," he said.

Somewhere around one, Janet showed up at Oscar's with Ntango.

"Ntango took me on a tour," she said. Her mood had improved dramatically. "I think I found out something." Once more she bubbled with enthusiasm. Bubbling until she spotted Betsy drooped over the end of the bar watching her. She stiffened like the old alley cat coming upon an arch enemy. How she knew I had anything to do with Betsy was completely beyond me. But I felt like she'd just walked in and found us in the sack.

"But I guess you're busy," she said.

"No, I'm not."

"You're an asshole," Janet said. She swallowed her drink in a gulp, took Ntango's arm and walked out, returning Betsy's smile with an icy stare.

〜〜〜

At the end of my shift, I closed out the register. Oscar usually pushed the limits of the closing law, and we often stayed with a dozen or so regulars and the lights down low until five, even later. This night, I told Oscar to take over and left with Betsy.

As we walked up Broadway, I told Betsy, who had somewhat sobered up, that I needed to go home because I had to get up early.

"It's alright," she said sadly. "Your new girlfriend has really latched on, hasn't she? Maybe we could just have a cup of coffee."

"I don't think I even want that," I told her. But I did walk her home and kissed her goodnight in front of her building.

"This is quite gallant of you," Betsy said. Then, when she had opened the door, she grabbed my arm and said, "I almost forgot. The other day when we were talking about who might have killed Angelina, after you left, I remembered that once, when I was in Reuben's apartment, I saw a clipping from an old newspaper about a woman who had been murdered. It was long before all this happened. I was just looking through some books and it was inside one of them. It was old and brownish and crumbly, from *The Journal-American*."

"Do you remember the date?"

Betsy shook her head. "I just put it back. It made me feel creepy. Why would someone have an old newspaper article about someone being murdered?"

↩ ↩ ↩

In the morning, I went to the 42nd Street library on the off chance the newspaper clipping Betsy found was about Reuben himself, and called Janet from a pay phone there to ask if she'd like to go to Brooklyn with me. I did it without thinking. I'd never brought anyone with me before.

"My, you're up early," she said.

"I've been up for an hour," I told her pointedly. "I left Oscar at the bar and went home right at closing."

"Alone?"

"Of course."

She agreed to meet me in the main reading room at noon, so I went to look through the back issues of the *Journal-American*. I'd gotten through about a dozen copies, going backwards from the final issue in 1966, before I realized that the paper was probably indexed. The idea was good, but there wasn't an index. So I kept slogging through the microfilm, but found no Reuben Foster. A bunch of Fosters over the years for various accomplishments and defaults, but nothing on Reuben, and nothing on a murder.

Janet found me among the wooden desks and creaking chairs in the silence of the reading room. She moved through the room toward me, rustling in her dress and October coat; her demeanor was reverent enough for the place, like someone who was used to it might tiptoe through a church at a pretty brisk pace.

She sat down next to me, and I told her what I was doing and about drawing a blank on the index. I made it clear that I was talking with Betsy only to gather information, so she should be ashamed of herself for thinking otherwise. But she saw right through my story.

"Oh yeah. Have you ever been to bed with her?"

I didn't answer.

"You have."

On the train out to Flatbush, Janet told me what she'd found out and wouldn't tell me the night before.

"A bartender at a place across the street from Hanrahan's said Angelina used to come in there sometimes to meet an older man." The train was noisy, so she had to lean close to tell me this. I leaned even closer until her mouth brushed my ear.

"Oh?" I asked when she moved away from me.

"Maybe we should find out who he was."

"We should. But Angelina met a lot of men a lot of places."

"You're downplaying this because I found out about it and not you."

"Jesus," I said. "All right. Let's find out. Did you ask the bartender?"

"Of course. He didn't know who the man was."

"What did the guy drink?"

"How should I know?" Her expression suggested I might be dumber than she'd originally thought.

"The bartender would know if he came in any way regularly," I said patiently. "Bartenders know people by what they drink."

"I'll find out."

Janet was relieved that we were picking Kevin up at my father's apartment, and she wouldn't have to meet my ex-wife. "I couldn't think of a more awful experience. What's she like?"

I didn't know why Janet was interested in this, but she seemed eager for an answer. "She's normal. She works for the telephone company, takes good care of Kevin, goes to church. She has a boyfriend, a neighborhood guy. He works for the phone company, too. Kevin likes him. Maybe they'll all have a new life. I certainly hope so."

"Did she leave you or did you leave her?"

"We didn't have much in common. We got married because she was pregnant. I thought that was the right thing to do. She had a miscarriage. But we stayed married anyway. I thought it was okay. I could be married and still chase around a little on the side. Sort of the open-marriage idea."

"Did she chase around?"

"The theory was she could, but I don't think she did. It got so I was never there, so I finally figured out I should leave. After I left, she told me she was pregnant. But she wouldn't let me come back...."

I stopped because I realized this was self-serving talk, soft, looking for pity. Kevin was the one who needed an explanation. If I couldn't give one to him—not one that would make things right—then I had no reason to explain to anyone else. "This isn't something we should talk about," I said.

Janet looked me over pityingly, like I might be dying of something.

~~~

For the first few minutes in my father's apartment, I wanted to leave. Kevin had grown sullen as he entered his teen years. He was playing a stupid video game he'd attached to my father's television. He didn't act glad to see me, and he wasn't friendly to Janet. This was his prerogative. He didn't owe me anything. Most of the time, though, we got along. Besides the fact he was my son, I liked him. He liked the Grateful Dead, peace better than war, felt sorry for poor people without thinking they had done something wrong to make themselves poor, didn't like Yuppies, thought Republicans sucked. I liked him a lot, even now when he thought himself too cool to hug.

"This boy's brain is turning to mush," my father said. "He sits there shooting beams of light at little figurines for hours at a time. When he gets tired of one set he puts it away, then takes out another and sits there shooting beams of light at different figurines."

"You're just mad because you can't do it," he told his grandfather. My son had a nice face still soft with youth, and his eyes, green like mine, were shy and gentle looking.

"Can I try?" Janet asked politely. I thought he would immediately see through this ruse of the new girlfriend making friends with the sullen son. But he stood up, gracious as Sir Galahad, and let her sit down. She whooped and giggled and laughed like a ten-year-old. He cheered her on, and showed her some tricks of the trade. They talked back and forth, engrossed in one another and the game.

Pop puttered around the apartment, back and forth to the kitchen, making some coffee, looking for a coffee cake he thought he had, and finally finding it. He has surprisingly good-sized shoulders and an almost-flat stomach. He was in better shape than I was and looked respectable if not distinguished. He kept his hair crewcut short, and his clothes were plain and neat, a cardigan sweater over a sport shirt and gabardine slacks, the same kind of clothes he'd worn all his life. Like his movements, his blue eyes were quick and alert. He poured me some coffee, and I told him about Angelina's murder, about the Boss and the cops on the take. I asked him about the *Journal-American*, and Reuben.

"Newspaper indexes, except for the *Times,* don't exist or are incomplete. They miss things. But somewhere there should be the clip files and someone who remembers…and the *Times* sometimes would cover a murder if they thought it was important. Let me make a couple of calls."

I liked how my father worked. I watched as he opened his flat ancient metal alphabetical file of phone numbers, sliding the clip along the side of the metal book until it lined up with the right letter, then pushing the clip so it sprang open. He'd had the phone book since I was a baby; many of the numbers still began with exchanges like MU 6 or BU 8. Watching him now made me quiver with the same excitement I felt as a kid. I loved watching him work then, even if it was only making a phone call. I thought he did it better than anyone else in the world ever did. I brought the same faith now, as I waited for him to get the information, as I did when I came to him as a kid with a math problem or a question of history, when I knew he did everything I'd ever learned a good father should do only to be shunned by the neighbors, fired from his jobs, and disowned by his friends and relatives.

"November 18, 1952," my father said when he put down the phone. I stared at him. "Don't write down the date," he said. "You can call me back from the library when you forget it."

He joined me at the round dining room table after attempting to warm up the coffee and boiling it in the process. I couldn't remember a time in recent years that he'd heated up the coffee without boiling it. He sputtered and muttered but poured it out anyway. It tasted like a brew of old shoes.

Even though he had a nicely furnished living room, which was neat as a pin, life took place around the dining room table. When I came to visit, we sat at it to talk. On the nights I stayed over, I came out from the bedroom to find him reading at the dining room table. I remembered that years before, when I visited him in North Carolina where he was organizing for the Furniture Workers Union, we sat at this same round dining room table. Besides a bed, it was the only piece of furniture in the small house he rented down there.

He patted the volume of Lenin he was reading. "His meanings are twisted by his followers. Like Freud, Darwin, even like Shakespeare. If you want to learn about something, read the originals, not their interpreters."

"Lenin interpreted Marx," I reminded him.

"You can't make sense of Lenin without reading Marx; that's what I mean." His face tightened and his eyes hardened; he wouldn't be made fun of. But I could see in his eyes that once more the quixotic hope of rescuing me from failure had taken hold of him.

"Most murders are committed by ordinary people," he said. "Usually someone the victim knows."

Janet pulled up a chair at the table. Kevin watched from in front of the TV, interested now that the subject of murder had come up, the figurines given a breather. When my pop spoke like this, you felt like you should sit at his feet and listen.

"If you want to find out who killed the girl, you need to know everything there is to know about her: What did she do? Where did she go? Who did she talk to and why?"

"Why?" I asked. "Why bother? What difference does it make if we find the killer? It doesn't bring Angelina back to life." At this moment, everything seemed futile. I couldn't think of any reason to do anything, so I took it out on my old man.

As usual, he had an answer, whether I wanted one or not. "Taking a life is wrong. Wars, executions, crimes of passion, or just plain neglect, all of it is wrong. Life is the only thing we have. Instead of doing what it takes to prevent murder, our society's response in these barbaric times is to track down and capture the culprit. We think this makes up for not doing what we might have done to keep the murder from happening in the first place. But maybe it's a step in that direction, a recognition that life is sacred."

⌐ ⌐ ⌐

Janet and I took Kevin into Manhattan. He wanted to see the Star Wars movie.

"It's not what you think, Dad," he said, patronizingly, standing on the corner of 41st and Broadway in his black jacket, his shoulders hunched, one hip thrust out—a stance learned on the street corners of Brooklyn.

"Oh?" I said. "And what is it that I think?"

"That it's violent and pro-capitalist and anti-working class."

"Is that what Grandpa said?"

"That's what he says about everything: TV, movies, my school books."

"Maybe he's right."

Kevin's sullenness broke; his face shone with that kid's earnestness too often missing. "Everything isn't terrible, is it? Something is good, isn't it?"

All of a sudden, he was young again, eager, earnest, hopeful. Watching him, I remembered the night I talked with Nigel about his not seeing his father for so many years. It made me wonder if I might be driving Kevin away with my own bleak take on life. I thought again how lucky I was—even if I was a lousy father—to have my son. This was one of those moments when just because I was with Kevin I was filled up with this whatever it was—joy, or something ridiculous like that.

I tousled his head. "Sorry, pal." I said, then, as brightly as an ingenue, "Let's go to the movies…"

He laughed, then grimaced. It was a line from *Annie,* a movie he loved when he was little—something he was now too cool to own up to.

━ ━ ━

When we'd walked up Broadway a block or so, Kevin stopped me. "I got an idea," he said. "Her and I can go to the movie. You go to the library."

This was okay with me, and seemed to be even better than okay with both of them. We agreed to meet later at my apartment, so I gave Kevin a quick hug and handed Janet the key to my apartment, kissing her quickly on the lips as I did, figuring she wouldn't make a scene and slug me in front of the kid.

I'd gone a half block east on 42nd Street toward the library when Kevin trotted up behind me. "We decided to stay downtown. Meet us in front of the theater at 5:15." Then, as he turned to leave, he almost smiled. "She's nice," he said and trotted on into the crowd.

━ ━ ━

In the library, I found the *New York Times* from November 18, 1952. From thirty years past, on paper now yellowed, bound in one of those pebbly black hard back covers that pre-date microfilm, a blurred picture of a young, strong Reuben Foster looked stonily out at me. He stood between two gray-suited detectives, both surely retired by now if not dead. He'd just been convicted of manslaughter for the murder of his wife Dorothy, the story stated matter-of-factly. Murders weren't happening three to the day in 1952, but even so I was surprised he got a write-up in the *Times* until I realized his wife was white. Fascinated, I read the news story over and over, expecting it would tell me something about why Reuben killed his wife, about what their lives had been like. But it told the story without really telling me anything, just facts and figures.

〜〜〜

Later at Nathan's, where we'd gone on my insistence, Janet told me something I would have known myself if I watched TV and went to more movies: a manslaughter charge meant you killed someone without having intended to in advance.

"What now?" I asked after my hot dog, french fries, and beer.

"God, what a lame supper," Kevin said. "Let's walk around until we get hungry and eat something decent."

We browsed through record stores, bookshops, and a couple of glittering electronics stores, meandering our way uptown. I sucked in the hum of the street and the glaring lights, the unending rush of people picking us up like a conveyor belt, rushing us forward until we got off at our next stop. The energy electrified me. I took strength from the city on nights like this; chaotic life made sense for a time.

Around 9:00, we ate a late dinner at a Chinese on Broadway in the Nineties. Kevin stayed at my apartment that night. Janet agreed to have breakfast with us the next morning downtown and go to the comic bookstore across from the Strand on Broadway near Twelfth.

The first thing Janet said when we slid into the booth across from her in a coffee shop on Eighth Street the next morning was, "The older man with Angelina drank Jack Daniels."

"That's a start," I said. "But lots of people drink Jack Daniels." What I didn't say was that Ozzie was one of them.

After breakfast, I thumbed through Tin Tin books in the comic store, more pleased than I would let on that Kevin told Janet about how I used to read them to him and that he still had his copies home under his bed, along with his Madeline and Babar books.

"Reuben Foster killed his wife before I was born," Janet said as we browsed through the Strand after dropping Kevin and his armload of comics at the subway.

We had lunch at a Mexican restaurant on MacDougal Street and, following my father's advice, decided we were going to talk to every single person Angelina knew. The race was on. At the moment, Reuben challenged Ozzie for the pole position, but Ozzie held on to the lead. We were barely into the first turn with the field crowded and the track sloppy.

Thinking through what my father said about knowing everything I could about Angelina, I wondered why she'd chosen the Upper West Side of all the neighborhoods in New York. If she'd been Jewish, a classical musician, a leftist, a former Barnard student, a serious acting student, it would make sense. If she knew one of the above, it would make sense.

"Why did Angelina come to New York," I asked Janet again.

"Excitement, I guess. She wanted to be an actress or a singer. And she wanted all the glitzy and trendy things of New York, too. She wanted to dress in high heels and wear make-up. She wanted to date men who wore three-piece suits instead of guys in dungarees with grease under their fingernails. She wanted to marry a millionaire. Why? Don't thousands of girls come to New York for the same reasons?" Her dark eyes clouded as she tried to peer deeper into mine.

"Why did she come to the Upper West Side then? Why not the East Side?"

"What's the difference?"

"The East Side is trendy, not the Upper West Side. The East Side is where she'd find the guys in the suits and the millionaires. Did she know anyone in New York?"

"No one I could name." Janet wrinkled her brow, not even noticing the guacamole salad the waitress put in front of her. I, however, noticed my bottle of Dos Equis. "But she might have. She went to New York a few times. Then, one day, she decided she'd move. I wondered, then, if she might have met someone."

"But she said no? She didn't seem to know anyone when I first met her."

Janet said, "Looking back now, I wonder…" I pointed to her guacamole. When she returned from her memories, she took a bite and said, "Angelina was smug and secretive when she was moving, which she never was with me. There was something about New York she wasn't telling me."

"Is there anyone around Oscar's you might have seen before?"

"No."

"Anyone who'd ever been in Springfield or wherever it is?"

"No."

"Anyone who knew more about Angelina than you expected?"

"Why do you ask all this?" Janet pushed her plate away; her eyes flared at me. "What are you getting at?"

"I don't know. When Angelina first started coming into the bar, I sometimes got the feeling she was looking for someone. All of a sudden, she had a lot of money. She said she had a sugar daddy. I thought she was kidding, but maybe she wasn't. She got a really good job. I thought the money must come from that. But it seems to me now she might have had too much money for even that good of a job. A kid with no experience shouldn't make that much money, not even if she's as pretty as Angelina."

"Where do you think she got the money?"

"I'm not thinking. I'm wondering."

Janet searched my face, as if she suspected I was keeping something from her. I wondered, too, what she might be keeping from me.

"Anyway," Janet said when she had looked at me long enough. She had an orderly business type mind and the ability to stick to the question through thick and thin. "To answer your question, the person who seems to know most about her besides you is Nigel. And also Carl. You should know how well she knew them."

I tried to remember when Angelina met Carl or Nigel. It seemed she'd known Carl as long as she'd known me, although I couldn't remember when she first met him. I did remember when she first met Nigel. He wasn't around when she began coming into Oscar's. When she did see him, though, she really latched on. Then everything cooled off fast. Maybe he'd become insanely jealous. But, Nigel, as weird as he was, didn't seem the insanely jealous type. He'd stayed friends with her, pined after her, hung around and made a pest of himself. But I'd seen enough insanely jealous, control freak drunks to know he wasn't one of them. Besides, Nigel told me he was in Connecticut that night.

"Do you think we should find out more about Nigel and Carl?" Janet asked, interrupting my reverie.

"I just happen to know that Nigel was visiting his father when Angelina was killed and Carl was working."

"Oh," Janet said, looking up abruptly from her salad. "How do you know?"

"They told me."

"Maybe they didn't tell the truth." This tone of hers, suggesting I was an idiot child, was getting on my nerves.

"Nigel was with his father. He wouldn't lie about that."

"That should be easy enough to check," said Janet smugly. I was sure we were having an argument, but I didn't know about what. She took a notebook out of her shoulder bag and stood up. "What's his last name and where does he live?"

"You're going to call Nigel's father, now?"

"Now," she said.

I nursed my enchilada and slugged down a Dos Equis while I waited. She came back quickly.

"This amazing thing happened. I got the number from information, then dialed the number in Connecticut, and Nigel's father's office answered the phone in New York."

"How about that?"

"He's very busy. But he'll see us." She began gathering up her things.

"Now?"

"Yes."

"Shit." I had just drunk my third Dos Equis and needed a nap before work. Besides, I didn't want to talk to Nigel's father. Since I was a kid, I never got along with anyone's parents. On top of this, it was invading Nigel's privacy. It violated whatever friendship or acquaintanceship we had. Already, I'd dug into Reuben's life. Whatever happened to Do Unto Others? I certainly wouldn't want anyone digging into my life.

⌐ ⌐ ⌐

Edwin Barthelme occupied an office-living suite in the Olympia Towers, neighbor across one street to Rockefeller Center and across another to St. Patrick's Cathedral. After a concierge announced us—this concierge assisted by two sub-alterns, who, were they dressed differently, might easily be mistaken for goons—we took an elevator to the twenty-ninth floor.

When the elevator door slid open, we stepped out into Mr. Barthelme's plushly carpeted, elegantly appointed tax write-off. Himself, giving the impression of tallness, grayness, suaveness, and indifference, looked up from the far end of the suite, where he stood gazing over the city from his floor to ceiling window. He'd left the door between his office and the anteroom open and now walked across the room—about a quarter mile—stretching out his hand toward me when he got within hailing distance. All of this, given the expensive cut of his gray suit, the contrasting grays of the sky and buildings beyond the window, the gray blue of the carpet, and the wide, gray expanse of the room, was an event in itself.

I watched raptly; it was better than any number of movie entrances I'd seen. Janet caught her breath. I expected I'd have to peel her off the double pile carpet.

In those few seconds, Barthelme took us both in. His eyes, though shining brightly enough in greeting, gave us to know, distinctly and beyond a shadow of doubt, that our relative wealth, social standing, and, more importantly, the amount of claim we might have on his time and interest had been measured. The results had been announced too, for those discerning enough to recognize them. We would not be taking up much of Mr. Barthelme's time.

"Edwin Barthelme." The man grasped my hand firmly, his steady gray eyes meeting my undoubtedly bloodshot ones. In spite of myself, I looked away, and my self-esteem immediately dropped nine stories. Janet, though, I was happy to see, held up our end of the contract, going after him handshake to handshake, steady gaze to steady gaze.

He was one of those people not comfortable with being tall who tried too hard to get down close to the people smaller than him. It had left him with a permanent stoop to his shoulders. He also had that drastic thinness of the rich that suggests overbreeding, but his face was etched with lines of the toughness that comes from the hard hustle and that you don't see in those born to wealth, while the wrinkles at the corners of his eyes suggested he might have a sense of humor about the whole chase for a buck.

When we'd seated ourselves on chairs and couches grouped around a clear glass coffee table, Mr. Barthelme looked expectantly at me and, when I looked somewhat sheepishly back at him, at Janet. It was clear he was in charge. He would define the conversation, set the mood, establish the permissible. How the hell were we going to ask him where his son was that night, the question bringing with it the implication that we suspected Nigel of murder?

Janet knew how. "It is very unpleasant to have to ask you these questions," she said. "And of course, you're under no obligation to answer." Her voice wavered a little here, and her eyes began to mist over. "I could never even bring myself to do this, except I have to do everything I can, no matter how unpleasant, to find out what happened to my sister." And there on the brink of accomplishment, she lost her composure. Her voice cracked; she stopped in mid sentence. Her faltering might have been forgivable if it hadn't put me on the spot. Sure enough, Barthleme turned to me, as if now that this woman was out of the way, we men could get to the point.

"I'll tell you what we're doing, Mr. Barthelme," I said, stiffening my upper lip. "We're trying to find out everything we can about Angelina and everyone who knew her. Your son Nigel knew her."

"I understand," said Barthelme, "that a young woman with whom my son was acquainted was killed. I gather that her sister is distraught and understandably so. I don't know why you brought her here. I don't know what your role might be. Or mine. Or my son's."

"Me neither," I said, letting the "you brought her here" crack go.

Realizing I wasn't getting us anywhere, Janet regrouped. "We're asking about every single person that Angelina knew, not just Nigel. Can you understand how important it is for me to know what really happened to my sister?" Janet's face was appealing, showing that vulnerability in it again that on her was so fleeting.

"I understand sorrow far better than you could ever imagine… as does my son," said Mr. Barthelme. "I understand your concern for your sister, but it's difficult for me not to resent your maligning my son." His face didn't show anger exactly; it was more indignation. The rich have cornered the indignation market.

"Nigel said he was with you. We just want to make sure he was," I said.

"If he told you, that should be sufficient. It would be for me."

We stared at each other. One stare too many from Mr. Barthelme. I'd had enough of his superciliousness. "I'm sure it would be....Would you mind telling us why you hadn't seen your son in ten years?"

A momentary start, an involuntary movement of his eyes. The overmatched challenger landed a surprising left hook and jarred the champ. Barthelme recovered quickly. But some of the arrogance was gone. Like the champ, he was more careful now, keeping his guard up, protecting himself while his head cleared. "It would be impertinent," he said, but his voice held echoes of sadness. No longer imperious, he became a man. It was like a moment on the stage when real emotion breaks through, and you're held spellbound, audience and actors alike.

"I do understand sadness," he said to Janet. "I wish there were some way to undo what happened to your sister, and I should understand that asking these questions gives you some satisfaction. And if you understood my life...but we all know there's not nearly enough understanding to go around."

She looked at him gratefully. Now that we'd brought him down from his high horse, I was a little unsteady myself.

"My son came to see me that night a little over a week ago for the first time since he left home ten years before. It was the end of much bitterness and a long misunderstanding, a happy event for both of us, one of the few...."

"The night my sister was murdered?" Janet's voice was very quiet.

"I'm sorry." He cast his eyes down, his face that of a sad, aging man.

"Uh, about that ten years, Mr. Barthelme?" I asked, interrupting the solemn silence.

He swung around to face me, and his eyes suddenly flamed with rage like I had landed a punch below the belt after the bell.

"I wondered why you hadn't seen Nigel in ten years," I said.

"That's our business, sir. It doesn't concern you."

⌐ ⌐ ⌐

The three of us waited for the elevator in strained silence. Janet paid our thanks. Edwin Barthelme stood beside her by the elevator door. I was struck by the equality we had achieved. No longer propped up by mystique, he seemed as bewildered and overcome by life as the rest of us.

As soon as the elevator doors closed, Janet moved to the far corner and glared at me. "You're awful," she said. "How could you be so awful?"

"Awful?" I had no idea what had happened.

"How can you be so unfeeling?"

"Unfeeling?"

"You just trampled right over that man's feelings. You belong in that skid-row bar with your bums for friends. You don't know how to act among decent people."

"Being rich makes you decent?"

"You just can't get over that, can you? You can't forgive anyone for being successful or well-to-do."

"I thought we wanted to find out something."

"We did. You didn't have to act like a thug."

"Thug? Mr. Suave back there is tougher than all the thugs on Broadway. He'd chew them up and spit them out, then go out to dinner at the Four Seasons. You're the one with a problem." My voice rose in opposition to the descent of the elevator. "You're the one who thinks that asshole is better than the folks I know on Broadway because he's rich. He's rich off the backs of his workers and the old ladies he dumps into the street." I was puffing when the elevator touched ground. The doors opened and Janet stomped out, through the lobby and off down Fifth Avenue. I gave her the finger from the doorway.

Then I walked across the street to Rockefeller Center to look at the murals of the workers. Mad at myself for getting mad, I moped through the building where Diego Rivera had attempted to memorialize Lenin. Rockefeller's dad made him take it down. I remembered the poem by E.B. White that ended, "But after all, it's my wall....'We'll see if it is,' said Rivera."

⌐ ⌐ ⌐

The next morning the phone, clanging like a fire alarm, woke me at ten-thirty, approximately four hours after I'd passed out on my bed. The night before, Ntango and the Eritreans held a reunion at the end of the bar, and Ntango kept tightening me up with blow. Consequently, I drank too much and stayed up too late, and couldn't fully remember coming home.

Janet came directly to the point. "I want to see the movie you picked up that night in Rocky's cellar," she said.

At first, I didn't say anything because I was afraid of what my voice would sound like.

"Are you there?"

"I'm here," I croaked.

"What's the matter?"

"I'm sick."

"Did you get drunk?"

"I don't remember....Why do you want to see the movie? Angelina isn't in it."

"How do you know what's in it?"

⌐ ⌐ ⌐

I told her I'd meet her at three in front of Oscar's and went back to sleep. When I woke up again I still felt shaky and sick. Nonetheless, I called Carl to ask him to set up the projector in the cellar, this being Rocky's weekend in Staten Island, but Carl hung up on me.

I called Eric the Red, told him I had some porno flicks and asked him to pick up Rocky's movie projector and meet me at Oscar's.

After poached eggs and bacon at Tom's, I walked down the street a few blocks and found Eric and Janet standing in front of the darkened Oscar's. I wasn't sure what Janet was after. But I was pretty sure the Boss had already gotten rid of the films with Angelina in them, so I wasn't that worried.

"Why isn't Oscar open in the daytime," Janet asked as I unlocked the door.

"He used to be but no one came in. Our customers only come out at night."

"For good reason," said Eric.

Eric set up the projector; the joint was dark enough to run the film on the wall. The first figure that appeared when the film came into focus was Carl van Sagan, wearing only a leering grin on his face, otherwise bare-ass naked but with his engorged penis at full salute, walking toward the camera and a dark-haired woman in a supine position, whose hair and back were all that were visible. The camera switched angles quickly to show the woman's face. She was young and waifishly pretty, and looked familiar. Her expression was enthusiastically lewd, suggesting she couldn't wait for Carl and his penis to arrive, but the sadness and fear in her eyes belied the enthusiasm.

"Isn't that Carl?" Janet sputtered in a shocked tone of voice somewhere between a whisper and a gasp.

"Jesus," said Eric, in a whispered gasp of his own. "You can't. Where the fuck did you get this? Turn it off, man." He reached for the projector.

I said, "No!"

"You don't understand, man," Eric moaned.

"My God!" This time, Janet really shouted. There in front of us, his brilliant white teeth shining through his black beard, his body hairier than most bears', his weapon, as they say, at battle ready, was Eric the Red. Janet covered her face with her hands, sinking down in her seat. I shut off the projector.

"I told you, man. This is crazy," said Eric. "You nuts?" He went behind the bar and poured himself a half a glass of vodka, which he threw down in one slug. "Why you do this? I'm embarrassed."

"I didn't know you and Carl were movie stars."

"You should mind your own business." He poured another shot. "Just once..." Eric said. "Someone didn't show up.... The

Boss and Rocky gave us about a pound of blow. We all got naked to have a party. Rocky took pictures."

"Can we watch the rest of the movie," Janet asked.

Eric blushed. I could see the red through the black of his beard.

"Who was the girl?" I asked Eric.

"I don't know. She worked for them. She'd been in here a couple of times—not that night. Oscar told me she gave Rocky blow jobs for nose candy."

I remembered her, then. Mannequin-thin with big brown eyes. She came on to me the first night she was ever in the bar. But I didn't want anything to do with her. She scared me. I thought she was crazy.

My memory formed a picture of her; then it formed a picture of Nigel. It was a couple of weeks after Angelina had arrived in town. Nigel came in to Oscar's with her. The skinny girl watched him and Angelina, stared at them for a long time, then this girl began screaming at Nigel and pointing, coming at him from the far end of the bar, screaming. I grabbed her and wrestled her out of the place. She'd come at him with her claws. "You raped me," she screamed at Nigel.... "He did," she screamed at Angelina, who like all of us watched her in shock. "He raped me," she screamed. Nigel weathered the accusations totally unruffled except for the sick expression on his face. He kept telling her to calm down, asking her name, trying to talk to her.

Reuben grabbed Nigel around the neck, as if he would run out the door. But Nigel had only been smiling sickly and trying to talk to the girl. It was the kind of situation where, if you try denying it, you only begin to look guiltier. The girl's hysteria and the fact that she wanted to fuck almost every man in the bar before her encounter with Nigel didn't do her argument any good. She was about falling-down drunk and didn't make sense.

Reuben took over as her protector, so no one else cared very much. She didn't want Reuben as a protector, it turned out, and since he made it impossible for her to get rid of him, I finally pushed her out the door and into a cab. The whole thing was weird. Sloppy drunk and zombie-like, as if she'd done too many Quaaludes, she tried to pull me into the cab with her, holding on to me and kissing me. I remembered she looked so bony she should feel hard like a bag of sticks; instead she felt soft and yielding. I wanted to go with her. But she really was too crazy.

An hour later the cops showed up in the bar and took Nigel out. The next night Nigel was back. Someone, not her, had called the cops. So they checked out her story, Nigel told us, and decided she was wacky. She never came back to Oscar's. Remembering how she felt in my arms, I'd actually hoped she would come back, but I never saw her anywhere again.

I didn't tell any of this to Janet because I didn't want to set her off after Nigel, and if Eric remembered, he kept quiet about it. "Do you think you could find out her name?" I asked Eric.

"She was pretty wasn't she," Janet said, no longer giggling.

"Too skinny," said Eric. "Like a rope."

I'd had enough of skin flicks for the day, so Janet and I walked up Broadway to have lunch at Tom's.

"Does that make Eric and Carl suspects now?" she asked. She was serious.

"Not Carl, he was working." We walked some more. Out of the corner of my eye, I noticed a fleet of squad cars in front of Betsy's building. "Come to think of it, not Eric either. He was with me."

"Oh," said Janet, her tone suspicious again. "Where were you?"

I started to tell her I was with the fluegelhorn player, and had left Eric in the sack with her friend, but I thought better of it. "We were drinking in Oscar's," I said.

"Any other witnesses?"

"No." Maybe Eric had gotten up and gone for Angelina. Maybe Carl had sneaked away from his post for a half-hour. No one told the truth, not even me.

"A likely story," said Janet, once more in that superior tone that suggested she sullied her reputation by associating with me.

The fact that the cop cars were in front of Betsy's apartment building finally dawned on me. I got really scared as soon as I realized what it might mean. I began running.

"What?" Janet screamed after me. "What happened?"

I ran as fast as I could. It couldn't be, I told myself. Not Betsy, too. Pictures of her grumpy, sad, and cheerful face ran through my memory. My lungs hurt. I think I'd forgotten to breathe while I ran. In the doorway, I ran into Sheehan. His face was grim.

"Your pal Ozzie bought it," he said.

At first, his words went right through me. It took a while for Ozzie's death to become real. Soon it did sink in, and sadness for Ozzie replaced the sadness for Betsy.

I walked away without another word to Sheehan. Maybe he expected my compliments on a job well done. But, in truth, I felt just as bad about Ozzie as I did Angelina. Poor pathetic Ozzie shooting it out with the cops seemed just as much a cold-blooded murder as Angelina's.

Forgetting about Janet, I walked away, too depressed and disgusted to even be angry, across Broadway toward my own apartment. It was over. Janet had her vengeance. I didn't feel any good at all about catching Angelina's murderer. I'd fingered Ozzie. I should have figured the cops would come down on him like storm troopers and one way or another scare him to death. I wasn't cut out for rooting out the bad guys. I never could tell the bad guys from the good guys.

Except this wasn't what happened. Breathless, Janet caught up with me at the door to my building. "Where are you going? Why didn't you wait?"

"I can't stand this shit," I said. "I liked Ozzie, the poor bastard."

"Who do you think did it?"

"What?" My head spun. I sat down on the doorstep.

"Are you all right?" For a moment I only noticed the concern in Janet's eyes, and how pretty they were.

"No. I'm not all right," I said. "What happened?"

She looked perplexed. "Someone murdered Ozzie. Didn't you listen?"

"Who?"

"No one knows."

"The cops didn't?"

"Of course not."

But as my head cleared, I still wasn't sure. I told Sheehan that we might have something on the Boss. The Boss gets a tip. I tell Sheehan Ozzie might be the murderer or—as I should have known and didn't and Sheehan would have figured out—knew who the murderer was, and Ozzie gets bumped off.

Chapter Eight

I kept my suspicions to myself, not so much because I wanted to keep anything from Janet, but the suspicions were insubstantial, unformulated, like daydreams; they hadn't come together enough to be formed into words. I did tell her that when Sheehan told me Ozzie had been killed, I thought he meant he was shot when the cops came to get him.

"Why would they come to get him?"

"I told Sheehan Danny saw Ozzie in the building lobby the night Angelina was killed."

Janet's eyes widened. "You don't think—"

"What I think is whoever killed Angelina found out Ozzie saw him or her. I don't know if the cops announced this. But I give you eight-to-five they grab Danny again."

That night a harried and angry Max Christianson showed up at the bar around nine before the winos had arrived and while the small dinner crowd was munching away on Eric's Calves Liver Grandmère, the liver and onions his grandmother used to serve him back in Yugoslavia.

Max's face was thin and haggard to begin with, his body as taut as one of his guitar strings. On a good night, he broke a guitar string four or five times. On this night, he looked like one of those strings wound to the breaking point.

"The cops just picked up Danny again. The fuckers. He pushed one of them, so they knocked him down the stairs." Max's eyes darted around like a pinball. "Handcuffed, the bastards."

Peter Finch showed up a few minutes later to meet Max. He ordered a martini. I used the mixing glass and stirred the drink with the bar spoon, the spoon not the handle, until the glass frosted over, then poured it in front of him, the amount in the mixing glass filling exactly the stem glass I'd placed there. Both he and Max watched me mix the drink and pour it. It felt good to be able to do something correctly and precisely.

"Very good," Peter said after taking a sip. "I'll take a six pack."

"That bad?"

"Worse. They're charging him on two murders. Now he has a black eye, so they're adding resisting arrest. It won't be so easy to get him out this time."

"He didn't resist arrest." Max turned on Peter.

Peter looked at him over his martini. "When the cops slap you around and it shows, they charge you with resisting arrest."

"Are they saying he killed Ozzie?"

Peter nodded, then finished his martini like he really meant to drink a six pack. I made him another.

"How was Ozzie killed?"

"He was shot twice—executed—while he slept. They found a gun in a sewer grate near Danny's apartment building."

Max shook his head. "Danny never had a gun. The gun he used to fire would have taken the building down."

⌐⌐⌐

When I told all this to Janet on the phone in the morning, she wanted to call Peter to get the story straight. I'd already told her the story straight, so I didn't know why she needed to do that. The next thing I knew, she called back to tell me she was having dinner with him that night.

"I thought you were supposed to be helping. So now Danny can rot in jail while you to go off to a fucking fancy restaurant to have dinner!"

"Everyone eats dinner," she said primly. "Besides it's my first date since I've been in New York."

"What about me?"

"You weren't a date. You picked me up."

⌐ ⌐ ⌐

That afternoon, by accident, I found Reuben at the West End. I just wandered in that direction, but I must have had a hunch he would be there looking for the Barnard girls. Half the degenerates on the Upper West Side claimed to have fathered children by Barnard girls over the years. This said something about aspiration in America. Reuben was genial, sober, and alone so I sat down and took my chances, asking him a couple of questions.

"Why do you think Ozzie was killed?" I asked for openers.

"How should I know?"

"I was just wondering why anyone would kill someone," I said as if to myself.

Reuben sipped his drink, staring straight ahead.

Since I couldn't figure out how to lead up to the questions I wanted to ask, I considered for a few seconds of silence what advice my father would give. I was sure he would say, "If that's the question you want answered, ask it." So I did.

"Did you ever kill anyone?" I asked.

Reuben turned toward me with thirty years of pain cascading through his eyes. He didn't answer, just stared at me. I didn't want to make him lie, but a perverted form of discretion kept me from saying I knew he murdered his wife.

"May you never know how it feels," Reuben said, throwing back the three fingers of dark rum in his glass.

"Danny's been arrested again."

Reuben nodded. "When I first came to New York, this was one of the few bars in the city where whites and blacks drank together." We surveyed the bar together. The West End wasn't much to look at. The bar loomed in front of you as soon as you opened the door. It stretched off into the distance, made the far turn like the track at Yonkers and circled back, leaving room against the side wall for a few narrow booths and space for the standees. A workingman's steam table lunch counter stood to the left of the door; tables and game machines lined the back wall. Sometime in its more recent history a jazz room had been added by breaking through the wall to what had been the store next door. The jazz was real, the West End a historical monument.

"The Beats used to drink here," Reuben said. He looked away. "I met my wife here."

I knew without asking which one he meant.

"Didn't the cops check you out? Oscar told them you were the killer."

He looked at me over the top of his glasses. "If Oscar told them, they figured I didn't do it." After sipping his replenished drink, he went on. "They did check me out. Maybe I'm the fall guy if they can't pin it on Danny. I was home in bed. No one saw me." He drank. I signaled the bartender for another round.

"I hit her once," Reuben said.

My blood stood still. I thought he was talking about Angelina.

"But I hit her hard. She caught the corner of the sink with her head." His thick body softened; he seemed to melt into himself.

I wished I didn't know Reuben killed his wife. Invading people's lives burdened you. Like that picture of Dorian Gray, you start picking up the ugliness from them when they let go of it.

I left the West End not knowing much more than when I got there. After sharing his secrets, I didn't know if I felt closer to Reuben or more distant. I didn't know if he'd killed Angelina or not.

Finding out about everyone's past was shattering whatever illusions I had about goodness in the world, but hadn't brought me a step closer to finding Angelina's—and now Ozzie's— killer.

I was discouraged because I couldn't figure out anything. What had Ozzie seen? He'd been scared to death to tell me. But he'd started to tell me something. If only shit-headed Nigel hadn't happened along. Why was he so scared when he saw Nigel? As far as I knew, Nigel was the last person to see Ozzie alive. I wondered if the cops knew this. I didn't know how they would, except if Nigel told them himself. Or I told them. I should have asked Reuben where he was last night, too. I wasn't doing so well at this sleuthing business.

~~ ~~ ~~

Carl showed up that night at Oscar's. He hadn't been in since our escapade with the Boss, and I hadn't spoken to him since he hung up on me when I asked about the movie. He looked ready to meet his fate when he sat down. I couldn't help grinning.

"So you showed her the movie you palmed from the Boss. Did she like it?"

"She wanted to keep watching, but I made her turn it off."

"I decided when I gave up being a Catholic that sex was not immoral."

"What about inflicting pain?"

"I'm not sure."

"What about murder?"

He stared at me.

"Did you make any movies with Angelina?"

"No. But I saw one of them. A rare beauty. She should have sex with the gods. She transcended the sordidness. They didn't know what to do with her. No movie, no characters, only Angelina—everything else disappeared. The movie should be a classic....I can't believe the jerk burned it." Carl's face flushed when he finished. He'd said more than he'd meant to. Drink does that. His enthusiasm for his fantasies about Angelina was embarrassing.

"So," he said, when he'd regained himself, "how goes the sleuthing?"

For the first time, I was cagey around Carl. How did I know he didn't leave his post for a half-hour to go into the park with Angelina?

"When did you first meet Angelina?" I asked.

Carl hesitated. "I don't remember. Around the time she began coming in here."

"Did you ever sleep with her?"

For a few seconds he looked angry. "No. It seems like she would sleep with anyone else in the world except you and me." His cynicism and wit overcome, his eyes reflected truth. Then he looked over my shoulder as the door to the bar opened and Nigel came in. "Even him."

For the rest of the night, as Carl sank slowly into his stupor, loquacious and intent on the conversations he held first with Nigel, later with Max and Peter Finch, who had stopped in for a quick one and stayed for hours. Then, as the night closed toward the small hours, drinking his scotches faster and faster, absorbed in deep and profound discussion with Ntango, whose cab waited with the hood and trunk open in the bus stop outside the door, and Eric the Red, who once more made it only as far as the bar when he closed up the kitchen—for that night, I watched Carl, who was as close as I got to a friend, and kept picturing him walking with Angelina down 104th Street toward Riverside Park.

I couldn't bring myself to ask him anything else. I settled for Nigel, with whom I decided to eat breakfast at the greasy spoon. This time, I tried to ask questions methodically.

"Did you talk to the cops yet?"

Nigel nodded.

"You did?"

"You've been in bars too long," Nigel said between dainty spoonfuls of his rice pudding. "It's not a crime to tell things to the police. Despite what you believe, they want to catch murderers." He paused between spoonfuls. His eyeballs looked gigantic behind his glasses. "Besides, I walked Ozzie right up Broadway. Why should I hide anything? Any number of people could have seen us. Just like they could have seen you run across the street to talk to him."

"Did you tell the cops that?"

"I might have mentioned it. What do you care? You have an alibi. I can even vouch for you." He chuckled.

"You weren't in the bar."

"Are you kidding?" Nigel said. "I was there till closing."

I tried to remember, but it was too blurry.

"I came down right after I dropped Ozzie off."

"I don't remember," I said. "I don't even know where I am half the time."

Nigel laughed.

"Why did Ozzie look so scared when he saw you?"

Nigel sat back and raised his eyes from his rice pudding. "Ozzie was afraid of his shadow. How did he look when you ran up to him?"

Nigel had a point there. Ozzie wasn't any more scared of Nigel than he had been of me. "Did he say anything on the way home?"

"He blabbered most of the way. But I have no idea what he was talking about."

"Do you know where he was coming from?"

Nigel shook his head. "He sometimes stops off in the Village for a few on the way uptown after work."

I remembered what Janet had said about Angelina meeting someone at a bar near Hanrahan's. "Does he stop off down around Lincoln Center, too?"

"I think he might. He used to stop off to see Angelina at Hanrahan's."

We sat for a few minutes longer. I realized I liked having Nigel around. Somehow, without my intending it, he'd become part of my life. He helped shore me up. We didn't talk for a while, and it must have been that he was lost in thought, too. He looked at me for a long time. Then he said,

"These are sad things to talk about, aren't they? Your life goes along its usual route. It's ordinary. You might even think boring. You think nothing will ever be different. You don't even notice you're growing older. Then something tragic happens and all the ordinariness is gone. You don't feel safe anymore. Did you ever think your friends would be murdered?"

⌐⌐⌐

The next morning, Janet called to tell me she was going to help Peter get some information that might help Danny. I wondered if this meant she'd spent the night with Peter. She had some things to do, she said, and would call me later at my apartment. I felt that sinking feeling I get when I realize I'm being supplanted, like the guy coming home and finding a pair of men's shoes in front of the couch. I didn't expect I'd be seeing her later.

Well, it wasn't the first time, and since she'd already woke me up, I decided to do something useful rather than sit around feeling sorry for myself. I sat around for a few minutes in a stupor of sorts, finally settling on a plan that included getting a handle on Angelina's life at Hanrahan's and then visiting Pop and talking things over.

Angelina's reputation at Hanrahan's was a bit better than her uptown one. Not so surprisingly, she wasn't the only one who went slumming above 96th Street. She'd been a day waitress for the most part, so getting there in the quiet time when folks were setting up, but before the lunch rush, was the best time to try to find out something. The day bartender and I had a couple of mutual acquaintances, both in the bars and in the theater. He was a big handsome Midwesterner, like ninety percent of the male out-of-work acting profession in New York. But he was pretty serious about his acting— and his bartending. Hanrahan's was a good, union job, and he handled it well. He'd also had enough luck off-Broadway that I'd seen a couple of his plays. We talked about this and that, and he even owned up to having seen me on the stage in one of my rare appearances.

His name was Bob Lewis, and he wasn't a bullshit guy, so I leveled with him. And it seemed he leveled with me.

"The cops asked a lot of questions about her," he said, once the preliminaries and my first cup of coffee were finished. "I don't think I told them anything very important."

"Who'd she hang out with? Any of the other waiters or waitresses?"

Bob Lewis shook his head.

"Did you spend any time with her?"

He shuffled around, looking a little sheepish.

"You slept with her?"

"Just once."

"Did anyone else."

He didn't know. "Most of the waiters are fags, so I doubt it."

"Any special customers?"

"The cops asked me that. I told them, no. But there was one guy who came in pretty regularly for lunch—an older guy."

"Wear a suit?"

"I think so."

"What'd he drink?"

"Jack Daniels on the rocks."

"Did he stand up all the time?"

Bob Lewis looked perplexed. "Stand up? I don't remember."

When I got to Pop's house in Brooklyn, I went over everything I'd found out since I'd seen him last. I told him I was stymied. Nothing I found out led me anywhere.

Pop put on the coffee pot to heat up, and we sat down at his dining room table. "Most reporters already have the lead in mind when they go to get the story," he said. "They already think they know what the story is about and what they should be finding out. It's like finding proof for your theory. Sometimes they're wrong. But most of the time it beats stumbling around in the dark."

I wasn't so sure. "It sounds to me like you're still stumbling around in the dark. You just pretend you know where you're going."

Pop digested this with some difficulty. Then, he jumped up to run into the kitchen to remove the boiling coffee from the gas-jet flame. He came back muttering and swearing at the pot and poured out two cups. I sipped my burned coffee, rubbing my fingers against the dark mahogany of the dining room table. On the sideboard that didn't quite match the table was a picture of my mother when she was young, holding a curly-haired child whom my father said was me. Next to this picture stood my high school graduation picture: a truculent youth with Vaseline slicked-back hair and a sneer for a smile. My father was watching me when I drifted back to the present. I realized he must be lonely.

"Unless you have a better idea, why not follow a hunch? Pick someone. Investigate him. Try to trap him. If he comes out clean, go on to someone else."

I didn't like this plan. I didn't like my father proposing it, either. "Do you think that's fair? Isn't that what happened to you?"

His face blanched. I felt like I'd slapped him. He sat still, leaning on his dining room armchair, as if only those wooden arms kept him from sinking. Even for these informal discussions, my father sat in his designated chair at the head of the table.

When he spoke, his voice was hushed. "You can't tell anyone your suspicions. You can't accuse anyone until you're certain. Those people—the slime from the FBI—didn't investigate me. You've got that wrong. They set out to destroy me. They had no interest in finding out the truth."

"I wasn't trying to compare you...." My voice shook. We'd never talked like this before.

"You think you know what happened during that time?" he asked sadly.

"I was here."

Tears formed in his eyes. He made no attempt to wipe them away. With all my heart, I wanted to get up from my chair to go to him and put my arms around him. But years of restrained emotions held me back. The McNulty men, poor Kevin, too—no emotions on our sleeves—full of all this love and not able to get it out.

⌒ ⌒ ⌒

Later that afternoon, in a somber mood, I opened my apartment door for Janet. Seeing her surprised and comforted me. I wanted to put my arms around her too, but again I held back.

"The police found a bloodstained jacket in the garbage chute at Danny's building on Amsterdam," she told me before I'd even closed the door. "It's his. Danny said he'd lost it. Peter said he might have lost it at Oscar's the last time he played there."

"Nice to see you, too," I said.

"Peter said it's a set-up," Janet went on, ignoring what I said. "Ozzie was shot in bed. Why would Danny have gotten blood on his jacket?"

"It might be worth finding out when he did lose the jacket," I said, walking her into my living room.

Janet nodded absently as she walked. We both knew the last night Danny played at Oscar's was the night Angelina was killed.

"I told you you can't trust the cops," I told her. "They plant evidence."

"You don't know it was the cops. It could have been anybody."

I didn't trust Sheehan. Janet did. I was still smarting over the Boss finding us in the cellar. And I kept thinking it was my fault Ozzie got killed because I told Sheehan about him. The cops didn't tell us what they knew. Why should we tell them anything?

Now, I wondered if the cops kept a record of the complaint the porno actress made against Nigel. Did they decide to drop it because Nigel was the wrong guy? Or was it that cops are underpaid and overworked, and this girl wasn't important enough to jack them into using up their time? I'd have liked to get my hands on the police report. But I didn't want to send Janet to Peter to try to get it. I didn't want to seem like I was making accusations against Nigel again. Whatever I thought of Nigel, it wasn't right. Accusations were dirty stuff that followed you around, making you an outcast whether you deserved it or not. Just like someone accusing your old man of being a Communist.

"I checked into Hanrahan's," I told Janet instead. "It looks as if there was an older man she was involved with there, too. But I don't know if it means anything. I didn't think to ask the bartender if the guy still came in to Hanrahan's."

"You mean if he stopped coming in after Angelina's death, then...?"

"Or after Ozzie got killed. I don't know. I just should've asked if he still came in."

"Are you sure it was Ozzie?"

"I would be if I'd remembered to ask."

Janet plopped down on the couch, sighing and looking exasperated. "We have so many different possibilities I don't know what to do. This person at Hanrahan's may not have anything to do with anything. But we should still find out; don't you think?"

"We should. But that reminds me—" I gathered up about a week's worth of the *Daily News* so I could sit down beside her. "Can you get the court records from the time Angelina was molested when she was a kid?"

Janet cleared her throat loudly enough to make me stop my gathering and turn toward her. Her eyes narrowed with worry. Getting up from the couch, she began pacing, not looking at me. She looked like Eric did the night he came out of the men's room to tell me he'd accidentally dropped my packet of coke into the toilet.

"It wasn't reported," she said very quietly.

I stared at her, grappling with my armload of newspapers.

She sat down again and fidgeted with her fingers in her lap. She spoke looking down at them. "My mother didn't file a complaint, so the police dropped the charges."

"Why didn't she file a complaint?"

"It was a college boy who molested Angelina. His father paid her a lot of money. He said my mom could use it to send Angelina to college. But, really, he had my mother figured out. He gave the money to her. Angelina never got it. A couple of years later, Angelina was raped again. This time by a friend of my mother's. Angelina kept trying to please everyone." Janet cried while she told me this. The longer she talked, the harder she cried, until she wailed like a baby, her face blotching red, her eyes swimming in tears.

This valley of tears, my mother used to say. I stood awkwardly over Janet while she hid her face and cried. I told her once or twice that everything was okay.

She turned her blotchy and tear-stained face toward me accusingly. "My sister's dead," she screamed. "How can that be okay?"

"It isn't," I said, then left her alone to cry and went into the kitchen to make coffee. I sat at my small kitchen table watching the water boil until she joined me.

"It's hard to admit that I come from such an awful family," she said.

I couldn't answer her; I wondered if my own son would say that someday. Again, I was reminded I owed him something, like maybe making sure he knew he had folks who cared about him more than Angelina's cared about her.

"What's with your mother anyway? Didn't she know she was supposed to take care of Angelina?"

We sat across from one another drinking coffee until the red blotches were gone from her face and her eyes became clear. "My mother thinks she's perfect. Because she's perfect, everyone else has to be also. That's what was wrong with my father: He wasn't good enough for her...and then Angelina was her little doll. When she was little, Mom even tried to make her a child model. Then, this thing happened....Angelina was abused, so she was tainted. She wasn't perfect anymore, and my mother couldn't stand her....Pretty awful, eh?"

"What about you?"

"I'm her last hope, the accomplishment in her life. I'm a success, she thinks, so she is also."

Janet didn't hide the bitterness, so I wondered, without asking, what her success meant to her. The more you find out about people, the more tangled up you find their lives really are. I got this awful feeling I might be normal, after all.

When I thought Janet had calmed down enough, I asked again about Angelina's rape, which even she had trouble putting the right name to.

"What was this college boy's name?"

"I don't know."

"What did he look like?"

"I never saw him."

"Maybe you could ask your mother."

Janet shook her head slowly.

"What do you mean, no?"

She winced but continued to shake her head. "The arrangement was that mother never divulge his name. I'm not even sure she knows."

"She must know what he looks like."

"Maybe."

"Maybe?" I snorted. "Maybe she wouldn't remember the person who raped her ten-year-old daughter?" I glared at Janet, as if it were her doing. But she hadn't raised her eyes from her lap and didn't see me.

With a good deal of effort, I convinced Janet that she had to go back to Springfield and find out all she could about what happened, no matter what she thought her mother would say. But there was a price to pay. Janet demanded I go with her. I tried to squirm out of it but finally agreed to go on Tuesday, my night off. Maybe something would break in the meanwhile. We'd teach the horse to talk.

In the meanwhile, I asked, apologetically, if she'd find out a couple of things about Carl for me.

"Why?" She acted like I'd kicked a baby.

I was embarrassed myself. I didn't really think Carl killed Angelina, and I wasn't accusing him of anything, so I thought it was okay to turn Janet loose. "I don't want to, myself," I said. "I don't want to find out things about him he doesn't tell me himself. It's not the same for you. You only have to tell me things if it's relevant, which I don't think it will be."

"If you don't suspect him, why are we doing this?"

I tried to be placating. "We have to check out everyone if we're going to do this right," I said in what I thought passed for a reasonable tone. "What you shouldn't do is accuse anyone, talk about your suspicions, or tell anyone what you find out." I sounded very wise to myself.

Janet rolled her eyes like she knew I was full of shit but went off to call her mother and make arrangements to go to Springfield and to find out what she could about Carl. I went over to the dope store on Amsterdam to buy a couple of joints for work and ran right into him. Despite the fact that he looked more sinister now that he was under investigation than I ever would have thought possible, Carl was just as friendly and distracted as ever.

"I've got some information for you," he said brightly.

"Oh?"

"The girl in the movie with Eric the Red and me. Her name is Sharon Collins. She used to work at the Buffalo Roadhouse in the Village."

"Maybe she still does?"

"Maybe, but I haven't seen her there."

Now why did he tell me that? I wondered as he walked away.

I didn't drink that night at work. The next day, I couldn't reach Janet on the phone, so, to take my mind off everything for a while, I took in a Rip Torn movie I wanted to see and went to work feeling virtuous. When I got home, there was a message from Janet telling me things were set for visiting her mother on Tuesday and she hadn't found out anything about Carl but would call when she did.

The following day, I couldn't reach Janet, and she hadn't picked up my message by that evening. I began to worry— less that something had happened than that she was now shacking up with Peter Finch.

To avoid drowning my sorrows in the Terrace, I took the train to the Village that afternoon. The Buffalo Roadhouse, made of glass and blonde wood, looked like a joint you could make a buck in. The brunch crowd filled all of the tables; the bar had a good crowd, too. Whenever I ate brunch, I got filled up on sugar and booze and felt waterlogged, then went to sleep for the rest of the day. I ordered a soda with lime.

"I'm looking for Sharon Collins," I told the bartender when he put the drink down. He ignored me. I pushed the change from my five into the rail on his side of the bar.

"She doesn't work here anymore. She went back home a couple of months ago."

"Where's home?" He looked me in the eye. The change from a five was a good tip, but not enough to sell out a friend. "I'm not after her for anything. She's a friend of mine. I work uptown at a place called Oscar's."

He'd heard of it. His name was Jack, and he knew David from the Terrace. We shook hands.

"Some place in Connecticut. A nice kid, but she burned out on the city real fast."

"Where in Connecticut?"

He shrugged.

I took a guess. "Stamford?"

"That sounds like it. I thought it was in California."

While I was downtown, I thought I'd try to trace Ozzie's travels the night before his murder, so I walked a couple of blocks up to the Lion's Head, where I knew Ozzie drank sometimes after work. I knew the day bartender slightly. He was another actor, named Willie. We'd worked together for a short time at Tavern on the Green.

He didn't know Ozzie by name but recognized the guy who drank Jack Daniels and water and never sat down.

He also remembered a big guy—maybe a light-skinned black guy—who drank straight rum who came in with Ozzie.

"Often?"

"Not very often."

"The last time?"

"I think so. I didn't pay much attention."

"Try to remember."

Willie wrinkled his brow. He still thought so but wasn't positive. Tall and handsome in a really traditional way, Willie was nonetheless dumber than a bag of hammers. Already, though he was a lot younger than me, he looked middle-aged, like he should be settled down with a family and running a hardware store in Peoria. He was filled with that middle-west contentment that New Yorkers associate with cows.

What pissed me off was that he didn't pay enough attention to things to be a really good bartender, expecting, no doubt, he would soon make it as an actor and forget his sordid past. Every time I leaned forward I found myself sticking to the bar. My thinking was that if he was a lousy bartender, he'd be a lousy actor, too. Not that that would stand in the way of success, of course.

$$\sim\sim\sim$$

When I got home, I had a message from my answering service that told me to call Janet. I was relieved to hear her voice. She was quite excited.

"News," she said, "on two fronts."

"What?"

"Eric the Red is an illegal alien."

"So are ninety percent of the other kitchen workers in New York."

"Oh," said Janet. "Well, he's involved in a phony marriage with a woman I think is a prostitute. Suppose Angelina knew about it and was blackmailing him?"

"The marriage is so he can get a green card. Anyway, does turning him in sound like something Angelina would do?"

"No." Janet kind of hummed to herself while she thought things through. "I guess it doesn't mean anything, does it?" She brightened. "I have more. I found out that Carl used to work in Easthampton during the summers."

"So?"

"Angelina went to Easthampton two summers ago, so I rented a car and took a quick trip out there." She paused. "Some of what I found out you're not going to like." I waited. She went on. "Your friend Carl has been lying to you. He knew Angelina before she ever came to New York. They worked together in a hotel in Easthampton two summers ago."

"Oh," I said, trying not to sound disappointed that one more of my friends was not to be trusted. I remembered that Carl went out to Long Island for a couple of summers. I hadn't thought much about it because that kind of coming and going wasn't unusual in the neighborhood. Someone fell in love and moved to Brooklyn or got a summer stock part in Connecticut or a teaching job in Ohio for a year. Carl used to work as a chef in the summer. Most everyone came back after a time; others disappeared forever into a new life. That Carl knew Angelina in Easthampton was a pretty big surprise, though, and his keeping it from me a pretty big secret, as secrets go.

"How did you find out?"

"After Eric told me Carl worked as a chef in Easthampton, I went there and found the hotel Angelina worked at and talked to the manager, who remembered both of them by name and description."

"Okay, I believe you. Now what?"

"Well, I guess we know now why Angelina came to the Upper West Side instead of some other part of the city." Her voice was soft. "Should I tell the police?"

I hemmed and hawed. I didn't want her to. But I didn't know how to say so. "You can if you want," I said grudgingly.

"Do you want me to wait?"

"Maybe...until I talk to him."

"Okay." She didn't hide the reluctance in her voice. "There's something else about Carl that isn't directly connected but I think you should know." Her voice took on a whispery, secretive tone that I didn't like.

"If it isn't directly connected, I don't want to know."

She itched to tell me; I could feel it even over the phone. The silence now bristled with disapproval. "It might be important."

"You decide. If it's important, tell me. If not, don't, until you're sure it is."

"I understand."

"Will you come to Oscar's tonight?"

"No," she said and hung up.

A minute later she called back. "I will come in later, with Peter."

⌐⌐⌐

Peter and Janet, in their casual dress, had the aura of young professionals about them; I had to admit they matched each other. Anyone's grandmother would take one look and say "nice couple." I let them sit at the bar for a good few minutes before I took their order.

"You're in your usual good mood," Peter said.

"Bartenders are supposed to be surly," I told him.

"Danny sends his regards."

"What do the cops say?" Despite being a defense lawyer, a defender of blacks, and a progressive, Peter got along well with the cops.

"They know the case sucks. I'm going to meet with the ADA who has the case on Monday."

Janet smiled a little self-consciously, sitting beside Peter. I could tell she was pleased to be with a hot shot New York criminal lawyer.

"We're going to Springfield on Tuesday," I said. Just to let Peter know he wasn't the only one who did things with Janet.

Janet's eyes opened wider. "Are we still going to do that?"

I nodded.

Peter raised an eyebrow in mild interest. "To see your mother?"

Janet nodded.

"It's probably a long shot," Peter said. "But a good idea."

Meanwhile, empty glasses cluttered the bar and the winos were getting restless. Troubled faces bent forward, looking my way as if for a lost son. One or two of the better fortified of the group had the temerity to bang an empty glass on the bar until I shot a withering glance at them. A couple of snarls and snaps of my whip and they all quieted, waiting patiently while I slid along the bar, replenishing the scotches and bourbons, the gin and tonics and vodka martinis, sliding a drink here and there to a regular, knocking on the bar in front of him in lieu of payment, the frowns becoming smiles. In less than five minutes I'd recovered my former standing. I returned to Janet's corner of the bar and was pleased as Punch to note that Peter was saying goodnight and Janet would hang on for a while.

Ntango's arrival a few minutes later gave me an idea. I suggested Janet ask him to take her downtown to visit a couple of places around Hanrahan's to ask questions. Since he drove a horse hire, Ntango didn't have to account for where he was or how many trips he made. I handed him a twenty out of the cash register as Oscar's contribution to the investigation.

"For Danny?" he asked. I didn't know how he knew, but I nodded. When they left, I figured out Janet must have told him. She hadn't learned well enough yet about keeping her mouth shut.

Before I left that night I asked Oscar if he remembered if Nigel had been in the bar the night Ozzie was murdered.

"Yeah," Oscar answered without hesitation. "He was here." Then, closing one eye, he looked at me shrewdly with the other.

"Are you sure?" He hadn't even thought about it for a second.

"I'm sure," Oscar said. "One hundred percent."

Chapter Nine

On the bus ride to Springfield, I remembered the cab driver who'd brought Angelina to the West Side that first time and later tried to break into her apartment. I'd totally forgotten about him. I wondered if the police knew. Finding him would be next to impossible, unless he was a legitimate driver who kept a trip log. I told Janet about him, and she said Angelina told her about the crazy cab driver in a letter. She didn't remember if Angelina mentioned his name. But she would look for the letter when we got to Springfield.

Janet also told me about her previous night's trek through the bars near Hanrahan's with Ntango to see how the regulars at those places stacked up against Oscar's first team. Most of the places didn't remember Angelina, much less anyone she hung out with. But one bartender did remember her. And a hefty, light-skinned black guy who drank straight rum also stood out in the crowd, as did a scarecrow-like guy with a southern accent who drank Jack Daniels. Both Ozzie and Reuben, it seemed, visited Angelina at Hanrahan's and drank with her at a couple of other joints in the area.

Janet also caught up with the bartender who remembered Angelina coming in to The Pub across the street from Hanrahan's with an older man, who, she said, was probably Ozzie, too.

"How do you know?" I asked her.

"He drank Jack Daniels," she said smugly.

"Did he stand up all the time?"

"I don't know." She looked worried. "Why? Do you think it wasn't Ozzie?…Who else would it be?"

"I don't know who else it would be. I just wanted to know if the guy stood up. I forgot to ask last time."

I went back to reading my book, a Ross Macdonald mystery I'd picked up at Port Authority. Lew Archer figured things out a lot more quickly than I did. I told Janet this in some perplexity.

"Maybe he's smarter than you," she ventured. "You just don't like to admit the very real possibility that the person who killed Angelina came from Oscar's. You'd like it if someone respectable was the killer, instead of one of your bum friends."

Janet quieted down after this ringing defense of respectability, quieting down into her nervousness. As we got closer to Springfield, she practically danced in her seat from her nerves, every five seconds speculating about what her mother would do or say. When she ran out of her own speculations, she asked me for answers. When I said I didn't know and tried to read my book, she pouted.

"I don't know your mother," I said patiently. "I don't know what she'll say. I hope she tells us what happened."

"Do you think she'll be mad?"

I tried to read my book, but Janet demanded attention, by her frenetic bouncing around if nothing else. "I don't know," I said finally.

"Do you think we should come right out and ask her?"

"Maybe."

"Should we tell her what we already know?" Her jitteriness made her voice shrill; she was becoming a nag.

"Jesus, Janet. I don't know. Tell her what you want."

"We should have a plan."

"How can we plan if we don't know what she'll say?"

"God," said Janet. "I hate doing this."

Her face shone white in the subdued light of the bus. High-strung and wired, she had that tension in the way she held her neck and shoulders that you see sometimes in a thoroughbred who really wants to run. Her cheeks were pink with excitement and the make-up she wore for the trip.

I thought about what might happen after we talked with her mother, when we would be alone together for dinner and then would find a hotel—when there might be some release of all the tension. We hadn't slept together since that first time. I thought about dinner at that German restaurant Carl and I had found, a bottle of wine, a joint for later in the hotel room. I forgot, for the moment, that Janet lived with her mother and might just stay in her own room by herself.

Her body a few inches from mine in the narrow bus seat, her thigh once or twice brushing mine, the slight scent of her perfume, I absorbed being next to her. Just north of Hartford, she started to doze off. I put my arm around her shoulder, pulling her gently toward me until she nestled her head in against my chest. I kissed her hair.

We picked up her car, a shiny red Toyota, at a gas station near the bus depot. On the drive to her mother's, Janet pulled herself together. When we arrived at the small wooden frame house, she marched decisively up the walk, rang the doorbell, and then put her key in the lock and opened the door before her mother got to it.

Mom was twittering around in the cramped foyer as we entered. She brushed at her hair and her dress, complained that her house was a terrible mess, chastised Janet for not calling her, and kept saying, "I don't know what Mr. McNulty will think of us," implying that if I had my head on straight I would figure out they were high-class people, despite any appearances to the contrary. In short, Mrs. Carter struck me as a phony, all appearance, anything that might reveal truth tucked away and protected like the family heirlooms. Maybe a life works out that way: you learn to protect yourself at all cost, show nothing but a false front to strangers. None of this attitude had rubbed off on Angelina, though. Maybe, because she could never get behind that impregnable wall of her mother's appearances, Angelina opened herself to everyone else, to me, to the college boy when she was ten, to the person who murdered her before she'd altogether grown up.

"It's not something I like to talk about," Mrs. Carter said after we were seated in a cramped, stuffy living room, and I asked her to tell me about the time Angelina was molested. Mrs. Carter's hair was black going on gray and pulled back severely. She was controlled and conscious of herself, treading as carefully as if she were walking across a tightrope.

"She knew the boy. They had become friends." Her challenging expression when she said this suggested I should realize I didn't know as much about things as I thought I did. "She liked him. He didn't jump out of the bushes and attack her. Angelina was always boy-crazy. She was a little flirt, maybe because she had no father."

"Mom," said Janet. "She was a child. She was cute. She wanted attention. All kids do. You're making it sound like it was Angelina's fault."

Mrs. Carter shot a sidelong glance at her daughter. Janet bounced back in her chair as if she'd been whacked.

Having put Janet in her place without much effort, Mrs. Carter went on with her story. "The boy was heartbroken. Even I could see that he hadn't meant to hurt her." She took me into her confidence, ignoring Janet, indicating by this attempt at sincerity that I would understand the nuances of the situation she described, even if her daughter didn't. "It was a tragedy for him, too. He was very nervous. I wouldn't be surprised if he was having a nervous breakdown. His father was devastated. The boy had great promise. The family was wealthy." She looked at me significantly then said again, "It was obvious they were cultured and wealthy." Perhaps not obvious to an asshole like me, her tone suggested, but obvious to someone who understood such things.

"How did Angelina feel about being molested?"

This shot got inside the armor. She took some time to answer. "She was too young to know all of what was going on. I don't think she realized what had happened. It was better for her that we kept it that way and didn't make much of the whole situation."

"What was the deal you made?" I asked.

Janet's mother turned on her daughter so fiercely I thought she'd spring from the couch and go for her throat. "There was no deal," she said. "Did Janet tell you there was?"

"They gave you money..." Janet snarled.

Mrs. Carter smiled faintly to show that she could rise above the perfidy of her daughter. "It was never that. Not money for a deal." She shook her head to ward off the accusation. "I understood the boy needed treatment. He wasn't a criminal. He'd gotten carried away...made a mistake... Angelina went along with it, you know?"

"Mother!" Janet shrieked.

Unruffled, Mom went on. "You know what I mean....It was wrong but it wasn't an attack." She looked at me again. "The family was rich and could provide the help the son needed. He would go to a hospital and be treated. What good would it do for him to be sent to jail? Angelina consented to whatever happened. I'm sure she didn't know what she was doing. But she might have led him on....Boys at that age, you know...."

I stared at this woman in amazement, but she didn't notice. She was floating on a cloud with her eyes closed.

"I agreed with the boy's father that prison wouldn't help anyone. Angelina least of all would want the boy to go to prison. They were grateful that I saw it wasn't really a criminal matter. That was all of any deal."

She tried to look saintly as she said all this. It didn't work on me but seemed to on her. Her eyes closed again like a child's when she drifts off to sleep.

Keeping my tone soft as befit the mood she'd established, I whispered, "And the money?"

Her eyes sprang open. The corners of her mouth curled. I thought she would spit. "The family wanted to do something for Angelina, for all of us. Money meant nothing to them. I had no husband, Mr. McNulty. I couldn't make ends meet. Should I have let my pride impoverish my family?"

Actually, I didn't disapprove of the things she was most defensive about. Sick people should go to hospitals instead of jail; rich people should give money to poor people to make their lives better; poor people shouldn't be ashamed to take it. Yet the entire episode reeked of betrayal and selfishness. Everything had been done to satisfy greed: the boy's greed for the little girl, the family's greed for their good name; Mrs. Carter's greed for money, and her willingness to sacrifice her daughter because of her greed for the good opinion of the rich. I realized nothing in the world could make this woman admit she'd sold her daughter down the river for a few bucks. I understood how much Mrs. Carter needed the falsity that surrounded her. The truth would drive her screaming over a cliff.

The tension between her and Janet was near the exploding point. It looked as if there had been some unspoken agreements about things they wouldn't talk about, but Janet was talking about them. Mrs. Carter was furious and all during our conversation cast pointed glances at her daughter, while Janet, for the most part, kept her eyes averted.

"Did you ever hear from or about the boy again?" I asked Mrs. Carter.

She shook her head.

"Where was he from?"

"They never said. He was attending college near here."

"What was the boy's name?"

Mrs. Carter gritted her teeth and tightened her face, as if to say torture wouldn't get the name from her.

I played my trump card. "Was his name Nigel Barthelme?"

"No," she said. "That wasn't it."

Janet stood behind her, looking like she'd just discovered a body. She recovered herself quickly though. "Was his name Carl van Sagan?"

"That wasn't it either," her mother said haughtily. "I'm certain he's no one you would know."

"Mother, you must know his name or the family name. You have to tell us. This could be the key to everything."

Mrs. Carter blustered up like Foghorn Leghorn. "Don't be ridiculous, Janet. How could something that happened so long ago have anything to do with Angelina's death? She was in New York, for God's sake. In those terrible slums, doing the Lord knows what, associating with low lifes. How dare you bring all this up! How dare you divulge our family affairs in front of this—this…"

"Low life?" I ventured.

⌐⌐⌐

Janet went to her room to pick up the letters Angelina had sent her from New York. I stood alone with Mrs. Carter for an uncomfortable few minutes.

"Aren't you staying?" Mrs. Carter asked Janet when she came back.

"No, I'm going back to New York. I took a few days off."

"You have phone calls and messages. Don't you want to see them? Mr. Riggs from the bank?" Her tone was loaded with not so subtle hints of a gentleman caller, not just a colleague.

"I'll be back in a few days, mother. I wish you'd think over being more helpful. Whatever you promised that family, I'm sure it doesn't bind you in this situation."

"You haven't been at the bank long enough to go traipsing off for a few days, even if there has been a family tragedy. Someone in an important position like yours is expected to carry on in the face of difficulties." Mrs. Carter was pointedly ignoring me now, talking above and beyond me, implying I was of the elements dragging her daughter down.

〜 〜 〜

Before we got down the front steps, Janet climbed all over me with questions. "Why did you ask about Nigel? Do you know something?"

"Just a guess. He's the right age. He comes from a rich family."

"But you had a reason…. Tell me."

"He doesn't drink. I don't trust people who don't drink." She almost smiled through her peevishness.

"In fact, we should have a drink right now," I said. "I know a great German restaurant in Springfield near the bus depot."

"The Student Prince. How did you know that?" I put my arm around her, but she walked out from under it as we headed toward her car.

Lew Archer got paid expenses. He wouldn't even track down a murderer except if someone paid him. I had to come up with expenses myself, and this dinner wasn't going to be cheap. Maybe I could ask Oscar to put me on a per diem to clear the joint's name. Maybe Danny could hock his bass guitar.

Angelina's suitor, the cabbie—Janet found his name in one of her letters—was, fittingly enough, named Romeo. He was Romanian. She read the letter at the restaurant while we waited for dinner, and cried again, while I drank a gigantic glass of Wurtzburger from the tap. I didn't know if Janet cried because the letters got her to thinking about Angelina again or because the recent episode reminded her how awful her mother was.

"Mother's pretty hard to take sometimes," she said in answer to my unasked question. "She can be so cold. That's how she was with Angelina, just so cold…"

"Why do you still live with her, if you don't mind my asking?"

Janet blushed. "I don't know, really. I lived away from home for years, in Boston. The position at the bank in Spring-field is recent, or fairly recent. I planned to stay with Mother for a few weeks until I found a place. At first, it was fun because Angelina was there, and I spent some time getting to know her again as an almost grown-up. Also, she and mother fought all the time, and I was a kind of buffer." Our dinner came and Janet looked it over like it was leftover stew from Sam's hash house. "Since Angelina left, I've been meaning to move out. But I guess I feel sorry for my mother. She's sad and lonely."

"Meanness does that to you."

Midway through dinner, Janet pointed to a gray-haired man in a blue suit who'd tucked away three martinis while I was drinking my beer and who I expected was now about to go face down in his wiener schnitzel. "That's the DA," she said. "Rumor has it that he's been coming in here and getting drunk every night for the past ten years."

"Was he the DA when Angelina was raped?"

"Probably."

"Let's go say hello."

Janet hesitated, her eyes narrowed with worry. "I don't think people are supposed to notice when he's drunk....The bank is very sensitive...our position in the community..."

I waited. She stood and walked to his table.

"George," she said, as he raised his gaze. He reminded me of a basset hound. "This is Brian McNulty." She raised an eyebrow in my direction. "He's a private investigator from New York."

I raised an eyebrow myself. But I did have a suit on—albeit borrowed—I was fortified by the Wurtzburger, and had finished the first third of a Lew Archer book. What the hell!

"Pleased to meetcha," he garbled, holding out his puffy, pink hand, and looking at me droopily with his bloodshot eyes. "What can I do for you?"

"A number of years ago," I said in what I imagined was a hardboiled tone—I really needed a hat and a cigarette to bring this off—"a number of years ago, a ten-year-old girl was molested by a college student. Do you remember it?"

"No," said the DA, hovering over his martini like he suspected I might steal it. We might have gotten along better if Janet had introduced me as a bartender.

"Try," I said. "I doubt they'd bury that kind of case without you knowing about it. Maybe you keep a file of cases that never got prosecuted."

"Not if there were no charges," he said.

I didn't get it.

"We can't force parents to file charges, can't force a kid to testify if the parents say she's too traumatized, they just want her to forget it and get on with her life." The DA's eyes shone with cunning through the red lines and puffiness. "Ask her." He nodded toward Janet. "It was her sister."

"I know. I want the name of the suspected molester."

"No can do." He dismissed me with a wave of his hand and returned to his martini.

I didn't take the hint. "Can you tell me what you remember?"

He rolled his eyes toward Janet, hinting that she should take me away. But he did answer. "Something allegedly happened between the boy and the girl, but both families got involved. They agreed something happened. But they agreed also that nothing criminal had happened."

"Was the girl examined by a doctor?"

"I don't know." He turned on Janet. "Tell your friend who doesn't take hints to ask his questions during office hours. I come here to relax."

Janet began sputtering an apology.

"Just a friendly chat," I said.

"Good. Nice to see you." Genial, nary a slurred word, he held his liquor well, polishing off another martini while we spoke.

"Our dinner's waiting," I said.

"I don't have anything to hide," the DA said as we walked away.

⌐⌐⌐

Janet wanted to leave for the city. This time she was driving back and keeping her car. But, optimist that I am, I talked her into spending the night in Springfield and driving back in the morning. We found a hotel a few blocks from the restaurant. It was connected to an inside shopping mall, so after we registered we walked around for a while browsing in stores.

Janet asked again why I'd become interested in Nigel, but I didn't have anything to tell her. It was the sort of feeling I'd had about Danny's innocence. And it had to do with the girl Sharon Collins who'd accused Nigel of raping her. Since her accusation was probably false, I didn't want to tell Janet.

"Tell me everything you know about the night Angelina was murdered," I told Janet when we'd found our way back to the hotel and to a small lobby bar.

"She left Oscar's with the band," Janet said.

"Right."

"She went with them to that person Max's apartment on 114th Street where they jammed for an hour or two. Maybe they drank and did drugs. The police lab found alcohol and marijuana in her blood."

"But not much."

Janet let the information register. She was tired; it showed in her eyes. The tension was gone, yet not from any release, just weariness. It took effort for her to go on. "She left with Danny."

"They went for breakfast," I said.

"Right. That was in the laboratory report also." She rubbed her eyes and rested her face in her hands. "They walked up Broadway, right? I'm having a hard time remembering."

"Right. They'd been in the park."

She leaned back in her chair, closing her eyes. "How do you know?"

"Danny said that's where they'd been. Angelina wasn't wearing a sweater."

"Where were they heading?"

"Danny said he walked her home and left her in the lobby."

She sat up in her seat again, alertness returning to her eyes. "Why wouldn't she bring him home with her?"

"That's strange, isn't it? Angelina wasn't shy about bringing men home."

"Maybe she was tired."

"Maybe someone was already there."

Janet's eyes registered surprise. "Who?"

"Good question. Less than two weeks later, Ozzie gets killed in the same building, in his own apartment. How did the murderer get in?"

"The police said there was no forced entry." Janet sat back in her chair. She hadn't touched her drink. "Ozzie must have opened the door."

"Maybe."

"Maybe he forgot to lock the door."

"Maybe."

I ordered one more cognac for each of us. "I feel creepy," Janet said. "It seems like we must almost know who killed Angelina. Yet we don't."

"We've pretty well narrowed the field," I said, sniffing my brandy instead of taking a drink. What I didn't tell her but expected her to realize anyway was that the closer we got the more likely it was that the murderer would know it.

◂◂◂

Janet and I shared a double room. To cut down on expenses, she'd said. I'd had grander plans.

"It's funny," Janet said, having changed in the bathroom into a wooly, floor-length Planned Parenthood nightgown. "You're the most disreputable person I know. Yet I feel totally safe sharing a hotel room, despite your tough guy facade and your alley cat sexual morals." She looked at me apologetically. You might say, with sympathy. "I don't trust you romantically. I can't bring myself to be with you that way again...not now.

I don't expect you to understand. But I know you'll accept what I say."

Talk about deflating romance. I tried to see through her words to find the passion hidden by some fear, reluctance that might be overcome with patience and gentleness. But it was like looking into an adding machine. After a tentative embrace, Janet hung her head, said she was tired and needed to sleep. I didn't have much trouble sleeping either, despite my plans coming to naught.

⌐ ⌐ ⌐

When we got back to New York, I went to try out a theory I'd developed on the way home. It followed from my thinking about Romeo the cab driver and led to my remembering how one gets an apartment on the Upper West Side. Janet went to see what she could find out about Romeo. I walked down Broadway to 103rd Street, turned east, and found the building Angelina had first lived in, a five-story walk-up in a Spanish neighborhood. I dug around in a few cellars until I came up with a super who took care of most of the buildings on the block.

"Any apartments?" I asked. He shook his head and mumbled something in Spanish that suggested he knew nothing of apartments and didn't recall ever having heard the word before.

"My friend Carl at 811 West End said one might open up. I got three hundred dollars."

The super smiled. "Maybe for next month," he said.

"Remember the girl Carl sent? The blonde?"

The super nodded sadly. So did I.

⌐ ⌐ ⌐

I walked back uptown, remembering something I overheard my father telling my mother once. It was during the Inquisition in the Fifties, and he sat at the mahogany dining room table while my mother tried to persuade him to give up. He was drooped over the table. I can picture the tired and defeated look on his face. "It's worse when you know too much," he said. I didn't know what he meant then, but it was so different from what he always told me about the importance of knowledge that it stuck in my mind.

‑‑‑

When I got back to my apartment, I knew right away someone had been in it. I noticed something wrong as soon as I turned from the foyer to enter my room, before I even saw my bedroom. My bureau had been torn apart, my books tossed all over the floor, Tolstoy dumped on his nose, the bookcase black and empty where he had stood. The gun gone. I'd never wanted the fucking thing in the first place; now it had gone off on its own to haunt me.

To begin with, someone could still be in the apartment. Through the door beyond the foyer was the kitchen, behind the wall in front of me my living room, off to the other side of my room the bathroom. Someone might be hiding in any one of those places. I flung myself against the wall of my bedroom, sliding along with my back arched against it—for God knows what reason—until I reached the bathroom door, slamming it open and diving through—in hopes, I suppose, of catching my would-be assailant in the middle of a before-murder crap. The bathroom was empty. I went out along the short hallway to the living room, yanking open the hall closet door on the way. No one in the closet or the living room. This left only the kitchen. Unless, of course, the assailant was doubling along behind me, hiding now in the bedroom ready to leap into the bathroom as soon as I got to the bedroom again. No one in the kitchen.

Instead of circling my apartment again, I went for a drink at the Marlin. When I came back, the eeriness hung from ceiling and walls, filling my apartment—the only place I ever felt completely safe—with fear as thick as fog.

I went to work and came home to the same awful feeling of fear and violation. Chills ran up and down my back when I opened the door; once more, I searched the apartment.

Someone had taken my peace, like Macbeth had killed sleep. I lay awake listening to every sound from the street, every opening of the lobby door, every groan of the elevator starting up. I stayed awake until the morning, hypnotized by the clattering of cans and the groaning of the sanitation trucks, the grumbling hiss and roar of the M 104 bus on its way up Broadway. When I did finally fall into a rigid, fragile, wakeful sleep, the phone screamed out of the false twilight like a tortured banshee, and I dove straight up into the air and hit the floor running.

It was my ex-wife telling me Kevin was on his way over and to be sure and call her if he wasn't there by eleven.

"He can't come over," I said.

"Don't be an asshole, Brian. He's been waiting for this since Christmas. I'm going to Florida. He has to stay there for two weeks."

"He can stay at my father's."

"Your father is in Chicago."

"What the—" My street level window rattled and began to slide open. I dropped the phone, grabbed my baseball bat from behind the bed, and charged toward the window. Kevin's head appeared over the window ledge. Just in time, I checked my swing.

"Jesus, Dad…" he said.

"Are you crazy?" I shouted at him.

"I didn't want to wake you up." Fear wrinkled his lower lip, not so much from the bat, I realized, as from, more likely, the murderous expression he saw in my eyes. "This is how I came in last time." This was true. Then I had thought him cute and enterprising. I held my tongue.

"Go tell your mother you're here okay," I said, nodding toward the phone.

"Hi," he said into the receiver. Then a pause. "Yeah, except Dad tried to brain me with a baseball bat." Another pause. His twinkling laugh. "No, Ma. It's fine." He hung up.

"You gotta go someplace else," I said. "It's too dangerous here."

His lip quivered and his dark eyes went darker with the deep anger he got only when he was deeply hurt and feeling rejected.

"What do you mean I can't stay here? I'm supposed to stay here. You forgot I was coming..." His face—his god-damn face—his lower lip puffed out, the same expression he had when he was a baby just about to cry. That lower lip would puff out, ten full seconds before he began to wail.

And he had me. Boing. Right on the money. He'd been waiting to spend this week with me for months, so first I forget he's coming and then I try to send him away. What did the poor kid do to deserve this crap? I was turning into Angelina's mother.

I tousled his hair. "I'm just being a jerk, Kevin. My nerves are shot."

"No," he shouted. "You're just mad you can't invite women over and get laid when I'm here."

"Kevin!...Sit down," I said, and told him the whole story—or most of it. "Now, do you see what's going on? Why I'm worried about you staying here?"

His face lit up. "Someone's after you?"

"I'm afraid for you....I'm afraid for me."

"But I'm your son. I'm supposed to stick with you when things get tough."

I put my arm around him. "Kevin. Kevin. Kevin. What would I do without you?"

"So?" he asked, a prosecutor's glare in his eyes.

"Okay. Okay. You can stay. We'll just need some backup now and again. You can hang out with Eric and maybe Janet this afternoon, and I'll find someone to stay with you tonight while I'm at work."

"A babysitter? I don't need no babysitter."

"Not a babysitter. Backup. You're my backup and you need a backup when I'm not around."

Pop was at a Communist party convention at a borderline seedy hotel in Chicago. I called and had him paged out of a meeting.

"You've got to come home," I said.

"Oh," said Pop. "Did someone die?"

"No, but I might. Kevin is here. Someone broke into my apartment last night and stole my gun."

"Since when do you have a gun?"

"It's a long story." I told him part of it. He said he'd be back tomorrow.

I called and asked Eric the Red if Kevin could visit him for a while. Then I called Janet and asked if she would meet Kevin at Eric's and take him out for the afternoon. When she said she would, I went looking for Sam the Hammer and found him drinking coffee on a bench in the middle of Broadway at 107th Street. He didn't look surprised to see me.

"Nice weather," I said.

He nodded, not inviting me to join him but not sending me away either. I seemed to blend into the day for him. There was the sun, the sky, the traffic on Broadway, and now someone standing in front of him making conversation. Sipping his coffee, he took it all in with equanimity.

"That gun you gave me a few days back," I said. "Someone stole it from my apartment."

Sam grimaced.

"Did someone know I had it?"

Sam shrugged his shoulders, hunching a little further into his Yankee windbreaker.

"How would they know where to look?"

"In your bureau?" Sam guessed. "Behind some books in your bookcase?"

My expression gave me away. "What should I do?"

"Forget it."

I sat on the bench next to Sam. He looked at the world of Broadway in front of him. I did, too. This thing had gone far enough. My kid might be in danger; I certainly was. Only one person probably wanted me dead. And like a fool I kept looking for him.

"Why was Ozzie killed?" I asked Sam.

Sam watched the cars coming up Broadway. He looked at the foot-high cement wall recently installed along the curb between the island and the street. "They put those things in so Broadway would look like a race track and everyone would drive faster," Sam said. After a suitable pause, he went on. "I talked to the Boss. He'll lay off you unless he hears that his movies have become famous."

"Does the Boss kill people?" I asked in all seriousness.

"Naw, he's a shoe salesman." Sam punctuated his statement with a couple of hunches of his shoulder, body language telling me to go away.

"And a gentleman," I said. "How can I find out who killed Ozzie?"

"What did Ozzie know?" Sam did not shift his gaze all this time.

"Who killed Angelina."

"What do you think happens to the person who knows who killed Ozzie?"

"Is that who stole the gun?"

"No one knew you had it unless you told them."

"Not me," I said. We sat for a while longer watching the traffic. A panhandler came by. Sam gave him a quarter.

"I need you to take care of my kid tonight," I said when the panhandler shuffled off.

"I'm a fucking babysitter?" Sam said, taking in the view, as if he sat on the back porch of his mountain retreat, watching the Great Smokies roll off into the distance, instead of yellow cabs and gypsy cabs battling for position with delivery trucks.

"Not a babysitter. Backup."

"Huh?"

Sam saved my life once when a lunatic came into Oscar's after me with a gun. A bartender had been sleeping with his wife. He'd gotten the wrong bar and the wrong bartender but was too distraught to make distinctions. Everyone dove for cover, except Sam who sat in his place drinking his coffee. When the maniac got close, Sam stood up and reached into his pocket.

"Take that gun out and you're dead," the man said.

"Yeah," said Sam, "and so are you. We'll go together tonight." I saw Sam's eyes and knew he meant it. The irate husband stood facing Sam for what seemed like hours. Finally, he walked away.

Once more, I was afraid and needed help.

"You got a television?" Sam asked.

"Yep, but it's a small scratchy black and white. I could borrow a different one."

"Naw, maybe I'll read one of your books." He thought some more. "Does your kid play chess?"

Once more I was taken aback. "As a matter of fact, he does. Do you?"

Sam glanced at me contemptuously before going back to his coffee.

He showed up just as I gathered myself together to leave for work. Kevin noticed *The Racing Form* under his arm.

"I've been to the track," Kevin said.

"How'd you do?" asked Sam.

～～～

Noticing Reuben at the bar as I came in Oscar's door, I wondered for a moment if he waited to kill me. Oscar trotted back and forth between the dining room and the kitchen. Neither the waitress nor Eric had shown up. Janet came in five minutes behind me to tell Oscar Eric was on his way. Oscar asked if she wanted to be a waitress for a night. Before I could stop her, she said yes.

"I need some drinks," Janet hollered thirty seconds after she'd taken over her new position. I was talking to Reuben at the other end of the bar. Waitresses never hollered at me. I didn't keep them waiting for drinks either. I always knew who needed what at my bar. In this case, there wasn't such a big hurry, and Janet wasn't a waitress. She drummed her fingers on the bar while I finished talking with Reuben. Then, I sauntered over.

"You don't have to call me," I said. "I know when you're at the service bar."

"You weren't looking."

"I would have looked."

"But you didn't." She had a mildly crazed look in her eyes.

"Have you ever been a waitress before?"

"Once," she said sheepishly. "At Friendly's."

"What?"

"What?" she glowered at me.

"What?…What do you want?"

She thumbed through her notepad at a frantic pace and ordered hesitatingly: "A beer, a vodka martini, a Coke, another beer, a whiskey sour."

"That's not how you do it," I said.

"Stop lording it over me, just because you're the bartender." She held her notepad like a rock she was about to throw.

"Order liquors, mixed drinks, stirred drinks, shaken drinks, wine, beer in that order. Group your drinks. Get your own glasses and ice."

Janet fumed. Fury darkened her eyes. I wasn't trying to piss her off. This was how things were done. The bartender was the boss. Waitresses shouldn't argue, particularly waitresses who didn't know what they were doing. All this I knew, yet I couldn't shake the feeling that something was wrong. Janet gritted her teeth and did what I told her. Totally flustered, always behind herself, she grouped her drinks, iced her glasses, and waited at the bar until I came to get her order. I'm fast; I didn't keep her waiting. I thought I was helpful and charming. She continued seething. When she finally did have a break, I told her she was doing fine.

"Go fuck yourself," she said, from the waitress station section of the bar where, like a wounded animal, she rested, breathing heavily, her eyes filled with pain.

"Why are you mad?"

"You act like I'm a slave."

"No," I said. "It's to be efficient. The bartender controls the bar."

Her face took on this momentary look of horror. "You really are a Neanderthal."

⌐ ⌐ ⌐

Reuben and I talked about this and that, politely ignoring the topic of murder. While we talked, I got the impression he wanted to tell me something. He would be saying one thing, but the distant expression in his eyes suggested he thought about something far beyond what he was saying.

I had just given him his third rum on the house, which would bring his total intake almost to double figures, when he got around to saying it. "Do you remember a long time ago when a girl started screaming at Nigel that he'd raped her?"

I froze with the rum bottle in my hand. I couldn't get that girl off my mind.

Reuben took his glasses off and cleaned them with a bar napkin for about the fifteenth time that evening. "I saw her a couple of times at the Buffalo Roadhouse. She never changed her story."

"Did you tell the cops that?"

Reuben slugged down his shot of rum and shoved the empty glass toward me. "C'mon, McNulty. I can't go tell stories to the cops."

Rum sometimes worked like truth serum. Other times, the rum produced mouthfuls of lies. Maybe Reuben was trying this out on me so I could steer the cops away from him. I pushed my luck. "Did you go to the Buffalo Roadhouse after work?"

He weighed his answer before he spoke; his eyes narrowed into meanness. "Sometimes."

"Where else in the Village?"

"The Fifty-Five. The Lion's Head." He answered each question with a jerk of his head and an inflection at the end that said "so what?"

"Did you go with Ozzie?"

Even though he'd seemed to be waiting for it, the question hit him pretty hard. It took a while for his eyes to clear.

When he spoke, his voice was quieter and the truculence was gone. He seemed to sense more was coming. "I'd see him there once in a while."

"In both places?"

"More often in the Lion's Head. I don't remember him in the Roadhouse."

"Did Nigel ever go to any of those places?"

"No." Reuben drew himself up and slugged down another rum. "I told him if he went near that girl, I'd break his head open."

"Did you see Ozzie the night he was murdered?"

"No. I spent the evening in the law library at Columbia, then came here after midnight." Reuben finished up what was left of his drink and picked up his change from the bar, leaving a couple of bucks for me. As he usually did when he felt the drink coming on him, he pulled himself up and out of the joint before his composure slipped. He had a jug at home to help him finish off the night.

I wanted to tell Reuben about my talk with Willie, to give him a chance to correct himself. Then I wanted to ask if he were in the law library preparing his defense.

Reuben knew what I was thinking. "I was reading about divorce and alimony," he said, as he steadied himself on his feet to leave.

⌐⌐⌐

Janet and I continued to grate on each other's nerves for the rest of the night. Later, over breakfast, she continued to berate me. "I just don't believe you," she said. "I don't know how any waitress puts up with you."

"You don't know anything about being a waitress. Just because it's not a professional job with bankers and business-men, you think it's easy. It's not. Anybody can be a lousy waitress—but not a good waitress."

Janet continued to fume. "You just don't care at all about embarrassing me in front of people."

"I didn't do that," I said softly.

"Yes you did."

"I didn't."

"You did too."

I ate my eggs in silence. Once more, things had turned on me. I'd started out the veteran professional bartender breaking in the novice waitress. Now here I was, eating humble pie with my greasy eggs.

Explaining the standards of excellence I adhered to as a bartender seemed silly now in the fluorescent light of the Greek's restaurant at five A.M. Once, having those standards made perfect sense; it meant doing things right. I couldn't explain this to Janet because now it sounded insignificant. But in not saying it I gave up something. Maybe it was small, but I felt it go.

Janet calmed eventually after we went back to my apart-ment and relieved Sam the Hammer, who was asleep in a chair with Kevin's chessboard in front of him.

When Sam left, we sat down in the living room. "Sergeant Sheehan found out about that cab driver for me," Janet said in a bruised voice. I waited. "Romeo has been in jail since a week before Angelina was killed. He beat up his wife."

"Beating his wife wasn't enough, he needed a younger woman on the side to beat up?"

Janet leaned back against the couch and closed her eyes. I felt sorry for her, for her grief, for her guilt about her sister, whatever it was. She might also be in danger now. Janet. Kevin, asleep in my bed. This all had to end.

"What if we're wrong?" Janet said. "Maybe it's not someone from Oscar's but a stranger, someone we don't know about.

What about the man the bartender at The Pub told us about. Maybe it wasn't Ozzie? Or maybe it's the gangsters after all, and they'll just come and kill us too."

Janet was right. Why concentrate on Oscar's? Why not suspect the Boss and his pals? Who was the man Angelina met downtown, who maybe stood up and maybe didn't? Did I stick with Oscar's because it was familiar ground? Or because most of Oscar's clientele were so obviously guilty of something, you couldn't help but suspect them? On top of this, I'd pretty much had it with sticking my nose in the Boss's business. I might already be on his to-do list for my last escapade.

Downtown was another matter. Hanrahan's and its environs were a part of Angelina's life I didn't know about. Downtown was where she found her gold mine and—I now remembered—her sugar daddy. If I could get my mind off the folks around Oscar's, it would be worth trying to find out if there really had been a sugar daddy. I wondered if the cops had found out.

"In those letters she sent, did Angelina mention an older man?" I asked Janet.

The question startled her out of her drowsiness. "What? An old man?"

"Never mind, we'll talk about it tomorrow. Why don't you sleep here?" I said since she was almost asleep anyway. There may be things to look into elsewhere, but in the meanwhile there was one giant question looming over me that I couldn't put off any longer. "I'm going out for a while."

"Where?" she asked, opening her eyes but not lifting her head.

"To see Carl."

Mumbling, Janet curled up on the couch. I threw a blanket over her and went in to kiss Kevin on his forehead before I left, then walked down Broadway in the pale light of morning toward Strauss Park and West End Avenue.

Chapter Ten

I grabbed some coffee and a couple of hard rolls at the donut shop at 109th Street. Then I stood outside 811 West End watching through the window. Carl sat hunched over his desk in his small cubicle, writing. I considered not disturbing him but screwed up my courage and went in. He didn't seem to mind stopping what he was doing.

We drank coffee and ate hard rolls. "Is that a poem?" I asked.

He picked up the notebook he'd been writing in. "I write different kinds of poems at night. When I'm tired like this, they're fragmented with these weird images. But not a poem yet."

I found myself pacing around his tiny cubicle. Carl's owl expression replaced the peaceful, pensive face I'd seen when he was writing. He watched me pace but didn't say anything.

"I don't know what to do next," I said finally. "I'm trying to figure out which one of my friends is a murderer."

Carl began very deliberately breaking up the plastic lid of the coffee container into tiny pieces. He nodded solemnly.

"What would you do?"

"I'd pretend I was Angelina. Why would she let herself get murdered?"

"What about Ozzie?"

"He let himself get murdered because he was too afraid to stay alive."

"Angelina?"

Carl stopped breaking up the container lid to brush the tiny pieces he had already broken off into two equal piles. He let his gaze travel back in my direction. Looking him in the eye made me nervous, so I looked at the walls. "Something was going on that we didn't know about. I thought it was the porno flicks, but it's something else."

"Do you remember her talking about a sugar daddy? After she started working at Hanrahan's, she was spending money like a drunken sailor."

Carl carefully scooped up the piles of container lid chips and dumped them in his wastebasket. "A mysterious stranger, eh?" He nodded judiciously. "She never told me about anyone like that. But, then, she didn't very often tell me about men in her life."

"Well, she told me," I said defensively. "But, then again, everyone lies to me."

"You seem surprised."

"Where were you the night Angelina was killed?"

Carl's eyes flickered but his expression didn't change. "Here."

"The night Ozzie was killed, too, right?"

"Not much of an alibi, eh?" Carl said calmly, starting to work on the lid again. "I could have slipped away. The only way I could get tripped up is if someone tried to get in and I wasn't here to run the elevator. You'd have to check with every apartment in the building, though. That's a lot of work. And you still might not come up with anything because the odds are no one would be coming in the building at those hours."

"Did you find Angelina's apartment for her?"

"How'd you find that out?" Carl eyes opened wider.

"I asked the super."

"Good thinking."

"Why didn't you tell me you knew Angelina in Montauk?" I could hear the hurt in my voice.

Carl's eyes shot open again. "All right!" he said, the same tone he used to use for one of the Pearl's finger-roll lay-ups. "You are getting good at this."

"It wasn't me, it was Janet."

"Quite a team," said Carl, putting the remains of the second lid down on the desk and pushing it and the new pile of plastic bits away to the far corner of the desk. He pulled himself up out of the old wooden office chair he'd been sitting in.

"You aren't going to tell me?"

"I have to check the boilers." When he looked at me from the doorway, his eyes held that mournful Snoopy look. "What good would it do? You wouldn't believe me, so you'd have to investigate anyway."

I stared at him.

"Who else are you checking up on besides me?" He seemed to accept being a suspect without animosity.

I felt foolish answering him. "Reuben. Nigel. Maybe Eric. Maybe Danny, after all. It might be someone else we don't even know about. I'm going to see what I can find out about her life at Hanrahan's."

Carl raised an eyebrow. "It usually turns out to be the person you least suspect."

"I think that's only in books. In real life, I think it's usually the person you most suspect."

"You should still keep your eye on the people that look innocent."

"Why?"

"Brecht said the guilty have proof of their innocence in their hands."

⌐⌐⌐

When I woke up in the early afternoon, Janet was playing chess in the kitchen with Kevin. Over bagels, we agreed that we would continue to check up on everyone: Nigel, Carl, and Reuben from Oscar's, and anyone else we turned up from

Hanrahan's. Janet's first foray would be to Stamford to talk to neighbors and maybe the Barthelme's hired help and find out all she could about Nigel's younger years. Kevin wanted to go to Stamford with Janet. At first, I said no, but then thought better of it. Going with her was probably safer than staying in my apartment.

I walked Janet and Kevin to the subway and then called Peter Finch to ask if there was any way to check discreetly with Carl's tenants to see if any of them noticed if he was missing from his post on the nights of the murders.

"I could have it done by a detective agency if you think he's the man. I find that hard to believe though."

"Me, too." I wouldn't believe Carl was a murderer if I found him standing over the body with a smoking gun in his hand. "I just want to rule it out."

"I'll do it," Peter said. "By the way, Danny said he's sure he left his jacket in Oscar's, the one they found with blood stains. Do you remember seeing it?"

I thought back through a blur of nights and customers, trying to pick Danny out of a crowd, trying to guess what his jacket looked like. I didn't know if, without saying so, Peter was asking me to lie, so I hemmed and hawed.

"Don't worry about it," Peter said. "Even if you told the truth, they'd think you were lying."

⌐ ⌐ ⌐

Still high on my new determination, I headed up Broadway to the law library at Columbia. If bartenders knew people by what they drank, it followed that librarians must know people by what they read. Sure enough, the librarian who'd been on that Thursday night did remember a massive, aging, light-skinned black man wearing glasses who'd been poring over the Domestic Relations sections of the New York State statutes, remembered him just as certainly as if he'd been drinking rum. He stayed all evening, leaving shortly before midnight when the library closed. That still gave him time to stop off and kill Ozzie on his way down to Oscar's for a drink, but, even if Reuben had lied about seeing Ozzie earlier the night he was killed, he had at least told me some truth. Every little bit would help.

Next, I went looking for Nigel. I thought it might be better to talk to him before he found out Janet was snooping around in Stamford. The Upper West Side being a kind of French cafe society, I checked a few places where he might be before I made bold to call him at home. When I did, he invited me up.

His building, familiar as it was, gave me the creeps. The marble lobby was unpolished and worn and, even though the door had a security buzzer, the lobby felt haunted. Death had met Angelina in that lobby and walked with her to the park. Death had picked up Ozzie in the lobby another night, following him to his apartment. I looked over my shoulder while I listened to the elevator creaking toward me. I jumped when it shuddered to a stop and danced around nervously as it moaned and groaned its way to the ninth floor. It was tiny, like a coffin stood on end, and I couldn't get over the feeling someone was in it with me. The door opened onto a deserted hallway. I walked uneasily to 9D and rang Nigel's bell.

He led me down a narrow hallway lined with bookshelves to a small living room cluttered with typewriters and computers, with printers and drills and hand tools and various gauges and clocks. Had I been on the trail of the mad bomber, I was home free.

"What do you do anyway?" I asked Nigel.

"Install and program computer systems. All this is just a hobby."

The apartment had all the clutter of long inhabitancy and eccentricity. Nigel spent a great deal of time in this place and had built a life out of being alone.

"I'm trying to figure some things out," I said in a voice that sounded much more casual than I felt. "Maybe you can help."

"Try me." Nigel smiled ingratiatingly. Ushering me into this facsimile of a small appliance repair shop, offering to make coffee, he seemed both pleased and uncomfortable that I was there, reminding me of a little kid always willing to please and never able to. Maybe me as the little kid.

"Who do you think killed Angelina?"

Nigel pursed his lips and doubt flickered in his eyes. He sat on a straightback chair at a desk he used as a repair bench. "I hate to say this, but I think Danny did."

"And Ozzie, too?"

Nigel nodded.

"Where did you first meet Angelina?"

"In Oscar's."

"Where were you before you came to New York?"

Nigel's eyes stopped smiling. "I don't like the third-degree, Brian. This is the second time. What are you trying to do?"

"Figure out why someone would say you knew Angelina before she came to New York."

"Who said that?" Nigel's body tensed, his eyes hardened. He stood up and leaned over me.

I stiffened my back to keep from giving up. "Take it easy, Nigel," I said, but sank further into his sagging couch all the same. "Lots of things get said. I'm just asking you."

He calmed. I'd gotten better at lying than I thought.

"What else are you hearing?" He chuckled. The sound rattled around the room like the false laughter after a bad joke. He sat back down in his chair.

"About a girl named Sharon Collins."

Nigel had pretty good control of himself now. When I mentioned the girl's name, his expression didn't change, not even a blink. After a few seconds of looking thoughtful, he asked, "Who's she?"

"The girl who accused you of raping her."

"Jesus," said Nigel, sighing. "Is this coming from Danny? Or from Reuben?"

I didn't answer.

He stood up slowly. He didn't seem upset, bothered maybe, but not really agitated. "Danny's trying to save his own ass by frying mine?" His smile was bitter, his tone indignant. "Check it out, Brian, if that's what you're doing. It's better for me if you do. I don't want whispering behind my back."

"I'm asking you to your front."

"The girl was crazy. She never saw me before in her life. Ask the cops. They checked out the whole story." He shook his head. "You oughta know about people pointing fingers at other people."

A voice told me to let it go. Instead, in the hallway of the tall bookcases, as I was edging my way out, I said, "Ozzie was drunk enough to pass out the night he was killed."

"He did pass out. I dumped him on his bed, and he went out like a light." He looked at me steadily. "He was alive when I left him there, Brian." His eyes pleaded with me. "Come on. Three or four people in the building heard shots hours after I dropped him off."

While he stood in his doorway, and I stood in the lonely hallway, I asked one more question. "Suppose Danny didn't kill her, who did?"

Nigel didn't answer for a long while. "I have no idea. It could have been anyone."

The feeling I was being followed returned as soon as I got on the elevator. I expected a man with a gun to be standing facing me, inches away, when the elevator door opened.

As the door opened, I caught a glimpse of a gray coat and screamed. Betsy Blumberg screamed right back at me.

"Are you crazy," she yelled when the door had fully opened and we stood facing one another.

"This building gives me the creeps."

"Maybe you ought to give up searching around for murderers before you scare yourself to death." She looked me over. "Wanna have lunch?"

I did, so we went to Tom's.

In her daytime clothes, a gray suit and running shoes, with her dress shoes in her handbag, Betsy looked like one of the thousands of New York everyday working women you see on the streets of midtown. She seemed efficient and normal, and, for all that, I guess she was, in the context of New York being a pretty lonely place and everyone having his or her own store of secrets.

"What do you know about Nigel?" I asked, when we were seated in a booth.

"Is he your latest suspect? I thought Reuben was."

"I'm beginning to think it might be me."

Betsy wrinkled her eyebrows and pursed her lips before she spoke. "Nigel is strange. I guess he's really smart, and he's always Mr. Helpful. The old ladies in the building love him. He's always carrying packages and opening doors and changing light bulbs and fixing sinks. The funny thing is I think he really is nice like that. He's a do-gooder. But he's such a loner. And I don't know why he hangs around bars all the time if he doesn't drink."

"Do you know anything bad about him?"

"He doesn't seem to have a family."

"Do people visit him? Women?"

"No. But he goes to prostitutes."

"How do you know that?"

She wrinkled her eyebrows again. "I've seen him near my office where they live—or work, I guess. My block is a prostitute block. Not streetwalkers, the high class kind. I'm always being mistaken for one." Betsy eyed me suspiciously. "Do I look like a whore?"

"You look sweet and caring, and you're adorable, a true Rebecca of Sunnybrook Farm." I picked up her hand, holding it for a second.

"Thank you," said Betsy.

"What's the address of this house of ill repute?"

"Are you going there?" Betsy stared at me with her turkey sandwich halfway to her mouth.

"For information."

"Men are sick," said Betsy, dropping her sandwich back onto her plate.

⌐⌐⌐

Before work, I went downtown to check out Hanrahan's and The Pub, the joint where Janet had spoken to the bartender who remembered Angelina with the older man. The bartender, Frank, was an older man himself: A bartender from the old school, you could tell at first glance—starched shirt, immaculate tie, creased dress pants. He was freshly shaved, his half-bald dome shining. The bar was squeaky clean and his movements reminded you of a close order drill. He was friends with Eric the Red and had been in Oscar's a couple of times, so he recognized me.

"He drank Jack Daniels, right?"

"Yeh."

"And he stood, right? He never sat down."

"No. They used to sit together at a table in back." He pointed.

"A southern accent?"

"No southern accent."

"They came in a lot?"

"A few times," Frank said. "Angelina came in a lot but with different men. She came in with the guy in the suit a bunch of times but only for a short time."

"Why'd you remember then?"

"He didn't seem the kind of guy she'd be hanging out with."

Frank tried to be helpful but wasn't able to describe the guy, beyond his wearing a suit and looking like a capitalist. Since we're talking New York City here, arguably the business capital of the world, this information wasn't all that helpful. I tried to describe Edwin Barthelme to him, since he was the only capitalist I could think of, but, my powers of description being not much better than Frank's, got a blank look in response.

From The Pub, I went to Hanrahan's. The day bartender I'd spoken to once before didn't know the senior Barthelme. Angelina chatted and flirted with a lot of businessmen customers, he said. He didn't think she had a special relationship with any of them, didn't remember anyone who fit the description I gave him.

〜〜〜

That night at Oscar's, I got Michael the waiter to watch the bar for a few minutes around midnight so I could slip off to see Carl. I was pretty sure he knew about whorehouses and such things. Since he already approved of everyone—including himself—being investigated, I figured he might as well help.

"On 39th Street between Fifth and Madison." Carl knew the place right away. "It's a brownstone. Very classy place—and expensive. Two hundred dollars a shot. But the girls are beauties." Carl smiled. His eyes closed. He was a man with a vision—of the whores on 39th Street. "I went with Nigel once. He goes to an adorable little wench named Patricia. But I'm sure she'd never tell you anything."

We thought that over for a few minutes. I suggested a dozen reasons why she should talk to me.

"Those are all highly moral reasons. But this isn't a convent we're talking about," Carl said. "It's a whorehouse."

After another moment Carl began to smile mischievously; he had a plan.

"You're crazy," I said.

"No. This will work. You're an actor, right?"

Carl's plan was for me to impersonate a priest. This plan was based on his belief that a prostitute's morality would allow her to share confidences with someone else who abided by the seal of the confessional.

Carl knew the madam, Ms. Trinkle, and he knew the phone number. We practiced a couple of times, and I called her from his phone. I was the priest, and Carl would be Nigel if I needed him.

"I'm terribly sorry to trouble you, madam," I said unctuously. "But I am here in my office with a terribly troubled person. My name is Father John Henry."

"Good evening, Father," a cultivated voice said gently. "What might I do for you?"

"I know this is a terribly unusual request," I said, modulating my voice, speaking carefully in the tone of one used to addressing an audience of worshippers. I built my character around a large church in Manhattan, where I was a veteran, first-string curate. Holy though I was, I was a man of the people. I knew the score. I was a forgiver. That's why sinners came to me. I wasn't going to throw the first stone. "I would like an audience with one of your employees."

"I understand, Father," she said, softly and reassuringly. "We are the pinnacle of discretion."

I paused while that registered. "Uh, that's not what I had in mind," I said, almost losing my character. "You understand I can't reveal the concerns of my client. But if I can speak in complete confidence."

"Of course," said the woman, a little more cautiously.

"My client wishes me to speak on his behalf to a woman named Patricia."

"About what?"

"I can't say, madam, as you, I'm sure, understand. But it is of great importance to him and of little trouble to her, I can assure you."

"How do I know who's sending you?" Her carefully modulated tones were slipping a little too.

I whispered, "He's quite broken up, but you might have one word with him, if you're careful." I handed the phone to Carl.

He muffled his voice and tried to make it sound cracked and strained. "Yes," he said. "Ms. Trinkle. I'm Patricia's friend, Nigel."

He listened for a second. "Yes, please," he said. Then, I yanked the phone away and whimpered into it for him. A poet is not an actor.

Returning to my priestly role, I said, "I'm sorry, the poor man—perhaps I shouldn't have done that."

"Yes, Father," the woman said. "I know him. I'll ask Patricia. But it will be up to her."

In a minute she came back to the phone and told me Patricia would meet me at four the next afternoon in a lounge on Madison Avenue between 39th and 40th.

In the morning, I went to a wardrobe shop over on 50th to pick up a priest's outfit that I put on in their dressing room. Murray the clothier, a long-time friend, wasn't in the store. The new guy was a pain in the ass.

"Is this for a part?" he asked sharply. "You can't use my costumes for panhandling."

I showed him my Equity card.

The girl I soon spoke to in the living room-like lounge on Madison introduced herself as Patricia.

She wore a short yellow wool skirt that slid up her thigh as she sat down beside me on the couch and crossed her legs. She sat close enough for me to touch her, and I could feel immediately why someone might pay two hundred dollars: her legs were slender and muscular, her body taut, her breasts high and firm and bra-less against her maroon sweater. I also liked her smile, the way the auburn ringlets of her hair curled around her pale forehead, and her dark brown eyes. She looked quite young and being young talked easily about herself. She seemed flattered that a priest wanted to talk to her.

When she ordered a split of champagne for fifty dollars, I realized the lounge was a front for the pleasure palace around the corner. "You can drink the champagne," she said. "I don't really want it." Her leg brushed against my hand as she settled in comfortably beside me. She didn't wear stockings, and her skin felt cool.

"Me neither," I said. "I need to talk to you."

She stretched, so her breasts pushed against her sweater. She twisted in her seat to face me, and her skirt slid farther up her thigh. My priestly character was falling apart. I wanted to bury my face in her lap.

"I'm on duty in a little while," she said. "So this has to be pretty quick."

"What's on duty?"

"I need to move around the bar and socialize."

"Socialize?"

"Make men horny."

"Oh."

"It's my job." She smiled into my eyes.

"What if I want to spend more time with you?"

"You got a credit card? For a hundred dollars we can go in back in private for a while. Otherwise, I have to move around up here and socialize."

"I don't have a credit card," I told her honestly. "And I can't afford a hundred dollars." I regained my composure, handed her a twenty-dollar bill, and asked her to sit for as long as she could.

She talked easily about herself, no pretenses. It was as if she needed to tell her story. When we had talked long enough for me to have a good sense of her, I began to like her. She reminded me of Angelina. I wondered what might have happened if she'd become a waitress instead of a prostitute. She'd come to New York from New Orleans to be a dancer, she said. From a strict religious upbringing. Her father was a fundamentalist who, just before she left home, made her strip naked before he beat her. First, she was an exotic dancer. "Now I'm an escort," she said. "I'm not really a prostitute. I only go to bed with men I want to go to bed with." She seemed certain she was moving up in the world.

"Nigel?"

"My relationships are private," she said primly.

I told her about Angelina. She kept her eyes on mine while I spoke. When I finished, I was holding her hand. "I'm trying to find someone who killed a girl. A young pretty girl who wanted to be a star, just like you."

She nodded, her eyes narrowed into seriousness. Serious, she looked even younger.

"Tell me about Nigel," I said.

"Everybody gets their kicks in weird ways."

"Does he hurt you?"

"No, not really."

"But it's rough?"

"He takes me instead of me giving. He talks hard, but he doesn't hit me."

"What does he talk about?"

"Not much. He talks dirty for a while, yells right into my face about my being a prick teaser and a slut. Sometimes he pushes me. In the beginning, I was scared. But I got used to him. He tells me he loves me, and he says he's sorry. Sometimes he cries. Then we fuck."

"What do you wear?"

"Something like this," she said, lifting the edge of her little skirt to show me, "and no top." She ran her hand across her breasts. My mouth watered, but I had years of training. I kept my concentration.

"What does he wear?"

"Right," she said. "That is a little weird. He always wears the same old college jacket."

"From where?"

"I don't remember," she said after thinking hard for a few minutes.

"How often does he visit you?"

"Every Wednesday night."

Wednesday night didn't sound right. The answer came too quickly. Angelina had been killed on Wednesday night. "Are you sure?"

"I think so."

"He never misses?" I was badgering her.

"No."

"Never?"

"I'm pretty sure." She seemed hurt that I didn't believe her.

"Maybe you forgot."

"Maybe," she said in a small voice.

I sat with her for a little while longer, but I had to get out before I blew my cover. Something winsome and charming about her, a kind of openness I didn't expect, made me not want to leave her. I also imagined my hands wrapped around the firm young breasts beneath her maroon sweater. I put my hand on her leg just above the knee and looked into her eyes when she handed me back the twenty. "God, you're beautiful," I said.

"Do you think God understands?" she asked seriously.

"I'm sure he does," I said, removing my hand.

～～～

Janet and Kevin arrived back at Oscar's close to midnight Friday night when the place was hopping. I didn't have time to talk to them. I was flying, and I needed to make some money to pay back that fifty bucks for the horse piss champagne I'd shared with Patricia, so, since Pop was back in town, I asked Janet to take Kevin to my father's house in Brooklyn for the night. Ntango was at the bar, so I asked how much he'd charge to take them. It really was a hell of a fare from the Upper West Side to Flatbush.

"For you, Mr. Brian," he proclaimed in his half-teasing manner, "never a charge to go anywhere."

I still had the twenty the hooker returned to me, so I gave it to him. I planned to make the fifty back off Oscar anyway.

An hour later, Janet called to tell me Ntango picked up a fare to the airport from my father's building, and my father offered her the spare room. I could barely hear over the bellowing of the drunks, but I finally grasped that she would stay there overnight, and I should come out there in the morning.

"How about if I join you late tonight in the spare room?"

"Don't be silly," said Janet.

Since Janet wouldn't be around, I thought about going back to Patricia. The two hundred dollar nut talked me out of it, so I went home alone and fantasized about cuddly hookers, big brown eyes, short yellow skirts over long, slim legs, maroon sweaters lifting to expose firm pale breasts as white as lilies.

Around eleven the next morning, I took the subway out to Flatbush and found my father, my son, and Janet eating bagels at the dining room table.

"We didn't find anything," Janet said challengingly, as if it was my fault. "We went through court records and the *Stamford Daily News* clip files, but we didn't find out anything on Nigel. We couldn't even find a birth certificate."

"That happens," I said.

"Next time it can happen to you." She glared at me, urging me to say something else so she could berate me some more.

"Why are you mad at me?"

"We went to Nigel's father's house," Janet said.

"He turned the dogs on us," Kevin added. "Boy what a place, a big mansion like a castle. With a butler and everything." Kevin was excited enough to have misplaced his usual nonchalance for the time being.

My father cleared his throat for attention. "Your son is unduly impressed by the trappings of wealth."

"Yeah," I shot back, "well, your son spent yesterday afternoon in a whorehouse."

Janet choked on her bagel. Kevin's eyes opened wide. I never know what's going to impress that kid. Before Janet threw her coffee, I explained myself.

"That sounds like an excuse," Janet said. "We're wasting our time on Nigel."

I put some cream cheese on a bagel and asked my pop if he'd boil me some coffee.

"Ha, ha," he said.

"They didn't exactly let the dogs loose on us, but they do have dogs patrolling the grounds," Janet said when my father went to the kitchen. She told me that the butler took her message and came back with a lawyer's card, saying Mr. Barthelme wouldn't talk to me, and if I wanted anything else I should call the lawyer. "I called," said Janet. "But the lawyer wouldn't answer any questions....That's not unusual, you know," she went on, speaking rapidly, in case I'd mistakenly planned on disagreeing with her. "Don't think it means they're hiding something, because it doesn't. It just means Mr. Barthelme's interest isn't served by talking to us, and the lawyer's job is to protect his client's interest. So he said not to talk to us."

Janet was on a roll, lowering her head like a bull about to charge, leaning across the table to make sure she had my attention. "This has been all wrong." Why didn't I follow up on Carl? she wanted to know. What about Reuben? He'd had time to cover all his tracks. And maybe Danny did do it. How did I know that he was such a good guy?

"I'm not going to do what you say anymore. I'm going to do this on my own. You keep making me do the wrong thing."

She would not be comforted. I didn't understand her anger; maybe I didn't want to. She pissed me off, so I let her leave by herself. After she left, I moped for a while and then talked with my father, while Kevin's video game boinged and beeped in the background. I told Pop about Janet's mother's version of Angelina's rape.

He thought for a long time, then asked, "Did you ever learn why she came to New York or why you came to know her?"

I recapped what Janet had found out about Carl and my feeling that Angelina might have come looking for someone on the Upper West Side.

Once more, he thought for a long time. Pop wasn't self-conscious about long silences. "Have you considered blackmail?" he asked.

"No. Who's blackmailing whom?" We sat at the dining room table, Pop in his customary seat in the armchair at the head.

"The girl would be the blackmailer. Who do you think might have done something in the past they wouldn't want discovered?"

I did a quick count of Oscar's rogues' gallery. "Everyone, as far as I can tell."

"Two threads in the stories you've told interest me. The first is the businessman who doesn't fit with the girl's lifestyle, yet has drinks with her. I don't know why you haven't tried to track him down. The second is the girl who accuses the man of raping her and turns out to be from the same town as the one she accuses. This one I can help you follow up on. What was her name?"

"Sharon Collins. But I don't see the connection between her and the businessman."

"I didn't say there was a connection."

Pop went once more to his spring-open phone book and made two or three phone calls. "Sharon Collins went to New York six months ago. The captain said she'd been arrested for prostitution in Stamford. He didn't know she was back in town. Nigel Barthelme, he never heard of. He didn't know Barthelme had a son. Barthelme's long been divorced, lives alone."

Pop also called to make sure a friend of his still worked for the *Stamford Daily News*. "Go see him. Albert Hawkins." Pop's eyes took on the faraway quality they always did when he traveled back into his memory. "He's a fighter. He held one of the first half-dozen books from the Newspaper Guild. Blacklisted. Spent ten years laying linoleum and another ten covering Zoning Commission meetings, until they discovered affirmative action and made him an editor. He'd know what went on in Stamford."

━ ━ ━

I met Albert Hawkins in the *Daily News* newsroom Monday afternoon. I hadn't slept except for dozing for forty-five minutes on the train out there. Monday was my day off, so I was hanging in for the duration. Albert Hawkins had a broad black face that wrinkled around the eyes and mouth when he smiled, curly hair with gray specks scattered through like snow flakes, a soft southern accent, thick working man's hands. I'd met bunches of my father's former comrades when I traveled around the country in the Sixties to this peace demonstration and that anti-war conference, thinking I was part of a revolution that was much smarter than my father's had been.

The old comrades put us up, we with our long hair, guitars, and sleeping bags, feeding us and listening to our tales of tear gas and billy clubs, cheering us on in our battles with the establishment. They were the folks we went to for contributions for the April Days of Protest or for Summer of Peace, and the people we went to for bail when things went sour.

I told him about Nigel and Sharon Collins. Albert was a big man with a raspy voice, quick, intelligent eyes, and a brisk manner, as if he were used to getting things done. At first, he looked at me hard and long. Then, he chuckled. "You're Kevin McNulty's son all right. Your dad knows me all too well. Edwin Barthelme owns the floor you're standing on. He owns the paper." Albert cuffed me on the shoulder and grabbed his jacket off the coat rack. "I've got a file at home that might interest you."

Albert drove me by the Barthelme place before he took me to his home after work. He wouldn't hear of a hotel; he went back too far with my old man. I would sleep on his foldout couch.

A ten-foot-high stone wall wrapped around the Barthelme estate, which was at the Stamford-Greenwich border on the top of a hill overlooking a golf course and the town of Stamford beyond. We sat for twenty minutes or so in the driveway of another walled estate across the street and looked at the wooden gate that blocked the entrance to the Barthelme place while Albert Hawkins told me an incredible story.

"A deal with the devil, for sure," said Albert. "But in his case the devil took the form of God."

He looked steadily at the estate across the street from us. "Edwin was a copy editor at the old *World*," he began. "He might even have been there in your father's time. Not a particularly good editor, kind of nondescript. During the first Guild organizing drive, the publisher did a management shake-up. Bernie Ross, the managing editor, was a good guy, so I guess he didn't fight the union hard enough. One day we came to work, Bernie was gone and Barthelme had taken over."

Albert looked at me; he was holding back a smile. "That's only the beginning," he said cheerfully. "A few months later, I came into work to find that the publisher was gone and Barthelme had taken his place." Now Albert let go and laughed heartily.

"Some years ago, Edwin hooked up with a group of backers—rich, right-wing religious fundamentalists. He kissed their asses, and the money rolled in. He bought this paper, cut the editorial staff, brought on old war horses like me, who couldn't command big salaries, subscribed to news services instead of hiring reporters, and everybody got rich. Except the workers, of course." He laughed again. "They bought up small and mid-sized dailies like this one all over the country, using the same approach.

"Everything was fine until his son got in trouble, and I know for a fact that he did. The trouble had to do with sex and a young girl and would have ruined Edwin Barthelme. He'd have lost his backing from the holy rollers, so he squashed the story and disappeared his son."

Albert lived with his wife in a brick garden apartment. The walls of the living room and the upstairs hallway were lined with bookcases, overflowing with books, many of the same old International Publishers editions my father had on his bookshelves. We drank a martini before dinner, then ate pot roast, mashed potatoes, and collard greens. Afterward, we drank coffee and Albert looked through his file.

He sat surrounded by six or seven piles of that old brown newsprint reporters used to type their stories on in the old days. It was the paper my father had brought home from work for me to write and draw on when I was a kid.

"I got it," Albert shouted. The story was on one of those old sheets of newsprint. He handed it to me.

☜☜☜

"A Stamford man was taken into custody last night on a warrant issued on the complaint of the parents of a 12-year-old Glenbrook girl.

"Nigel Barthelme, 18, of Palmer Hill Road, has been charged with six counts of corrupting the morals of a minor and three counts of statutory rape. He is scheduled to appear in town court this morning for arraignment."

~ ~ ~

"There never was a court appearance." Albert laughed, humor mixed with bitterness, "and there never was a news story."

This was what I went looking for, yet it stunned me. The girl who'd accused Nigel that night in my bar told the truth. The charge was statutory rape, which meant he didn't use force; it was sex with a young girl too young to know what she was doing. The date on Albert's story was August 11, 1971, two years before the same kind of non-forcible rape happened to Angelina. My hunch on Nigel was borne out, just as my hunch on Reuben had held up. Reuben was a murderer. Nigel was a child molester of at least one young girl. Now what?

Before I left the next morning, I remembered Patricia the adorable hooker mentioning Nigel's college jacket and asked Albert if he knew anything about Nigel's college days—where he went to college, for instance.

He said he didn't but he'd see what he could find out.

Chapter Eleven

I called Janet when I got back to the city, figuring she'd gotten over being mad by then.

"I've found out a number of things," she said excitedly. "Your good friend Carl may be in the clear, after all. I think it was someone else."

"Who?"

"I'm not going to tell you because I'm not sure. But if I'm right, you'll be amazed."

"Let's not keep secrets from one another," I said, calmly I hoped. "It's too dangerous now to go nosing around by yourself."

"Talking about secrets, your father said you went to Stamford. Why?"

"Checking on something."

"I thought we weren't keeping secrets."

"Who's your suspect?"

"Never mind."

"Why is Carl in the clear?"

"I talked to him. All of what he told me makes sense, and it brings up the possibility of this other person. I'll have all the information I need by tomorrow night. Then we can compare notes. I will tell you one thing," she said. "Nigel Barthelme called the police to tell them Angelina had been with Danny."

"How do you know that?"

"Well, at least, I'm pretty sure it's him. Peter found out they had a tape of the call, and they let him listen to it. He said he recognized the voice."

"What are you going to do now?"

"You'll see."

"You're doing this wrong." My voice was rising. "It's too dangerous now to go off doing stuff alone."

"Now you want to work together. You don't want any help from me when you're talking to prostitutes. Why didn't you tell me about going to Stamford again?"

"You walked out before I had a chance."

She hung up.

I felt like a four-year-old who couldn't make anyone, particularly this pain in the ass Massachusetts banker, understand what I meant. I wondered what she was on to. I needed to see Carl to find out which way he'd pointed her. But, first, I wanted another crack at Barthelme.

⇌ ⇌ ⇌

Once more, I resorted to my borrowed suit and followed a group of pin stripes into Barthelme's building and onto the elevator. I didn't want to be announced by the concierge this time around.

I knew I'd have to move fast once the elevator door opened, so I tried to picture the layout of Barthelme's suite. The elevator opened into the reception area where Janet and I had met him. His office was beyond the reception area, and, if I remembered correctly, there was a reception desk that no one was at the last time, but someone might be at this time. The trick would be to get past and through his office door.

When the elevator door opened, I caught a glimpse of Barthelme's back as he went into his inner office. Taking my chances, I rushed across the reception area, waving my copy of Lew Archer. "Oh, Mr. Barthelme, you forgot—"

Before anyone could react, I was in. As soon as I got through the door, Barthelme turned on me, his face hard, his expression contemptuous. He was a lot taller than Nigel, taller than me, and I'm a shade over six feet and wear a hefty size forty-four.

"What do you want?" His tone suggested my answer had better be good. Dressed in gray this time, too, he bent forward at the shoulders toward me, although clearly this time he had no desire to get closer.

"Maybe to save your son."

"I don't know what you mean." His eyelids came down over his eyes like hoods.

"I'm speaking of your son Nigel, the child molester."

His eyes opened, registering the news without losing their imperiousness.

He stood behind his desk. I stood in front. "Who are you?"

"A friend of Angelina Carter's."

He leaned farther forward, peering at me more carefully. "You're that bartender."

"You should remember Angelina. You paid off her mother to keep her from pressing charges against Nigel a few years back."

His clear gray eyes never left mine, nor did his expression show anything except contempt.

"Was Nigel with you on that Wednesday night and Thursday morning two weeks ago?"

No answer.

"Do you know another girl named Sharon Collins? Did you know Ozzie Jackson? Did you go to visit Angelina when she was working at Hanrahan's? Did she put the bite on you again?"

His eyes bored into mine.

I was really glad I'd gotten a chance to talk to Edwin Barthelme. For some stupid reason, I thought he might answer something. What do you do when the guy doesn't answer?

What the hell? I tried one more. "It's hard to believe that a son you hadn't seen in ten years was with you on the very night he most needs an alibi. Was he with you the night Ozzie was killed, too?"

No answer, just the icy stare.

"Look, it's been really nice chatting, Mr. Barthelme. But I have things to do, as I'm sure you do." I smiled toothily. "We'll talk again sometime soon."

Riding down in the elevator, I considered what I'd done. Tipped Nigel's father that I was onto Nigel's past. Found out nothing at all that might help me. Like the man said, if I'd've had a third leg, I'd've kicked myself in the ass.

⌐ ⌐ ⌐

That night, after I'd eaten a steak, and, in pursuit of normalcy, had a couple of drinks with Nick at the Terrace, I stopped off to see Carl at his guard post on West End Avenue. He was busy for a good fifteen minutes with the elevator. Every time he came down with it, someone else was waiting to go up, so I sat in his cubicle looking over a book he was reading, *Diet for a Small Planet*. I was always amazed by Carl's wide-ranging interests, his primitiveness in learning what he himself thought he needed to know in life, and how little this kind of knowledge had to do with being successful in the world as most people knew it.

"Who are the crazy people running the world?" I asked him when he finally returned to his booth.

"You were looking at that book, eh? I know. We let people starve so we can eat overstuffed deli sandwiches. Our entire food chain is wrong. No one has to go hungry."

I watched my friend drinking his Coke and eating his hard roll with butter. He looked at me, then at his hard roll. "One must learn to practice what one preaches," he said.

I approached this conversation awkwardly, once more wishing I could avoid confronting someone with his failings and misdeeds. But now I was afraid someone else would be killed, that Janet might be, or me, so I probed when things might much better be left alone.

"What did you talk to Janet about?" I asked.

When he started involuntarily, I realized he hadn't expected her to tell me. "I told her some personal things I'm not sure I want to tell you."

"Oh," I said. Certainly in any civilized world he should have that right, but not now. "I'm afraid someone is going to die," I said.

"Who?"

"I don't know. Maybe Janet. Maybe me."

"That's a lot to be afraid of," Carl said. I knew nothing I could say would make him talk unless he decided himself, so I waited.

After a long time he said, "I told her about meeting Angelina in Montauk. I went there that summer to try to get my head together. Instead, it blew apart. I wound up coming back to the psych ward in Bellevue." Carl paused to look at me accusingly, his baleful expression suggesting how difficult it was for him to tell me this. "I didn't want everyone in town to know that I was in a nuthouse."

"I understand."

He didn't say anything, but his stance and his manner softened ever so slightly. He began playing with the Coke bottle cap, breaking off the thin metal fringe at the bottom of the cap.

"I didn't know Angelina very well in Montauk. But when they hauled me away, she came down to visit me every couple of weeks at Bellevue. That says something about her, doesn't it? She was the only person to come and see me. Actually, she was the only one I wanted to see.

"I knew you knowing about all of this wouldn't help find who killed her, and I didn't want to tell a hundred cops and district attorneys and lawyers and bartenders about it. It was my business." He went back to breaking up the thin band he'd peeled off the bottle cap.

I watched his fingers that were thick and stubby work on the cap. His movements were deliberate and precise as always. I was embarrassed. I would have liked to forget the whole thing and have gone back to the Terrace, but I went on. "Did Angelina come to visit you after you got out of the hospital?"

"When she still lived in Massachusetts, she would stay in my apartment for a weekend every now and again while she tooled around the city looking for a millionaire."

"Why did she move here?"

"I told you, to find a millionaire."

"A particular millionaire, or would anyone do?"

"I don't know."

"Why here on the West Side? Why not the East Side where the high rollers live? Because you were here?"

"No. I suggested the East Side or downtown. I even found a place for her on Tenth. But she wanted to live in this neighborhood."

"Did you find her an apartment?"

"The first one. The second one she got herself."

"Where'd she get the money?"

"I wondered that, too." Carl had broken up the strip from the bottle cap into tiny pieces that he now pushed together into two piles like he had done with the coffee lid the last time I'd visited him.

"Can you find out how she got the second apartment?"

"That's what I told Janet. I told her that I was pretty sure Angelina was set up with the apartment and with the job at Hanrahan's. Somebody made her Queen for a Day."

"Why?"

"You tell me."

"Blackmail."

Carl registered the word. His face took on that owl-like expression. "That might explain it," he said when he'd thought for a few minutes.

"What else did you tell Janet?"

"I gave her a name, Mario, he's the super for the building on 110th Street. He'd know how Angelina got the apartment."

It was around three by now. I went home to bed and slept for a long time. Checking my mail on my way out of my apartment late the next morning, I found a letter from the union telling me I'd won my grievance and should report to work at the hotel a week from Monday. The letter jolted me back to a life that had once been normal. Who the hell had I become?

When I opened the outer door, I saw Nigel in the doorway of the building across the street. He ducked back in. I would have left him there, but he came out himself.

"Hello, Brian," Nigel said. "Any new suspects?" He came on like a bully. Stood up close to me, his chest out. His eyes through those coke bottles of his were about the size of bar coasters. "Danny killed Angelina," Nigel said. "Ask the cops. It's all over."

"We'll see."

He laughed a tight rattling laugh. "Turn up anything on me?"

"No." I watched his eyes. "But I haven't found Sharon Collins yet."

His eyes moved, showing a glint of interest; he forgot about me for a split second. Then his eyes turned sad. I felt embarrassed for him. It's awful to have your secrets laid out for you, right there, a block off Broadway.

"Keep it up, McNulty," Nigel said. "You think you're going to prove I'm the murderer, but you won't because I'm not." He stared at me, and I caught a glimpse of his father's penchant for contempt. Like father, like son, after all. "You're a good person, McNulty, despite your attempts to bury it under your degeneracy. But you're not particularly bright."

What he said hurt my feelings, but I suspected he might have something there.

"By the time you discover I'm not the murderer, you'll have dug a couple of more graves. Your Massachusetts friend is worse. Why don't you take her to the Bahamas for a couple of weeks?" It sounded like a joke, but he wasn't smiling. "Let it go, Brian." His eyes began to mist over and his goggles to fog up. He walked off without another word.

I went back inside to call Albert Hawkins. When he answered the phone, he laughed his hearty laugh, so different from Nigel's.

"How 'bout Amherst College," he said. "Amherst is about twenty miles from Springfield, less than that from Chicopee. Nigel was there, a debater and a fencer, until 1973 when he left for health reasons. I found him by working my way through the ruling class schools. Somebody forgot to erase something." He paused. "By the way, how did you get along with his dad? He cut his day short yesterday and came home."

I needed to get to Springfield, then to Stamford, then back to New York in the same day. What I needed was a car, except I didn't know how to drive. I tried to call Janet, but I couldn't reach her. I left a message with her hotel for her to make sure I could find her tonight, then went looking for Ntango and found him having breakfast in La Rosita at 107th Street. He had the horse hire for the next twenty-four hours.

"I need to take a trip without the meter running," I told him while I sucked down a double espresso.

Ntango, his brown eyes soft and kind, said apologetically, "Mr. Brian, I haven't made my nut for the past two days."

"How much?"

He rested his elbows on the counter and leaned forward; his manner was patient. "Fifty for yesterday. A hundred for today."

No wonder Lew Archer had clients pay expenses. I'd settle for twenty-five a day and expenses myself. I needed a couple of hundred dollars fast. Only one person in our circle, so to speak, ever had that kind of money in pocket. I went looking for the Boss. He was always in Sully's from noon to five to collect from the numbers runners.

"I'll be right back," I told Ntango. "Don't take a fare even if it's to the airport." I ran across the street, hoping the mug I'd dumped into the elevator shaft had returned to Jersey for good.

The Boss looked up, but was not his usual gracious self. "Beat it, McNulty," he said.

"Sorry, man, I need a word." We walked outside.

"I want a deuce and a half."

The Boss, dapper in his fedora and sharkskin, stood on his little portion of Broadway sidewalk like it was his front porch. "A loan?"

"No, a grant."

He looked at me and then on either side of me. "What's that?"

"I want you to pay me to clear your good name."

With the decisiveness of a first-class businessman, the Boss took two C notes and a fifty from his wad. "You caught on," he said.

I also took a gram of blow on the cuff, figuring Ntango and I would be too wilted without it.

I handed Ntango the money, figuring the extra yard could keep him in rice and beans for a while, but held onto the blow.

We drove to the building Angelina had lived in on 110th Street. Ntango waited while I nosed around the cellar in search of Mario. I couldn't find him, so I decided to go downtown to Hanrahan's to see how Angelina got her job there. But on the way down Broadway, I changed my mind. The information about Nigel being twenty miles away from ten-year-old Angelina burned in my brain like the feeling I got at the track when I knew I had the sure thing. I told Ntango to head for Springfield.

"Which way, Mr. Brian?" he asked in his soft voice, looking at me in the rearview mirror, chuckling to himself. He didn't know Springfield from Ankara.

"North," I said. He glanced at me over his shoulder. "Uptown," I said.

He made a U-turn around the island at 106th Street and we headed north on Broadway, then across 125th Street to the Triboro and the New England Thruway. I told myself it was okay to skip Hanrahan's and not find Mario. Carl told Janet the same thing he told me, so she might cover that anyway. Why duplicate effort? Yet this icy fear began building around me. We were getting too close. I'd rather she wasn't off on her own.

Two hours and forty-five minutes later, Ntango and I cruised into Springfield and spent another forty-five minutes looking for Mrs. Carter's house. Ntango was patient and unflappable, circling the streets of Chicopee in ever-increasing circles like a lost dog until I recognized the 1940s window display and the bartenders' union hall.

When we found Mrs. Carter's house, I brought Ntango to the door with me for a witness in case I did get something out of her. Mrs. Carter, her eyes electric with cunning and fear, held the door in front of her like a shield, warding us off as if we were the Mongolian hordes, but I kept at her. Already cranked, I wasn't to be trifled with.

"Nigel Barthelme, do you remember that name?"

"I can't say," Mrs. Carter twittered, looking beyond me and Ntango for help.

"He may have killed your daughter. What kind of fucking principles are you running on?"

I held the door with my hand while she tried half-heartedly to wrestle it closed. "I'll call the police," she stammered.

"You missed your chance."

She began shaking.

"Answer one question, Mrs. Carter. For all the misery of your daughter's life."

The door went slack against my hand. "It wasn't my fault. It had already happened. It couldn't be undone." The challenge gone from her voice, her mask disintegrating, her eyes searching mine for pity.

"So you hated yourself, and you hated her."

Mrs. Carter let go of the door and stepped back from it. "I loved my daughter. It's just that everything I ever did was wrong." She looked hollow and lost like she didn't belong in her own hallway.

"Nigel Barthelme?" I asked with a lot more confidence this time.

She crumbled. "Yes. He was the boy."

She was still standing in the doorway when Ntango's cab tore out of her street, flattening me against the fake leather back seat. I lifted my hand in an awkward salute, but she didn't see. I wondered how long she'd stand there and what she'd do when she could no longer stand in the doorway.

We headed south on I-91 toward I-95 and Stamford. It would take us a little less than two hours to get there, so I needed to get my coked-up brain on-line. This would be my final visit to Edwin Barthelme.

Only one awful truth was missing, and that one came home to roost when I arrived in Stamford and called Albert. No laughter this time, pain in his voice. "A girl's body they found last night, it was Sharon Collins."

I guess I expected it, but I felt like crying all the same. "All my pretty ones," I thought. "Poor MacDuff."

"Where?"

"In some woods off Den Road." He anticipated me once again. "Not far from Palmer Hill."

I told Albert I wanted to try to see Barthelme again. I thought he might help me get in.

"He wouldn't let me in, either," said Albert. "You can't even get onto the estate, unless someone lets you in." He paused for a long time. "There's one chance. The superintendent, Tim O'Leary. He's also the chauffeur, a tough, ornery old Fenian, and a strong union man. Mention my name. His son is one of us, if you know what I mean. If you ring the gate bell and he's the one who answers, you might be able to persuade him."

A small Ramada Inn sat next to the golf course at the bottom of the hill below the Barthelme estate. On an off-chance, we stopped there. The scattering of leftover golfers didn't much like Ntango and let it show in the chilliness that dropped over the place like dew when we came in the door, but the bartender gave us both shots of tequila anyway.

I left the change from a ten. "We're looking for a guy who might have been in yesterday. A little guy with thick glasses and a mustache. He drinks ginger ale with lemon."

The bartender, tall and thin, dark-haired and handsome, with the nervous mannerisms of a gambler, looked blank. "Maybe he changed to vodka and orange juice," I said.

The bartender stopped wiping the bar and walked back toward me. He picked up the tip. "A really ugly drunk. But not yesterday. More like a couple of weeks ago." The bartender looked us over. "You can have him."

The facts didn't connect. My brain kept short-circuiting right at the main connection. "A couple of weeks ago, what night?"

The bartender shrugged. "During the week, that's when I work: Wednesday or Thursday."

"Alone or with someone?"

"Alone one night."

"With someone another night? What did the someone look like? What did he drink?" I leaned across the bar, I'm sure, with fire in my eyes.

"Drink?" The bartender looked at me blankly. "Jack Daniels."

"Did the guy who drank Jack Daniels stand up when he drank?"

"The guy who drank Jack Daniels was his old man," the bartender said.

None of this made sense, but I was on to something: I had to keep at it, despite the faint tinkle of the little bell, far back in the hallway, telling me to slow down.

⌒⌒⌒

I decided not to ring the gate bell. It was too much of a crap shoot. Someone else might answer. I figured if I got over the wall, I could get to Barthelme's door before anyone caught up with me. Ntango drove the cab up alongside the stone wall that surrounded the estate, and we followed the wall back down the hill until we were abreast of a grove of trees, stately and barren silhouettes against the pale sky. Ntango pulled in right next to the wall, so that from the roof of the cab I could jump to the top of the wall.

I saw some barns and two cottages not far below me with lights on in one of them. Everything else was quiet. So down I jumped—but I forgot about the damn dogs. Before I hit the ground they came flying. All I saw was shapes—big shapes like elephants—with teeth as long as daggers. One nipped me on the leg and then on the ass as I ran. The wall was too high from the inside to get back up, so I busted through the door of the cottage with the lights on, hoping I'd find the Fenian gardener. God those bites hurt. I'd been beaten up and I'd been cut, but none of it hurt like those dog bites. Yet, in one respect, luck was with me. I rolled on the floor in pain, while Tim, the gardener, shooed the dogs off.

He looked down at me, fear in his eyes.

"I'm a friend of Albert Hawkins," I said desperately. The pain and the coke had completely scrambled my brain. I moaned, while the gardener and the wife discussed my situation.

"He needs something for those bites," said the wife.

"A shot of whiskey," said Tim.

"Some iodine," she said decisively.

"Whiskey," I agreed.

When we were seated at the kitchen table, after the missus tended to my bites and the whiskey my nerves, I told Tim about Nigel and the rapes and the deaths. I also asked if Ntango could drive around and come in.

"Poor Nigel," Tim said sadly, after Ntango arrived and I finished the story. Tim's wind-roughened and callused hands rested on the tabletop; his eyes were wrinkled around the edges, and he squinted permanently against the sun, even now in the evening in the dim light of his own kitchen. His peaceful expression and lack of cunning reminded me of Ntango.

"When did you see him last?"

He looked behind me at a calendar on the wall. "Two weeks ago today, I saw him for the first time in ten years."

"You saw Nigel here two weeks ago? Two weeks ago on a Wednesday? Are you sure?"

"I picked him up myself," Tim spoke emphatically, though his eyes were still kind.

"Where?"

"In front of a brownstone on 39th Street, right off Madison Avenue, right around midnight."

"You're sure?" I asked again. Nigel's alibi held. My suspicions crumbled. Maybe Tim the gardener and Patricia the hooker had concocted a story together for Nigel. But I seriously doubted it.

The facts stood in direct opposition to my theory, yet something was not right. And like Miss Clavel, afraid of a disaster, I would run fast and even faster. There had to be an explanation.

"Was Nigel here yesterday?"

Tim wrinkled his brow thoughtfully. "I think I would have seen him had he been here. Mr. Edwin came back and used the car yesterday. I saw no sign of Nigel." The question startled him, though. I could see worry in his face and sensed that he thought about something beyond the answer he gave.

"Did you pick up Mr. Barthelme in the city yesterday?"

"I did. Mr. Barthelme was alone."

"Did you see him go out after you got back here?"

"He went out in the car." His tone was crisp, almost resentful; his face had tightened and the twinkle was gone from his eyes.

"Did you see him come back?"

Tim looked puzzled.

"Is all this unusual?"

"You might say so," said Tim quietly.

"Where's the car now?"

"By rights, it would be in the garage." He looked uneasily at his wife. I wondered if he thought about his job of forty years and his pension. This afternoon he probably raked leaves. Tonight, he's talking about murder. Somewhere between tea and supper, the world as he knew it had ended.

I waited.

"He worked in the fields with me. Before he went off to school, he was as good to us as another man. He'd come out in the morning and kneel down where I was pulling weeds, silent as a mouse. Or pick up a rake. Or putter around straightening up the shed. We'd let him drive the tractor when we picked up brush, and he was as happy as the day is long." Tim turned to face me, his expression full of sadness and perplexity. "You wouldn't think with all his money he'd need the likes of us to make him happy." He looked to me for an explanation.

I didn't have one, only another question. "Nigel broke with his family some time back. He told me he hadn't seen his father in ten years, until recently. Do you know why?"

The gardener glanced at his wife, who averted her eyes as if she were embarrassed. Not getting her attention, he looked back at me, pursed his lips and shook his head, his face contorted with this memory, whatever it was. "Ah, it went back years. Nigel was just a bit of a lad," he said. "It was the Italian chauffeur."

I tried not to look as bewildered as I felt. Tim was having a tough time getting the story out, and, as impatient as I was, I didn't want to push him.

"Something had been going on with the boy....He was out and gone in a day, the chauffeur, a young man, too, healthy and good looking..." Tim looked to his wife again. This time she watched him, but still said nothing. "...Mr. Barthelme called the staff together. He said the boy had been mistreated but would be all right." Tim shook his head sadly. "I don't think he ever was....The housekeeper, Mrs. Hutchings, she said that was why Nigel left home and never came back. He blamed his father for not taking care of him."

The kitchen with its checkered linoleum and its rough wooden cabinets and Formica table took on an ominous silence. We sat in the silence, listening to a clock ticking from somewhere back in the house. Tim's face held the shocked expression of an accident victim.

"The car," I asked. "What did you say about Mr. Barthelme and the car?"

"The car never came back," said Tim. "Mr. Barthelme came back but the car's gone and he never said a word about it."

⌐ ⌐ ⌐

I knew for sure that Edwin Barthelme had something to tell me, although I didn't know yet what it was. Ntango drove me to the big house, pulling up to the side of the front door. I hoped that Barthelme senior would think it was junior, home now that the shit had hit the fan. When the butler opened the door, I said, "Mr. Barthelme is expecting me."

"I think you're mistaken, sir," the stiff answered.

"Maybe he's not expecting me so soon," I said. "If you'll just tell him the bartender is here...."

That got me an eyebrow; Ntango coming up behind me raised the other one. We pushed our way in. "Never mind," I said, remembering the Fred Astaire movies. "We'll announce ourselves." Which might have worked if I'd had any idea which way to go. We were in an entryway inside the front door, a foyer of sorts, larger than most Manhattan studios; a small, polished oak stairway and another door separated us from the main part of the house. I gave up. "Look, pal," I told the butler. "We need to see Mr. Barthelme. Tell him I want a word before I go to the police. My name is McNulty. He knows me."

"No need," said Mr. Barthelme from the landing of the small staircase. Standing on that balcony, he once more looked vastly superior to the rest of us mortals, perhaps more so this time because he held a small revolver that matched the gray of his eyes. "You've broken into my house. You and a Negro, who's probably carrying drugs. I could kill you as trespassers."

He was right about the Negro, wrong about who was holding, right about getting away with shooting us—he probably had a fix with the judges.

"Now you want bodies on your doorstep?" I asked. "When's it going to stop?"

For a second, his eyes lost their glitter of superiority. Edwin Barthelme, newspaper magnate, Wall Street tycoon, philanthropist, political power broker, a mansion on the hill, a butler in the foyer, a gun in his hand, all that against a bartender and a cab driver with their cocaine highs wearing off.

"Your story isn't going to hold," I said politely. I wondered if my deferential tone came from my respect for his gun or from some primordial acceptance of his station in life, like my kid, unduly impressed by wealth. Whatever the reason, I spoke politely.

He looked interested.

"Your son called the police, Mr. Barthelme. The cops record all their calls. A technocrat like him should have known about voice prints."

It was a good bluff. But Barthelme senior had the nerves of a good poker player. "My son and I were here. I've checked my records and recall handling a rather complex financial matter on the phone that evening. A half-dozen unimpeachable witnesses can establish that Nigel was here and not in New York that evening."

"You must know about the girl's body on Den Road." I watched his eyes. "Maybe you don't. Sharon Collins. You bought her for Nigel, too." I could see some pain in his eyes. He wasn't going to get any weaker, so I went for him. "Let's reel your son in, Mr. Barthelme, before he does any more harm."

"Look to your own son, Mr. McNulty," he said, and froze my heart.

Then it hit me. "Shit!" I said. "It wasn't Nigel. It was you." The logjam cleared, the facts tumbled into place. The older man Carl saw with Angelina on West End Avenue wasn't Ozzie. Edwin walked Angelina to the park that night. And it wasn't

Nigel who shot Ozzie. Nigel just left Ozzie's door open for his old man, who did the dirty work. Then I came along and fingered Sharon Collins for him. What kind of jerk was I?

At this moment a long, gray-blue, steel barrel poked through the door from behind Ntango. "Mr. Barthelme," said Tim the gardener.

Mr. Barthelme lowered his gun and then let it thud to the floor. He knew his gardener well enough.

"Where's my son?" I asked, reaching for the gun on the floor. Ntango got to it first. Barthelme went once more to his well of contempt. "Where's my son?" I asked again. "What about my son?"

"The young lady was nice enough to call," Barthelme said.

I knew the questions but not how to connect them. If Edwin was the murderer, who had my son?

It had to be Nigel. But why would Nigel bring Kevin into this?

"Where is he?" I asked Barthelme again, knowing he wouldn't tell me—and understanding at that moment why interrogators tortured their prisoners.

Nothing. Then, "The Barthelmes' yacht in the city…it was opened up yesterday," said Tim. "The yacht club called to ask if it was okay. When I asked Mr. Barthelme, he said not to worry…Nigel would be using the boat now and then."

I didn't understand what that had to do with anything.

"The boat basin," Ntango said.

I still didn't get it.

"79th Street," said Ntango, and Tim nodded.

"What?"

"79th Street," Ntango said. "The boat basin."

I bolted for the cab, Ntango right beside me, except one of the dogs got his leg. I kicked in a fury and felt the animal sag against my foot. Ntango screamed from the bite, but jumped behind the wheel anyway. The fucking gate was closed. Ntango skidded to a stop, leaned the thick taxi bumper against it, dropped the Impala into low, and pushed like a bulldozer. The city cab took out the country fence, and off we went down a dark country lane toward the Thruway to the city.

I couldn't stop the dread that poured through me. How could I have gotten Kevin mixed up in this? How could I have left him alone? I thought of all the safe places he might be. All the reasons this couldn't be happening. But, every few seconds, I pictured Nigel, with an arm around Kevin's shoulder, walking him down a dock toward a rich man's yacht moored in the murky Hudson.

It was so easy now putting it all together. Angelina had come to the West Side to visit Carl, stumbled across Nigel, remembered the big payoff to her mother. She put the bite on Nigel for her share. He couldn't pay enough, so she went for the old man. Edwin had been around enough to know it was senseless to pay a blackmailer and was ruthless enough to do something about it. Now that we'd caught him, it should all be over. Instead, my stumbling around might have created another murderer—and this one might have my son.

Ntango pulled up to a phone booth in a shopping center across from the Thruway entrance. I called my ex-wife's number. No answer. I tried Janet at her hotel. No answer. I finally reached my father.

"Don't panic," he said, but his voice shook. "Kevin isn't here. I thought he was at your house." I told my father to call Sheehan and tell him about Nigel and the boat basin.

"Why would he take my son?" I asked my father in a choked off, sobbing voice.

"Mistakes," my father said. "We've all made mistakes. I got off the phone with Janet five minutes ago. She was on her way to meet Nigel Barthelme, and Kevin is with her."

"And Nigel's after her to dump her in the river. What should I do?"

"Find them."

I called Oscar, who babbled into the phone about firing me because I hadn't shown up for work.

"Is Janet there?"

"No," he said. But I knew she might be sitting right next to him. "My son, Oscar, has my son been there?" He had to be able to hear the terror in my voice.

"Last night," Oscar said. "He was here last night looking for you."

I didn't know whether to believe him or not. "Nigel," I said. "Has Nigel been in?"

"Come in or you're fired," said Oscar.

"Let me talk to Eric." Giving up on Oscar, who continually created his own reality, I now tried Eric, who understood about fifty words in English that didn't have to do with food, drink, or getting laid.

"I'm in trouble, man," I said and immediately, through the language barriers and across the cultural prisms, heard Eric settle down to help. Not much good at taking care of himself, he understood trouble better than most and how we all are required to take care of one another.

I told him Nigel might be after Kevin and Janet.

"What?"

"Keep Nigel away from my son and away from Janet. If they come in, bring them in the kitchen and keep them there. If Nigel comes in, call the cops and lock him in the walk-in."

"What's coming down, man? You mad at Nigel?"

"Nigel might kill Kevin."

Dead silence on the other end of the phone.

"Eric! Eric!" I screamed.

"This no good, man.…Man, Brian, I didn't know. Don't tell me this—"

"What? Eric, what's the matter?" I tried to keep my voice down, but I kept punching the telephone as hard as I could to get him to answer.

"Kevin's around, man. He said not to tell you. Last night, he stayed in your apartment."

The lights around me grew dimmer; I got colder and colder.

"Nigel's been around, too, Brian. He walked up with us last night. He knows Kevin's at your place."

"Janet?"

"I don't see her. I'll do something," Eric said. "I'll go look."

Back in the car, I stared into the darkness and at my reflection when the headlights from passing cars flashed it onto the window and thought about how easy it would be for me to give my life for Kevin's. I felt no anger, only terrible regret for getting him into this, and hope against what I knew to be terrible truth. Ntango stared grimly into the darkness in front of him and we flew.

When we hit Bruckner Boulevard, Ntango pulled over at another phone. It was after midnight. I called Oscar's. Eric was back.

"They're together, the three of them," he said. "Nick saw them getting in a cab in front of the Terrace."

Trying to keep my voice from shaking, I asked Eric to go downtown and ask the bartenders around 79th Street for a kid, a woman drinking bourbon and water, and a man drinking ginger ale—or perhaps vodka and orange juice.

Over the Triboro and across 125th Street to Broadway, Ntango flew. I craned my neck, bouncing from one side of the cab to the other, peering out the window.

"Try Riverside Drive," I said, and Ntango cut across 123rd. Six blocks later I wanted to go back to Broadway.

"We can get down into the park at 96th," Ntango said; his expression clear and resolute, but calm as always.

We drove by Oscar's. I hopped out. Sam the Hammer stood in the doorway. Freshly shaved, his hair slicked back, he was waiting for the Greek to go to the track. "That kid of yours," Sam said.

"Where is he?"

"With that broad and Nigel."

"Where?"

"Downtown, near 72nd Street." His face had gone tough, like he was ready for a scrape—and he was—but he wouldn't show me any sympathy.

A cab stopped in the inside lane on the uptown side of Broadway; Eric the Red came dancing through the traffic toward us waving and yelling. "They were in a burger place and Teacher's," he said, "near 83rd."

"We can get into the park at 79th," Ntango said.

Eric and Sam piled into the cab with me, and Ntango tore along Broadway, using the sidewalk for a half a block when the street got crowded at 86th Street. We drove into the park, under a stone bridge and in by the boat basin. The walkway along the river that ended up near 110th Street began there at 79th. I knew the walk was wide enough for a car because the cops used it, and the area was deserted, so we began following it. It was the walkway where, way uptown, they'd found Angelina's body.

The walkway curved away from the river about three blocks from the boat basin. Ntango navigated the twists and turns of the asphalt walk until, a hundred feet up the path, it became a two-lane white cement walkway with a grass island in the middle. Almost directly across from us was a gigantic tunnel-like structure that housed the railroad tracks running beneath the park and Riverside Drive. Nango turned, drove up against an entryway in the wall, and shone his headlights into the darkness. It was cavernous like a field house with a dirt floor and rows of railroad tracks. From inside, their eyes glittering red in the reflected light, a dozen rats looked back at us.

I told Ntango we should go back to the walkway, so he backed out and headed north. After a short distance, the path sloped down and ran beside the river again. There, far in front of us, specks appeared against the sky beneath the canopy of the bridge far in the distance. They were specks in motion, running every which way like the vanguard detachment of ants when you've kicked over their hill.

"It's them," I screamed, not knowing if it was or not. The cab groaned like a dynamo, hit passing gear, and shot forward. The noise froze the specks. But one figure began moving again before the headlights hit them, running north on the path. Ntango slowed for one split second while I rolled out of the car, then sped after Nigel. Kevin watched wide-eyed as I gingerly picked myself up off the ground after a couple of somersaults. I expected him to be in hysterics. He seemed unruffled, except perhaps a mite bewildered by his dad's entrance. Janet looked scared. I didn't know if Nigel had scared her, or if she thought I'd killed myself tumbling out of the car.

They were both all right, so I hugged and hugged Kevin instead of talking. When I reached out my arm for Janet, she came closer, holding a gun.

"Did you take that from Nigel?"

Janet looked down at her hand as if she had forgotten she held it. Then she dropped it. Lying on the ground it looked harmless enough. It was the gun I'd gotten from Sam.

"From my apartment?"

She nodded. "I had it with me. I've kept it since—"

"The key. You found the spare key to my apartment?"

She nodded again, this time without raising her head.

"Why...?" I began to ask.

Then the quick flash of hatred in her eyes when she looked up, and I knew why.

"You weren't going to use it," she said.

We began to walk quickly, following the path of the cab. Around one short turn, we saw its taillights at a strange angle, in against the fence next to the river, and I knew it had stopped. After a few more steps, I could see some figures. There was a struggle going on. It was dark. But there were dim streetlights scattered along the walkway and shadows, so I could make out who everyone was by the shapes. Ntango, even in the struggle, was regally straight, slim, and tall. Sam, thick, lumbering, massive like stone, slow-moving, relentless, outlined against hollow sky above the river. Eric, quick, slight, hunched into his tight pants and short jacket, his long-flowing beard twisting and turning like the silhouette of a shrub in heavy wind.

The smallest shape—weak and tentative in his movements—took on the attack of the other shapes, trying to run, flopping, scrambling to get up and run again. It was like watching when a pack of wolves have cornered a deer. The deer is fighting back but it's doomed, and you see the doom in the weakness of how it fights back and the strength of the pack as they rip at it with their teeth and the animal offers a feeble kick of resistance.

This was the dance I watched as Nigel struggled against Ntango, Eric, and Sam. These were hard men, who'd been in battles for their lives before. Nigel struggled and got away, but they caught him and held him. They dropped him to the ground. But he scrambled up again. Then, all at once, in his desperation, Nigel bolted from them, breaking away, blindly charging along the path in our direction. I braced myself; I'm not sure for what. Sam and Ntango came after him, not running, not even hurrying, yet coming after him relentlessly all the same. When Nigel got close enough to make out who we were, he faltered and tried to turn in toward the park, but fell. He scrambled to his feet, looked at me. He was close enough now for me to see his expression in the hazy light of the street lamp. I expected to see fear. I expected to see in his face an expression that asked for forgiveness, for sympathy, for help. But that wasn't what was there. Not panic, not fear. Was it anger? Resignation? Hate? I couldn't tell. But it was terrible, his expression. It was evil.

Then with a burst of movement, Nigel surged wildly toward the steel fence that ran along the river. He grabbed at it with both hands, then hand over hand, feet digging into the chain links, he scrambled up to the top, heedless of the barbed wire. For seconds, he froze at the top of the fence—standing, it seemed, standing up straight on the top wire at the top of the fence—and then flung himself—almost grace-fully—almost soaring—into the murky river. His initial plunge sent up a plume of water that cascaded back down stirring up the water all around him. Then his wake rippled out toward the middle of the dark river until the ripples began to shine and glitter from lights far across on the Jersey side.

Nigel took his dive not twenty feet in front of us. I don't know how long it was after Nigel plunged into the water before I was able to move. I didn't know what I was watch-ing—an escape, a death, a murder. When I could move, I ran to the place where he jumped and hoisted myself, feet kicking against the fence, hands grabbing the chain links, climbing to the top, ripping my skin, cutting my hands on the wire, then lowering myself onto the other side, getting my feet onto the stone wall that served as the bank of the river, stepping carefully, knowing I was dead if I slipped, reaching for Nigel and calling him. Calling all this time, I realized later, calling him the whole time I clambered over the steel fence.

Seeing him then in the water, struggling, sinking, still wearing his glasses, his face contorted with that same terrible look—knowing then what the expression was and hoping against hope that Kevin hadn't seen it. What I saw in Nigel's face was disgust, total contempt for life and everybody in it.

I called and he turned his face full toward me, those fogged-up Coke bottles pointed right at me as he went down and there again as he came back up and as he went back down again. He made no sound. I thought I should go in after him, to save him. But I didn't jump in. I don't know if I could have saved him, or if he would have taken me down, and I would have been lost with him. I don't know if he killed himself. Or if we killed him. I don't know if he would have been glad I saved him. But I didn't.

~~~

Before long, Eric came over the fence after me. He more or less lifted me, while I climbed. Then Sam the Hammer and

Ntango helped me down on the other side. We stood around with no one saying anything, watching the spot where Nigel had gone down. Pretty soon, we heard sirens in the distance.

Sam started to walk away. "Better for me not to be around," he said, casting his "you wanna make somethin' of it?" look at me. "It was his idea," he said, gesturing with a jerk of his head toward the river.

When we reached the cab, Ntango radioed the cops. But we could already see the blue and red lights coming toward us inside the park. Ntango's expression tried to tell me something, but I couldn't figure out what. "Ditch the blow," he said.

I chucked it over the fence, and the gun right behind it, hoping I wouldn't hear Nigel scream for help from the murky river, hoping, too, that his body wouldn't surface right in front of me, or come back to haunt me, since I'd driven it to its watery grave.

‿‿‿

Sheehan arrived with a convoy of police cruisers. Not at all disconcerted, he watched the river for a while with us. "I checked him," Sheehan said, as if we were sharing a professional confidence. "No record. How would I figure it? No one even put his father on the same block with her." Sheehan jerked his head toward the river. "Him and his old man, real Alibi Ikes. I give you five to one the old man comes up with a half-dozen witnesses for that night when we get to court."

"Rich people don't play by the same rules as the rest of us," I told Sheehan. "Nigel left the door to Ozzie's apartment unlocked. Ozzie passed out. He wouldn't wake up to let someone in. Maybe Nigel forgot to lock the door, I thought. But no way. Somebody in Dubuque may forget to lock his door. Nobody in New York would. Why did he leave the door unlocked? I had to keep wondering about the door.

"Angelina's mother's life was made out of lies. Why should I believe anything she tells me? But mostly that poor terrified girl, Sharon. I couldn't get her voice out of my mind. Ozzie could have identified Edwin Barthelme, and I'll bet Danny saw him that night, too. I know a doorman on West End who saw Angelina with Barthelme that night."

"We'll put a case together," said Sheehan. "Fuck the lawyers."

"There's a dead girl in Connecticut, and Barthelme's car somewhere. Maybe that'll mean something."

Later, we drank in Oscar's. No cook, no bartender, and the waitress got pissed off at Oscar's bitching and left, so he ran the bar, cooked, and waited on tables. Amazingly enough, he carried it off. When we ordered our second round of drinks, he went to get them, but after a minute or two behind the bar called me over to the service bar to ask me gruffly where the olives were. Then, while I looked in the bottom of the cooler, without saying anything, he left me behind the bar. A little later, Eric went back into the kitchen to put out whatever fire had caused a cloud of black smoke to gush from the place, and he stayed.

"Was Nigel going to kill us?" Kevin asked when things quieted down. He was a little kid again, sipping his Shirley Temple, working out his bad dreams, still young enough to think I took care of things.

"I don't know," I told him. "When you were a little kid, I told you never to go anywhere with strangers. Why would you go somewhere with him?"

"Nigel wasn't a stranger. He was going to take us out on the boat, and I'd never been on a yacht." Kevin's lip trembled. Monsters had shown up after all in his life. Nothing I could do would keep them away forever. "Why would he kill us?"

"Killing's a bad habit, like drugs. Once you start, it's hard to stop." I looked him over. "Listen to your father. Don't do drugs, and don't kill people."

"Thanks, Dad." Delight took him over again, almost a grown-up, perched on his barstool between Sam the Hammer and Ntango.

I honestly didn't know that Nigel would have killed Kevin. Leaving the door open on poor Ozzie was one thing, pulling the trigger something else. Edwin went off the deep end once he killed Angelina, arrogant enough to think he was entitled to kill those who got in his way—conscienceless. I wasn't sure that maybe Nigel did have a conscience and saw the murky Hudson a better alternative than facing up to Edwin.

"Nigel was really nice to me," Kevin said, "except he began drinking, and I'd never seen him drink before. I was worried he wouldn't be able to drive the boat. Then he made us walk into the park instead, and he said, 'Brian thinks I killed Angelina. He went to Connecticut where my father will take care of him. What can I do with you?'

"I felt creepy. He said, 'Your dad, dumb as he is, came out on top after all.' I think maybe he already planned to jump in the river."

I put my arm around my son's shoulder, thinking of the monsters that would invade his dreams. Thinking about Angelina without a father and Nigel with a father who cared more about the family name than the family, and my own distant and distracted father, I wondered what might be in store for Kevin. He didn't reach for me so blindly anymore; he was getting older and he expected more from me.

"Wait 'till I tell Mom," he said. There was enthusiasm in his voice. He'd be okay. His mom would work him through this. He'd been through worse things—like his dad leaving home. Watching him bounce back now from what he'd been through, I wished it were me who'd be working him through things. I wished he needed me as much as I needed him.

⌐⌐⌐

Carl van Sagan came in then. I was happy to see him and really happy he wasn't a murderer. "I just left my post," he announced. "It's pretty easy to slip out without getting caught. I don't know why I never thought of it before."

I poured him a scotch. "I knew you'd bring him in," he said when he'd sipped on his drink. "Where's Janet?"

"She's packing to go back to Massachusetts…"

He looked at me for a long moment over the rim of his scotch glass. "Back to the right side of the tracks, eh?"

To receive a free catalog of other Poisoned Pen Press titles, please contact us in one of the following ways:

Phone: 1-800-421-3976
Facsimile: 1-480-949-1707
Email: info@poisonedpenpress.com
Website: www.poisonedpenpress.com

Poisoned Pen Press
6962 E. First Ave. Ste 103
Scottsdale, AZ 85251